2. Best M8S

Kate Andrews

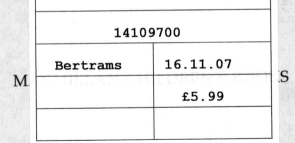

M... ...S

First published 1997 and 1998 in the Making Friends series as *Grow up, Amy,*
Go for it, Alex and *Tough luck, Carrie* by Macmillan Children's Books

This omnibus edition published 2005 by Macmillan Children's Books
a division of Macmillan Publishers Limited
20 New Wharf Road, London N1 9RR
Basingstoke and Oxford
www.panmacmillan.co.uk

Associated companies throughout the world

ISBN-13: 978-0-330-43650-2
ISBN-10: 0-330-43650-3

35798642

A CIP catalogue record for this book is available from
the British Library.

Typeset by Intype Libra Ltd
Printed and bound in Great Britain by
Mackays of Chatham plc, Kent

The cast of Friends 4 Ever 2

Alex

Age: 13

Looks: Light brown hair, blue eyes

Family: Mother died when she was a baby; lives with her dad and her brother, Matt, aged 14

Likes: Skateboarding; her family and friends; being adventurous; letting her feelings show!

Dislikes: People who make fun of skateboarding or her family; dressing smart; anything to do with maths or science; anything girlie

Carrie

Age: 13

Looks: Gorgeous long, dark hair, hazel eyes

Family: Awful! No brothers or sisters; very rich parents who go on about money all the time

Likes: Writing stories; wearing black (drives her mum mad); thinking deep thoughts; Sky's parents and their wicked houseboat!

Dislikes: Her full name – Carrington; her parents; her mum's choice of clothes; computers

Sky

Age: 13

Looks: Light brown skin, dark hair, brown eyes

Family: Crazy! Lives on a houseboat with weird parents and a brother, Leif, aged 8

Likes: Shopping; fashion; TV; pop music; talking!

Dislikes: Her parents' bizarre lifestyle; having no money; eating meat

Jordan

Age: 13

Looks: Floppy fair hair, green eyes

Family: Uncomfortable! Four big brothers – all so brilliant at sport he can never compete with them

Likes: Drawing (especially cartoons); basketball (but keeps it quiet); playing the sax (badly); taking the mickey out of his brothers

Dislikes: Being 'baby brother' to four brainless apes; Sky when she starts gossiping

Sam

Age: 13

Looks: Native American; very dark hair, very dark eyes

Family: Confusing! Both parents are Native American but have different views on how their kids should look and behave; one sister, Shawna, aged 16

Likes: Skateboarding with Alex; computers (especially surfing the Net); writing for the school paper; hanging out

Dislikes: The way his friends sometimes dump their problems on each other; his parents' arguments

Amy

Age: 13

Looks: Sickeningly gorgeous blonde hair, big baby-blue eyes

Family: Spoilt rotten by her dad, which worries her mum; two big sisters

Likes: Having loads of expensive clothes; making other people feel stupid; Alex's brother, Matt – she fancies him; being leader of 'The Amys' – her bunch of snobby friends

Dislikes: Alex, Carrie and Sky! Looking stupid or childish

Aimee

Age: 13

Looks: Very pretty, shiny auburn hair, striking green eyes

Family: Kind of normal. Nice parents and one younger sister

Likes: Being totally popular and influential at school; cool dresses; high-school guys

Dislikes: Alex, Carrie and Sky! Girls who aren't girlie enough (in her opinion)

Mel

Age: 13

Looks: Black hair, dark eyes

Family: Nice parents who work very hard to do their best for Mel

Likes: Her mum and dad; her friends — but should these be the Amys, or Alex, Carrie and Sky? Standing up for herself; reading horror novels

Dislikes: Amy, when she's rotten to other people; worrying about who are her *real* friends

Contents

Grow up,
Amy

The Wicked Mother
Another tale of unspeakable horror
By Carrie Mersel
(Note to myself: Keep hidden from Mom)

Heather's eighteenth birthday was a day she would remember for the rest of her life.

The morning dawned bleak and rainy in the town of Stony Brook. Heather awoke with a sense of foreboding, her mood as dark as the gray sky. She didn't understand it. She was turning eighteen. She should have been happy.

There was a knock on her bedroom door.

"Who is it?" Heather asked.

"It's your mother," came the reply.

Heather didn't want to answer the door. In truth, she had always suspected something was evil about her mother. All the signs pointed to wickedness: her mother's strange disappearances at all hours of the day or night, the bizarre company she kept—and most obviously, her fascination with witchcraft.

"What do you want?" Heather asked.

"I have a little present for you. . . ."

One

Clackety-clack went the antique typewriter keys.

Carrie Mersel was on a roll. She could feel it. She'd been hunched over her battered oak desk for the past hour, typing like somebody who was possessed. It was too bad she wouldn't be able to enter *this* story in a fiction contest. This was going to be one of her best. Yup. No doubt about it.

Of course, it didn't hurt that the house was empty. She always wrote better when nobody was around. It was like heaven in here. No TVs were blaring. No computerized gizmos were beeping. And it had pretty much been like this since Sunday. Her mom had been tied up with lame social engagements all week.

Monday, her mom had gone to some computer exhibition in Seattle. Tuesday, she'd helped design a dorky web site about old TV shows. Wednesday, she'd taken her gourmet cooking class. And today, Elizabeth Mersel was becoming an official member of some other weird club—her *fourth*. Carrie couldn't even remember what it was.

Not that it mattered, of course. The only thing that mattered was that her mother was out of the house.

Silence, Carrie said to herself. Once again, her fingers flew over the keyboard. Why did her parents even bother *living* here anymore? *She* was the only one who spent any time at home. She should just demolish this house and build another right in its place. One with big thick stone walls and dark stained-glass windows. One that wasn't swimming in the heinous colors of peach and white. . . .

"Hello, dear!"

Who the—?

Carrie nearly fell out of her chair.

Her mom was standing in the doorway with a wide smile.

"Mom!" Carrie gasped. She forced a weak grin. "You *scared* me. I didn't even hear you come in."

"Sorry, honey!" Mrs. Mersel sang out. She flipped on the light and marched over to Carrie's window. Her cream-colored linen pants *swished* and *swooshed* as she moved. She tossed her long blond hair over her shoulder, then tugged open Carrie's black velvet drapes, flooding the bedroom with afternoon sunlight.

Carrie blinked a few times.

"Uh . . . Mom?" she asked. "Do you really think we need to turn on the light *and* open the curtains?"

Mrs. Mersel sighed. "Carrie, one of these days, you're really going to hurt those beautiful hazel eyes of yours, you know that? You sit up here in the dark, squinting at that heap of junk on your desk—"

"Okay, okay," Carrie interrupted. She was definitely *not* in the mood to argue—especially about her typewriter. "So what are you doing home? I thought you had some meeting with a new club or something."

Her mom's perky smile abruptly reappeared. "I did!" she cried. She sat on the edge of Carrie's bed. "Today was more of a get-to-know-you type of thing than an actual meeting. But Carrie, it was *sooo* much fun."

I'll bet, Carrie thought. "What's the club again?"

"The Ocean's Edge Garden Club," Mrs. Mersel answered proudly.

"Oh." Carrie nodded, trying not to laugh. Her mom wasn't exactly the outdoorsy type. As far as Carrie knew, her mom didn't even own a pair of sneakers— much less any gardening tools.

"But here's the thing I just *have* to tell you," her mom babbled excitedly. "I met the most interesting woman there. And guess what? She has a daughter your age!"

Oh no. Carrie started shaking her head. *No you don't. . . .*

"Anyway, this woman has had a *fascinating* life," her mom went on. "She moved here from China in the mid-seventies, and she speaks five languages, and she loves . . ."

Carrie didn't even bother to listen. She knew exactly where this was heading. She was going to have to meet some lame, spoiled brat who was "her age." Her mom seemed to think that if she stuck Carrie in a room with any girl whose mom knew Carrie's mom, the two girls would become lifelong soul mates.

". . . So they'll be here tomorrow at four for tea. Isn't that great?"

Carrie's eyes widened. Tomorrow was Friday. And this Friday, she was supposed to be on Skyler Foley's boat with the rest of her friends, sailing around the peninsula— far away from *here*.

"Wait . . . did you say *tomorrow?*" she asked.

Her mom nodded enthusiastically.

"Mom—I can't be here tomorrow," Carrie protested. "I have plans."

Mrs. Mersel kept right on smiling. "Whatever they are, dear, I'm sure you can change them. This woman is going out of her way to bring her daughter—"

"Why did you just *assume* I'd be able to come?" Carrie interrupted. "I mean, shouldn't you have checked with me first? That *is* the polite thing to do, right?"

"Carrie, I don't ask very much of you," Mrs. Mersel stated. Her smile soured a little. "What are these plans, exactly?"

"Sky's parents are sailing their boat around the peninsula," Carrie explained. "They're going to have a cookout for all of us. Everybody's gonna be there and—"

"Carrie, *please*." Mrs. Mersel laughed. "You can go on a cookout with Skyler anytime. This is an opportunity for you to do something *new*. Honestly, dear, you need to branch out a little. You spend all your free time with the same old kids from the neighborhood."

"So *what*?" Carrie cried. Now she was *really* offended. "They're my *friends*, Mom. You like them, too. At least I thought you did."

"Of course I like them, dear," her mother said gently. "That's not the issue here. I'm just saying that it's important to have new experiences and meet new people."

Carrie shook her head. "No, you're saying that I don't have a choice," she muttered.

Mrs. Mersel laughed again. "I suppose I am." She stood. "But in any case, you *will* be here tomorrow at four. Understood?"

Carrie turned and faced her typewriter. She understood, all right. She was just too depressed to answer. It was really pretty amazing. In less than five minutes, her mom had totally destroyed Carrie's good mood.

"Oh—and Carrie, do me a favor, won't you?" Mrs. Mersel said, pausing in the doorway. "*Try* to wear something pretty—something *other* than black. Okay?"

The door closed behind her.

Carrie laughed once. Good old Mom. Sure. Carrie would *try* not to wear black. She just didn't know if she would try hard *enough*.

Her eyes flashed over the page sticking out of her typewriter. She wasn't sure if she could start writing again. Her concentration was totally shot. She wasn't very inspired, either—even though she couldn't help but notice how her mom's little visit sort of mirrored what was on the paper. Well, except for the part about witchcraft. But, hey, maybe that would be her mother's *next* club.

Yup. It was kind of a drag when real life imitated what happened in a made-up horror story. In fact, it totally stunk.

Oh, well. Carrie just hoped this girl—whoever she was—would be at least semitolerable.

That wasn't too much to ask, was it?

Melissa Eng

Dear Diary,

I don't believe it. For like the billionth time, Mom has decided to play social director with my life.

My life. Not hers. My is the key word. My Friday afternoon. My time. It's not like I force her to hang out with my friends' moms, right? So why does she force me to hang out with her friends' lame daughters?

I bet she thinks that I don't have enough friends. That's the only possible explanation. She thinks I'm unpopular. Me. It's such a joke. Mom obviously has no idea what "popularity" means. She doesn't understand that popularity has nothing to do with the number of people you hang out with.

Look at me: I only hang out with two other people on a regular basis, and I'm one of the most popular girls at school. I'm not patting myself on the back or anything. It's true. Why should I lie? Everybody knows that The Amys rule Robert Lowell Middle School. Ask anybody, and they'll say that the three most popular girls in school are Amy Anderson, Aimee Stewart, and me.

But Mom doesn't get it. She thinks that I'm lonely. That's why she makes me hang out with all these dorky kids. The pathetic thing is that <u>she's</u> the lonely one. The only reason she joins those stupid clubs —like the Ocean's Edge Garden Club, for example —is to hang out with as many different people as possible.

But it's her life, right? I don't interfere. Whatever makes her happy is cool.

So why does she interfere with me? I don't _need_ any more friends. Amy and Aimee are the two greatest friends anyone could have. They're enough. They're _more_ than enough.

All the complaining in the world won't do a bit of good, though. It's not like I have a choice. My Friday is going to be ruined. I'm going to spend it with some girl I don't even know, at some place I've never been, talking about stupid stuff. . . .

Blecch. It's beyond depressing. I just know that this girl is going to be a dork. I just know it

Two

I

"Why would your mom do something like this?" Amy asked.

"I don't *know*," Mel groaned.

"She knows that we watch our tape of *Days of Our Lives* at four," Aimee mumbled. "It doesn't make any sense."

Mel just shrugged. Aimee was right. It didn't make any sense—but there was nothing she could do about it now. Mel's mom had no understanding of the importance of *Days of Our Lives*. And in less than half an hour, Mel would be introducing herself to some loser while Aimee and Amy opened a fresh bag of Orange Milanos. . . .

"Let's go over to the corner," Amy said. "It's way too crowded here."

Mel nodded, following Amy as she pushed her way through the crowd on the front steps of Robert Lowell. Everybody seemed *much* too happy. Of course, it was Friday. School *was* over. But they didn't have to scream about it, did they?

Amy walked quickly, brushing her long blond hair behind one ear. "Do you know anything at all about this girl?" she asked.

Mel shook her head. "I don't even know her name. I don't even know where she *lives.*"

"Maybe she'll be cool," Amy said. "Maybe—"

"There's your mom!" Aimee cried.

Mel looked up. Sure enough, Mrs. Anderson's gray Jaguar was pulling up to the corner. Aimee and Amy broke into a run. Their hair fluttered behind them in the breeze. Mel was absolutely miserable. She almost felt as if they were running *away* from her. But who could blame them? She wasn't much fun to be around right now.

"Bye, Mel!" they both called at the same time.

The car doors slammed.

Mel frowned.

All right—just cheer up, she told herself. *It's only one afternoon of your life.*

Maybe Amy was right. Maybe this girl would be cool.

Yeah, right. And maybe Brick the bus driver would win the Mr. Universe contest.

II

"Are you sure you can't come with us?" Sky asked Carrie as the bus roared away from the school building. "Why don't you just skip the whole thing and make up an excuse later?"

Carrie hung her head. "Because my mom would kill me," she mumbled. "She has it all planned out. I'm supposed to become best friends with this girl."

Sky smiled sympathetically, but Carrie couldn't smile back. It was hard enough for her to be crammed into the long backseat with Alex, Jordan, Sky, and Sam, knowing that they were all about to whoop it up on a sunset cruise. Carrie glanced out the window. The day *had* to be perfect, didn't it? The evergreen trees were tinted with that beautiful autumn afternoon light, the kind of slanting sun that only came around at *this* time of year at *this* time of day.

"Maybe you could pretend that you

were kidnapped," Alex suggested. Her hopeful blue eyes peered at Carrie from under the bill of her green Supersonics cap. "You could say that these guys grabbed you right after school and tied you to a chair, but you managed to escape by chewing your way through the ropes."

Carrie laughed. "Yeah. Great idea, Alex," she said dryly. "The kidnapping rope-chewing excuse *always* works."

"Hey, it's not like you're going to be missing a gourmet feast or anything," Jordan said, leaning across Sky. "I mean, look at it this way. The Foleys' idea of a cookout is serving up cold celery sticks and vegetarian tofu burgers. No offense, Sky."

Carrie didn't trust herself to speak. She knew Jordan was just trying to make her feel better. But it wasn't working.

The bus slowed to a stop in front of Sky's dock. Carrie peered out the window at the houseboat. Sky's parents were running around the front deck, setting up the grill. A little moan escaped Carrie's lips.

"Don't have *too* much fun," she murmured. Sky glanced over her shoulder as the four of them headed for the door. "Hey—maybe you really *will* become best friends with this girl," she said enthusiastically.

"Maybe you're right," Carrie replied. "Maybe we'll become great buddies and room together in college and have a big double wedding and our kids will get married."

Sky shrugged. "You never know. . . ."

III

"You look so pretty, Melissa," Mrs. Eng said in her slightly accented, commanding voice. "I love your hair."

"Thanks," Mel mumbled. She glanced at herself in the rearview mirror as her mom parked on Whidbey Road. She didn't *feel* pretty. Her lips were curved downward and her black eyes were lifeless. She *was* wearing one of her favorite dresses, though—a really hip-looking purplish thing she had borrowed from Amy. Why she had wasted it on a day like today, though, she had no clue.

"Isn't this just a beautiful home?" her mom exclaimed.

Mel squinted up the long driveway at a sleek, modern white house, with its big glass windows. Something about this house was *very* familiar. Of course, it *was* right around the corner from Amy's place. . . .

"What's wrong?" Mrs. Eng asked.

"Uh, nothing," Mel said uncertainly. "It's just . . . I didn't know your friend lived in Taylor Haven."

Mrs. Eng nodded happily, clutching her shiny purse with both hands. "You know—I wouldn't be surprised if this girl went to Robert Lowell."

Neither would I, Mel thought.

She *did* know this house. The bus stopped here every morning. But she couldn't place *who* lived here. Of course, knowing the people who rode Bus #4, the possibilities were all pretty weak.

IV

Carrie's eyes roved over all the empty seats as the bus climbed Pike's Way. There were only five other kids on the bus besides her. Well, of course: It was Friday. Everybody *else* was going somewhere fun. Or at least their idea of fun. She knew at least three of the regular passengers were

17

doing something totally lame—namely, The Amys. They were about to watch *Days of Our Lives*.

The bus turned and jerked to a quick stop in front of Carrie's driveway.

Party time, Carrie groaned to herself.

"Why the long face?" Brick asked. He flashed a crazed grin from behind his dark glasses as she trudged past him. "It's the weekend, man! Time to let loose!"

"Not for me it isn't," she mumbled. "See ya later, Brick. Have fun."

"Always do, Carrie. Hey, cool threads by the way." He closed the door behind her.

Carrie waved as the bus pulled away. She allowed herself a little smile as she walked up the driveway. Her mom wouldn't think these threads were so cool. Carrie had deliberately chosen the blackest possible outfit: a black skirt and black T-shirt, with her favorite black sweater to cap it off—the one with the black buttons. And, of course, she'd gone with black nail polish and combat boots.

Perfect for meeting her future best friend, right?

"Carrie!" her mom called from the front

door. "Come on, honey. The guests are already here."

"You want me to leap for joy?" Carrie muttered under her breath.

"Carrie, I thought I told you not to wear black," Mrs. Mersel hissed in a low whisper. "The girl here is dressed so nicely—"

"Good for her, Mom," Carrie said, stepping into the hallway. She mustered up the biggest smile she could, then turned to face the two people sitting on the lone peach couch in the living room. "Hi—"

She froze.

Her jaw dropped.

No, she thought, utterly horrified. *Not her . . .*

Well, well, well.

One thing was for sure. She would *not* become lifelong friends with this girl. There would be no college rooming or double wedding.

She could rule out something else, too: The Amys were *not* watching *Days of Our Lives*. At least *one* of them wasn't.

Because Mel Eng—one of the three most heinous creatures on the planet—was right here.

Three

For a long while, Carrie couldn't move. She couldn't even speak. All she could do was stare.

"I knew it," Mel started muttering. She hung her head. Her black pigtails drooped over her shoulders. "I knew something like this would happen."

"So you two *know* each other!" Mrs. Mersel exclaimed. She marched across the front hall into the living room. Her heels clattered on the marble floor. "That's *wonderful!*"

Carrie started laughing. Wonderful? No— but she could think of a few other choice words.

"Well, don't just *stand* there, Carrie," her mother scolded. "Come here and introduce yourself to Mrs. Eng."

This must be some sort of bad karma or something, Carrie thought. She forced herself to walk toward Mel and Mrs. Eng. *Horrible things like this don't happen unless there's a*

20

reason. Did I do something bad? If I did, I'm sorry. I'm so very, very sorry. . . .

"It's lovely to meet you, Carrie," Mrs. Eng said. She gathered herself up off the couch and extended a hand.

Carrie shook it as politely as she could manage. "Nice to meet you, too, Mrs. Eng," she replied. She cast a sidelong glance at Mel, who was very deliberately avoiding Carrie's eyes by staring at her ultrastylish black suede shoes.

"Hello, Carrie," Mel groaned. She didn't look up.

"Melissa—is that any way to greet your hostess?" Mrs. Eng hissed.

Carrie smiled. Even after about three seconds, she could tell that Mrs. Eng and her mom were a perfect match. They were both really formal, they both wore the same kinds of expensive designer business suits, and they both liked to embarrass their kids in front of other people.

"Melissa?" Mrs. Eng prodded.

Mel rolled her eyes. "Fine," she muttered. She pushed herself to her feet and faced Carrie with a phony grin. "Carrie, it's so nice to see you for, like, the eightieth time today," she said in a flat voice.

21

"Speak for yourself," Carrie answered sweetly.

"Carrie!" Mrs. Mersel barked. But then she let out a nervous little laugh. "Uh . . . why don't you pull up a chair?"

"Good idea," Carrie mumbled. That would kill a nice ten seconds or so—anything to delay an actual *conversation*. She walked to the far wall as slowly as she could, picked up a hard-backed white chair, then lazily pushed it across the rug to the couch.

Tick, tick, tick went the clock.

"We were just talking about computers," Mrs. Eng said.

Perfect, Carrie thought. This really *was* bad karma. Not only did she hate computers, but she'd given away her own computer to Sam Wells. And her mom still didn't know anything about it.

"We can always talk about something else, though," Mel muttered.

Carrie slid into her chair. "Sounds good to me," she agreed.

"Oh, isn't this *funny!*" Mrs. Mersel chirped. She laughed once, squeezing in beside Mel's mom on the couch. "Carrie, you and Mel have something in common. You both have this strange phobia when it comes to—"

"Mom, *please*," Carrie interrupted. She forced another smile. "Didn't our guest say she wanted to talk about something else?"

"Listen, I do *not* have any phobia or anything," Mel muttered. "It's just that there's about a million other things to talk about that are about a million times more interesting than—"

"Melissa, you're being impolite," Mrs. Eng whispered sternly. "Enough."

"Oh, that's all right," Mrs. Mersel said with a breezy laugh. "Carrie also gets a little testy when we talk about anything computer related. That might be something else you two have in common."

Carrie's smile vanished. Testy? Something they had in common? That was *it*. She'd already had *way* more than she could take.

"You know what *else* we have in common?" Carrie grumbled under her breath. "Neither of us wants to be in this living room right now."

Mrs. Mersel's eyes narrowed. "Carrie, there's no need—"

"Why don't Carrie and I go to Carrie's room?" Mel suddenly suggested. "You two can talk about what *you* want to talk about, and we can talk about what *we* want to talk about."

There was another awkward silence. Carrie shot a quick glance at Mel. That wasn't such a bad idea. If they were alone, they wouldn't have to try to be polite to each other. They wouldn't have to do anything. They wouldn't even have to *speak* to each other. Besides, anything was better than being stuck in here with her mom.

"You know, I think that's a great idea," Carrie proclaimed, hopping to her feet.

"I bet you two want to talk about the garden club, right?" Mel added. "We'll just be in Carrie's room."

Mrs. Eng and Carrie's mom exchanged a bewildered glance.

"Bye!" Carrie called. She abruptly turned and marched for the stairs.

Mel followed close on her heels.

No, this isn't a bad idea at all, Carrie said to herself. Being alone with Mel was much better than hanging out with their mothers.

Besides, there was always a chance that she and Mel would be friendly, right?

There was an even *better* chance that she would ignore Mel completely.

24

Four

Black velvet drapes, Mel said to herself. *It figures. How cheesy could you get?*

Carrie slammed her door behind the both of them. Mel took a look around the room and shook her head. She should have known what it would be like in here. It was totally dark and depressing. The walls were covered with posters of lame grunge rock bands she'd never heard of. Everybody looked really pale and unhealthy and angry—as if they hadn't slept in weeks and were really mad about it.

"Nice room," Mel muttered sarcastically.

Carrie didn't answer. She sat down at a beaten-up old desk and immediately began poking at a typewriter.

Mel folded her arms across her chest. "Uh . . . hello?" she said, clearing her throat.

"What?" Carrie asked. She didn't even bother turning around.

"Sorry—but what am I supposed to do while you sit there and type?" Mel demanded.

Carrie lifted her shoulders. "Do whatever you want," she muttered. "Look at a book or something."

Mel raised her eyebrows. "A book?" She didn't even want to *think* about the kind of books Carrie Mersel read.

"Look, Mel—I don't want to talk to you and you don't want to talk to me," Carrie stated. "That's why you wanted to come up here, right? So we wouldn't have to talk?"

Mel laughed once. Carrie was right, *obviously*. But she still hadn't expected Carrie to pretend as if she weren't even *here*. It was so insulting.

"Make yourself at home," Carrie mumbled over the clacking of the typewriter keys. "Just don't turn on the light and don't open the shades."

Mel pursed her lips. *Why?* she wondered. *Because vampires melt in the sunlight?* But she kept her mouth shut. Carrie was right: *Neither* of them wanted to talk. With a loud sigh, she sat down at the edge of Carrie's unmade bed. Her eyes roved across the room. They came to rest on a stack of bookshelves near Carrie's night table.

Now *here* was something shocking.

Carrie Mersel actually had some halfway decent books.

Mel slid across the bed and peered at the top shelf closely. There were like thirty different books by Stephen King in there. She couldn't believe it. She'd always thought that *she* had a lot of Stephen King books. But this was ridiculous. She'd never even heard of most of them.

"*The Shining*!" she found herself exclaiming out loud.

The typing stopped.

"What about it?" Carrie asked, sounding bored.

"Uh . . . nothing." Mel glanced over her shoulder. *That* was embarrassing. Could she have sounded like *more* of a geek?

"Have you read it?" Carrie asked.

"No," Mel mumbled. "I've wanted to read it ever since my parents rented the movie, but I've never been able to find it."

"Oh." Carrie hunched back over the typewriter. "Well, the movie is totally different."

"A lot of Stephen King movies are," Mel said absently.

Carrie swiveled around in her chair.

"Wait a second," she said. "Are you trying to tell me you *like* Stephen King?"

"Yeah," Mel replied. She knew she sounded defensive, but she couldn't help it. "So?"

"No—it's . . . uh, nothing." Carrie laughed softly. "I'm just kind of surprised."

Mel rolled her eyes. "Carrie—you're not the only one who reads, you know. *Tons* of people like Stephen King. He's sold, like, forty zillion books."

Carrie shrugged. "I know. I guess I'm surprised because none of *my* friends like him."

"Well, none of *my* friends do, either," Mel shot back.

For a moment, their eyes locked.

Oh no, Mel thought. *Why did I say that? Mrs. Mersel was right. I do have something in common with Carrie. I should have never opened my big mouth. . . .*

Carrie grinned. "So which one is your favorite?" she asked.

"I don't like him all *that* much," Mel lied, clumsily turning back to the bookshelf. She didn't want Carrie to get any crazy ideas— like they had some kind of bond now or something. "I don't really have a favorite." Her voice fell to a low murmur. "Well, I kind of like *Carrie* . . . I mean, if I had to choose."

"What a coincidence," Carrie said dryly. "Me too."

Mel frowned. Carrie wasn't making fun of her, was she? She glanced over her shoulder.

But Carrie was still grinning. She raised her eyebrows. "I mean, it's kind of obvious, isn't it?"

Mel's brow grew furrowed. "What is?"

"*Duh,*" Carrie said. "It's my *name*, Mel."

"Oh, right." Mel's face grew flushed and she quickly turned away again. That *was* kind of obvious. Now Carrie probably thought she was an airhead. Great. And knowing how much of a smart aleck Carrie was, she would probably make some wise comment. . . .

"You can borrow *The Shining* if you want," Carrie said casually.

Mel hesitated.

"Or you can keep trying to find it in some really overpriced bookstore," Carrie muttered. She started typing again.

"Maybe I *will* borrow it," Mel said after a moment. She reached forward and pulled the battered paperback off the bookshelf. "Is it really okay?" she asked suspiciously.

"Sure," Carrie replied. She laughed. "I mean, I know where to find you—"

There was a loud knock on the door.

Mel whirled around.

"Carrie, that's not your *typewriter* I hear, is it?" Mrs. Mersel's muffled voice demanded.

Before Carrie could even answer, the door flew open.

"Mom!" she protested.

Mrs. Mersel stood in the doorway, shaking her head. "You're *typing* while you have company," she said in a tight voice. "You really have no manners at all, young lady." She glanced at Mel. "I'm sorry, dear. You'll have to excuse my daughter's rudeness."

Mel swallowed. *Jeez.* She actually felt kind of bad for Carrie. It *was* sort of rude to sit there and type, but still . . .

"It's okay, Mrs. Mersel," she found herself saying. She held up the book. "I was reading. We were just hanging out, doing our own thing."

All at once, a big smile broke on Mrs. Mersel's face. "Really?" she asked.

Mel nodded.

"Well, excuse me," she said, clasping her hands together. She was beaming now. "I'm sorry, Carrie. Look at you. This is just so nice. . . ."

Mrs. Eng's head appeared in the doorway. "How are you two doing?" she asked happily.

Oh, please, Mel grumbled to herself.

"They're like two peas in a pod," Mrs. Mersel chirped. "It's wonderful. They're already at the comfortable silence stage."

Mel's eyes widened. Comfortable silence stage? The woman *had* to be kidding.

Carrie started shaking her head. There was a sickly look on her face. "No," she choked out. "No, we're not—"

"What do you expect?" Mrs. Eng chuckled. "They're school chums."

"School chums!" Mel cried. Now *this* was ridiculous. "Give me a *break*, Mom!"

Mrs. Eng looked puzzled. "I don't understand. . . ."

Mel leaped off the bed and marched for the door. If she didn't understand, then Mel would just have to show her. Yes, things had gone far enough for one day. She and Carrie Mersel were not "chums"—and they never would be.

"What are you doing?" Mrs. Eng hissed as Mel brushed passed her. "What's going on?"

"I'm leaving," Mel stated, gripping the book tightly at her side. She hurried down the stairs. "You can stay if you want," she called. "I'm outta here. Thanks, Mrs. Mersel!"

"Melissa!" her mom shouted. "Come *back* here—"

Mel slammed the front door behind her.

There, she said to herself.

Then she realized something.

She couldn't go anywhere. She was stuck. After all, she needed a ride home, didn't she?

What did I just do?

That had been a really, really dumb move. She'd shown her mom, all right—but she knew right then that storming out wouldn't do a bit of good. Her mom was obviously going to punish her for being so rude.

Mel could just guess what that punishment would be, too.

She was going to have to do something incredibly lame—like apologize formally to Carrie Mersel.

Or even worse, she was going to have to come back here and spend another afternoon with Carrie all over again.

Saturday:

The Morning After . . .

EARLY MORNING
THE ENG HOUSE

Mrs. Eng calls Mrs. Mersel. She apologizes once again for Mel's rude behavior and suggests that the four of them get together Monday afternoon. Mrs. Mersel gladly accepts.

MIDMORNING
THE MERSEL HOUSE

Mrs. Mersel informs Carrie that she'll be spending another afternoon with the Engs this Monday. And no—Carrie doesn't have a choice. After all, Carrie must have given Mel a reason for storming out, right?

33

LATE MORNING
THE ENG HOUSE

Mel receives a call from Amy. Amy's mom is taking the three of them to the movies on Monday afternoon. No, she isn't. She's taking *two* of them. Mel will be spending yet another afternoon with Carrie Mersel. Yes, *the* Carrie Mersel. She'll explain later. She's *way* too bummed out right now.

NOON
THE MERSEL HOUSE

Carrie receives a call from Alex. Can she come over to her house after school on Monday? Carrie tells Alex the terrible truth: She has to hang out with Mel Eng. That's right—Mel Eng. She'll explain later. She's *way* too bummed out right now.

Five

I

"So what's Carrie's house like?" Amy whispered the moment Mel sat down for lunch. Her bright blue eyes sparkled. "Is it totally freakish?"

"Yeah," Aimee said eagerly. "Does it smell or anything?"

Mel hung her head, staring into her bowl of chili. Usually she looked forward to lunch on Mondays. She looked forward to sitting at their little table and getting in on all the juicy weekend gossip. She looked forward to planning a bunch of good stuff for the week ahead. But today, *naturally*, she was going to spend the entire lunch answering a lot of embarrassing questions about her stupid afternoon with Robert Lowell's biggest weirdo.

"You guys?" she mumbled. "Can we talk about something else? It's depressing enough as it is. I mean, I actually have to go *back* there this afternoon."

Amy shook her hair and laughed. "Just answer the question, Mel."

"Yeah, come on, Mel," Aimee pleaded. "I'm curious. Something strange *must* go on in that house."

Mel grinned slightly in spite of herself. "Well, it doesn't *smell* or anything," she muttered. "But her room is kind of a scary place."

The two of them shoved their trays aside and leaned forward. "Yeah?" they whispered at the exact same time.

Mel glanced at the two of them. Her grin widened. Maybe talking about her stupid afternoon *wasn't* so bad. They were hanging on her every word.

"Well, for starters, when I went in there, I could barely see a thing," Mel whispered. "She has these *totally* tacky black velvet drapes—"

"Black *velvet?*" Amy hissed, making a face.

Mel nodded. "Yeah. But get this. They completely cover her windows. No sun can get in at *all*. And she *freaked* when I asked if I could turn the light on."

II

"So, anyway, Mel comes into my room," Carrie said. "And she's all like, 'Hel-*lo*. What am *I* supposed to be doing while *you* sit there and amuse yourself?'"

Carrie took a deep breath. She felt as if she'd been ranting and raving about Mel Eng for hours now. But she couldn't stop. Everyone at the table was obviously *way* into this story. Jordan was laughing. Alex was shaking her head. Sky looked horrified, as if she had witnessed the whole thing herself. They hadn't even touched their lunches. Even Sam—the boy who hated getting involved with other people's problems—was gazing at her with wide black eyes.

This was actually kind of fun.

"What did you tell her?" Sky asked.

Carrie shrugged. "I was like, 'Read a book. Do whatever you want. Make yourself at home.' You know, just to be polite. There was no point in making a bad situation worse."

"And?" Alex prodded.

"And she was totally rude, of course," Carrie replied. "She was all like, 'I don't want to read any of your stupid books.'

But then she saw one that she wanted, and she started making this huge deal about how she couldn't find it anywhere. You know—she was obviously hinting that I should give it to her or something."

Carrie was beginning to realize something as she jabbered away.

Her story had very little to do with what really happened.

At first, she was only planning on exaggerating a teeny little bit—just for dramatic effect, of course. Every good story had to have *some* exaggeration. It wasn't as though she wanted to *lie* or anything. But the more she got into it, the more she got carried away. She couldn't help herself. Besides, she was entertaining her friends, right? That was what counted.

"Did you give her the book?" Sam asked.

"Of course," Carrie said evenly. "I had to do *something* to shut her up."

III

"And that was when things got *really* out of control," Mel whispered.

Amy and Aimee leaned even closer.

"So Carrie was typing this whole time,

right?" she continued. "She was acting like a total freakazoid and completely ignoring me. I felt like I was in a room with a psycho or something."

Amy raised her eyebrows. "You *were*, Mel," she stated.

Mel laughed. She was having a blast. It was unbelievable. The three of them were hunched together so closely now that their foreheads were practically touching. She'd *never* been the center of attention like this. Then again, it was kind of hard to be the center of attention when your best friend was Amy Anderson. Amy wasn't the type of person who enjoyed sharing the spotlight all that much.

"So I reach for a random book on Carrie's bookshelf," Mel breathed. "Just to kill some time. She has, like, a billion books—all by these weird people I've never even heard of. And just as I pull it out, she spins around and totally wigs out on me. She was like, 'What are you *doing* with that? Don't touch my stuff!' And I'm like, 'Excuse *me*. I'm not trying to *steal* it or anything. Just chill.'"

Amy leaned back and shook her head. "You know, Mel, I'm not surprised," she commented in a very serious voice. Her eyes darted over toward Carrie's table. "Carrie's insane. Really."

Mel hesitated. "Insane?"

"That's right," Amy said.

"Really?" Aimee asked excitedly.

"Really." Amy nodded. "I'm not joking. She's got a split-personality disorder or something. Remember that time she invited herself over to my house and wigged out on *me?* There was no reason for it. It was like she suddenly became a different person. I bet she's taking medication."

Mel didn't say anything. For the briefest instant, she felt the tiniest pang of something uncomfortable. It wasn't guilt, exactly. She *was* pretty much making stuff up as she went along—not that it mattered. Carrie was a dork. Still, she kind of doubted if Carrie was really, truly *insane* or anything. . . .

"If she's crazy, maybe that's why she wears all black all the time," Aimee mumbled.

Mel managed an awkward smile. "Maybe."

"So go on," Amy prompted. "What else?"

IV

Carrie lowered her voice to a whisper. She couldn't tell if The Amys were trying to listen in on her conversation—but judging from the way the three of them kept sneaking peeks in her direction, it was probably safe to assume the worst.

"Suddenly, my mom and Mel's mom literally *burst* into my room," she murmured. "And they see Mel sitting there with a book and me at the typewriter . . . and you'll never guess what my mom said."

She bit her lip, glancing around the table. Everyone's face was glazed with a totally rapt expression. Nobody said a word.

Carrie took a deep breath. "She said, 'Isn't this *wonderful!* Carrie and Mel are already at the comfortable silence stage!'"

Jordan started cracking up. "Come on, Carrie—"

"Shh!" Carrie whispered, but she was laughing, too. It figured that Jordan wouldn't believe the only true part of the story. "I swear, that's what she said. But that's not all. Because after she said it, Mel went off. I mean she *flipped*. She started yelling at her mom and then she stomped

41

out of the house and slammed the door."

Sky's mouth fell open. "Really? Mel always seems so calm and collected—"

"Believe me, she isn't," Carrie muttered. *That* much was true, too, at least. Well, she thought it was. Mel *had* thrown a huge temper tantrum. But Carrie had been adding so many little details that it was getting harder to remember what *really* happened and what didn't.

"I don't get why your mom is making you hang out with her again this afternoon," Alex said. "It's crazy."

Carrie shrugged. "Yeah, but my mom isn't really known for being sane."

"So, what do you think is gonna happen?" Sky asked anxiously.

"Who knows?" Carrie sighed. "But I'm looking at it this way. It can't get much worse than what happened on Friday, right?"

Six

Mel couldn't bring herself to get out of her seat.

Everyone was waiting. The bus door was open. The engine was quiet. She could hear birds chirping in front of Carrie's house. But she couldn't move.

This is the most humiliating moment of my life.

Coming back here was bad enough. But somehow, knowing that every single kid on Bus #4 was watching her . . . *Blecch*. She could just *predict* what would happen. Some loser was going to tell some other loser that Mel Eng— one of The Amys, one of the rulers of Robert Lowell—had gone to Carrie Mersel's house Monday afternoon. And by tomorrow, the entire student body would be convinced that Mel Eng and Carrie Mersel were best friends.

"Come on, Mel," Carrie muttered under her breath as she hurried out the door. "Move it."

"Yeah, Mel," Aimee teased loudly. She

gave Mel a nudge. "Your new best buddy is waiting for you."

Mel frowned. "Very funny," she growled. She lumbered to her feet.

"You're getting off *here?*" Brick exclaimed. "Wow. I didn't even know that you guys hung out together. I must really be out of it."

Amy and Aimee started giggling.

Mel shook her head. *Thanks, Brick.* The guy never had a thought that he didn't actually *say* out loud.

"Have fun!" he called. The door squeaked shut behind her, and the bus roared down Whidbey Road—right past her mom's little blue BMW.

"Great," she moped.

"What?" Carrie asked.

"My mom is already here. That means she's gonna make a huge scene and make me apologize, like, a hundred times and—"

"Look, I don't want that any more than you do," Carrie interrupted. The two of them paused at the front door. Carrie lowered her voice. "A big scene will be totally embarrassing for the both of us. So let's just say that you apologized at school, we made up, and that'll be that."

Mel thought for a second. It sounded good—but she doubted if that would work. Her mom always liked to make a big deal out of things. She brushed a few stray wisps of black hair out of her eyes. "Maybe . . ."

The door swung open.

"Hello, Melissa!" Mrs. Mersel cried. "I thought I heard you two whispering out there. Come in, come in."

Mel followed Carrie into the peach-and-white-checkered hallway and glanced into the living room. Her mom was standing by the couch, gazing at her sternly. So much for avoiding a scene.

"Melissa, do you have something you want to say to Mrs. Mersel and Carrie?" Mrs. Eng asked.

Mel swallowed. She could tell her mom was mad. Her mom's accent was always more pronounced when she was upset about something.

"Sorry?" she murmured hopefully.

Mrs. Eng shook her head. "Mel, you need to do a little better than that."

"She's already said she's sorry to me, like, a million times," Carrie announced. "And I

45

said I'm sorry to her. Everything's great. No hard feelings."

Mrs. Mersel tilted her head and smiled. "Well, that's fine, then. Apology accepted, Melissa."

A smile spread across Mel's face. That *had* been easy. Amazingly enough, Carrie had handled the situation pretty well.

"Well, I'd love to stay here and chat, but I really have to study for a math test," Carrie said abruptly. She marched up the stairs. "Mr. Engel announced a pop quiz for tomorrow, so . . ." Her voice trailed off.

Mel frowned. Now where did she think *she* was going?

"Carrie, you are *not* going to study for a math test when we have company," Mrs. Mersel stated. She was still smiling, but her eyes had narrowed into two angry slits. "Put your book bag away and come back here."

Carrie paused at the top of the stairs and raised her hands apologetically. "I *can't*, Mom. You *know* how much trouble I have with math. You're always telling me how I need to study harder. I can't *afford* to mess this up. I need to get my priorities straight, right?"

46

Mel rolled her eyes. She'd never heard a bigger load of garbage in her life.

But Mrs. Mersel was no longer smiling. Her lips were pressed into a tight line.

"Carrie, Melissa might be able to help you," Mrs. Eng suggested from the living room. "Math is her strongest subject."

Jeez, Mom . . . Mel put her face in her hands. This was *just* what she needed. Her mom might as well have said, "Carrie, Melissa is a major geek."

"Melissa?" her mom prodded. "You wouldn't mind, would you? You help your friend Amy with math all the time."

Mel's hands fell to her side. "What does *that* have to do with anything?" she cried.

"It has to do with thinking about someone besides yourself," Mrs. Eng replied matter-of-factly. "You know how grateful you are when someone helps you with your geography—"

"Fine," Mel grumbled. She was *not* going to get into a discussion about her geography problems in front of the Mersels. The whole thing was so ridiculous. If her mom only had the slightest clue, she would know that Carrie probably didn't even *have* a math quiz. She was just making an excuse to avoid the whole get-together.

"So?" Mrs. Eng asked.

Mel shook her head. She glanced up at Carrie. "Do you really want me to help you with your math?" she asked, feeling like a fool.

Carrie stared at her blankly. "Whatever." She turned and disappeared up to the second floor.

"Melissa, you'll have to excuse Carrie's behavior," Mrs. Mersel murmured. "Math is a touchy subject around here. . . ."

"That's all right," Mel said, sighing. She moved slowly toward the stairs. It was weird: Her own mom had once said the same exact thing about geography—that it was a "touchy subject." Her mom and Carrie's mom were like long-lost twins. No wonder they were trying to force Mel and Carrie to be friends.

But today was going to be the last day she *ever* set foot in this house.

Yes, today Mel was going to have a little chat with her mom. After all, if she spent any more time here, Carrie Mersel's weirdness might start rubbing off on her or something. . . .

And there was no way she was going to let that happen.

Seven

Why are they torturing me like this? Carrie wondered. She slouched down in front of her desk. She had been sure that the math quiz excuse would work. She was sure that the three of them would leave her alone. . . .

Mel sauntered into the room and closed the door without saying a word. She immediately spread herself out across Carrie's bed.

"Make yourself at home," Carrie mumbled sarcastically.

"Hey—I'm the one who's helping you study for your math quiz," Mel retorted.

Carrie turned to face her. "I don't *have* a math quiz, Mel."

"No kidding," she mumbled. She propped herself up against the pillows, then carefully flattened the wrinkles in her designer bell-bottom jeans and blue baby-doll T-shirt.

"Anybody could have figured *that* out."

"So why did you even bother coming up here?" Carrie asked.

"Because it's either stay in here with you or stay down there with *them*," Mel grumbled.

Carrie didn't say anything. "I guess you have a point," she finally admitted.

Mel's eyes briefly flickered over Carrie's face. "Our moms . . . they're like . . ."

" 'Like two peas in a pod!' " Carrie squealed in her mom's voice, adding the fake grin. She tossed her dyed black hair over her shoulders, imitating that irritating way her mom had of constantly primping.

Mel smirked. "Sure they are. They're garden club . . . *chums.*"

Carrie laughed once. Their eyes met. Then Mel blinked—and the next instant, she was wearing the same aloof and annoyed expression she always wore. Carrie sighed. Of course. Mel was obviously *way* too cool to admit that she had a sense of humor or anything.

"It *is* kind of freaky about our moms, though, isn't it?" Carrie asked after a minute, almost to herself. "I mean, they met . . . what? Four days ago? And it's like they've known each other their entire lives. Maybe they were separated at birth or something."

Mel frowned.

Oh, brother, Carrie thought. Now Mel was probably going to get offended that Carrie was ragging on Mrs. Eng so much.

"What?" Carrie demanded.

"Nothing, nothing," Mel murmured. She went back to straightening her pants. "It's just that I was thinking pretty much the exact same thing right before I came up here."

Carrie raised her eyebrows. "You *were?*"

A fleeting grin crossed Mel's face. "Yeah—when your mom said that math was a touchy subject. That's exactly what my mom says about geography. She actually makes me stay in on the weekends to study." She looked up. "Can you believe that?"

"My mom does the exact same thing!" Carrie exclaimed. "I had to sneak out of the house two weeks ago because my mom knew I had a math quiz."

"Well . . . math I can kind of

understand," Mel said. "Everybody has to know math. But *geography?* I mean, what's the point? If I really need to know where Tasmania is, I can look at a globe, right?"

Carrie snickered. "Come on, Mel. And if I really need to know the square root of one hundred eighty-nine, I can use a calculator, right?"

Much to Carrie's surprise, Mel actually laughed. "I guess you're right," she said. "I mean, when it comes right down to it, what's the point of even going to school?"

Carrie shrugged. "There *is* no point," she said dryly. "That's the great thing about modern society. You've got calculators, globes, dictionaries, encyclopedias. . . ."

"You've got everything," Mel agreed. She laughed again—and this time, it actually sounded sort of nice. "You know, somebody should tell that to Principal Cashen."

"Really." Carrie laughed, too. "Somebody should go up to him and be like, 'Look, buddy, I don't *need* your lousy school. I don't even need to get out of *bed.*"

"Can you imagine?" Mel said. She put her hands behind her head and leaned back into the pillows. "Maybe *I* should do that. Then once I stopped going to school, I wouldn't have to take any more geography tests. Maybe Mom would finally stop bugging me." Her voice flattened. "Maybe I'd even have time to join the Ocean's Edge Garden Club."

"And wouldn't that be *wonderful?*" Carrie cried.

Mel smiled. *"Fabulous,"* she stated, mimicking her own mom's voice. She let out a long sigh and shook her head. "Other kids' parents aren't as whacked-out as ours, are they?"

"None that *I've* met," Carrie mumbled.

Mel rolled over on her side and glanced at Carrie's bookshelf. "Maybe that's why I like Stephen King so much," she joked. "All the scary characters remind me of people in my own life. Namely my mom."

Carrie's eyes widened. *Whoa.* How many times had that exact same thought crossed *her* mind?

For a moment, she leaned back and stared at Mel, struck by the *weirdness* of what was happening in here. She was actually having a normal conversation with

Mel Eng. No, not a normal conversation: an *enjoyable* conversation. The girl *did* have a sense of humor. She had a frighteningly large number of things in common with Carrie, too. Sure—she was stuck up; she was spoiled . . . but she wasn't *all* bad.

"Have you started *The Shining*?" Carrie asked tentatively.

Mel nodded. She swung her legs over the side of the bed and sat up, then patted her slightly tousled black hair. "I read, like, the first thirty pages," she began. "It's really—"

"Carrie!" Mrs. Mersel called from downstairs.

Carrie rolled her eyes. "*What*, Mom?" she groaned.

"Are you studying?" Mrs. Mersel demanded.

Carrie glanced at Mel. They both started grinning.

"Yeah, Mom," Carrie stated flatly.

"Melissa—are you helping her?" Mrs. Eng chimed in.

Mel didn't answer. Her eyes bored deeply into Carrie's. They seemed to be asking: *What should we do?*

Carrie chewed her lip. *Hmm.* That was

54

kind of an important question. If their parents knew that the two of them were actually *talking*, then they might get the wrong idea. They might even think that Carrie and Mel wanted to do this again or something. And Carrie was *not* prepared to waste any more afternoons with Mel Eng—even if Mel *was* a Stephen King fan. No, it would be much better if their parents thought they weren't getting along at all.

"I think we're fighting," Mel whispered conspiratorially. "Don't you?"

Carrie nodded, smirking. "My thoughts exactly," she mouthed.

"Melissa?" Mrs. Eng called again.

"She isn't helping me, Mrs. Eng," Carrie shouted back.

"That's not *true*," Mel cried, getting into the act. "Carrie's lying. She's not studying at all. She's sitting at her desk, ignoring me."

"Come off it!" Carrie yelled. She was smiling now. "You've been acting like a jerk this whole time!"

Mel was smiling now as well. *"Me?"* she shrieked. "What about *you*—"

The door flew open.

Their smiles instantly vanished.

"What's going on in here?" Mrs. Mersel demanded, marching into the room. "Carrie—why aren't you studying?"

"I—I . . ." Carrie stammered, waving her hands dramatically.

Mel hopped off the bed. "I'm sorry, Mrs. Mersel," she said in a very cold and polite tone. "I think it would be best for all of us if I just left."

Mrs. Eng stepped through the doorway. "Melissa, what did I tell you about—"

"I'm *sorry*, Mom—but what do you want me to do?" Mel pleaded. "This *isn't* working out, okay? Can I please go home?"

Carrie's mom and Mrs. Eng exchanged glances.

Carrie held her breath.

"Maybe Mel should go home," Mrs. Mersel said slowly.

A sigh of relief escaped Carrie's lips. *Thank you, Mom.*

"And she can come back some other time," Mrs. Mersel finished.

Carrie's eyes bulged. "What?" she gasped.

Mrs. Mersel fixed Carrie with a frozen smile. "Some time when you aren't studying."

Carrie shot a horrified look at Mel, whose own face was wilting. "B-B-But—"

"Yes," Mrs. Eng stated. "I think that is an *excellent* idea."

"Mom!" Mel barked. "How can—"

"That's enough, Mel," Mrs. Eng continued, cutting her off. "There's no reason at all that you should keep acting so childish."

Carrie's heart sank. They just didn't get it. They didn't get that the two of them would never—no, *could* never—be friends. And if Carrie had to spend any more afternoons away from Alex and Sky and Jordan and Sam . . . well, they might start getting the wrong idea about her and Mel. Carrie swallowed. They weren't *already* getting the wrong idea, were they? She could just picture them hanging out at Alex's house and having an awesome time, wondering what she and Mel were really doing. . . .

"Whatever your differences are," Mrs. Eng concluded, "I just know you'll work them out."

Mrs. Mersel smiled broadly. "I couldn't agree more," she said. "You know the old saying: These things take time."

Mel

Dear Diary,
So . . . the nightmare
continues.

Our moms are obviously
in a state of denial. And
it's not like Carrie and I
haven't been trying. We
tried _everything_. Today we
even staged a major fight.
But the garden club
wonder twins still seem to
think that it's only a
matter of time before we go
skipping arm in arm into
the sunset together.

It's so incredibly . . .
I don't know. I'm more
frustrated than I've ever
been in my whole life. When
Carrie's mom said that
"these things take time" —
balaney, I wanted to _scream._

At least I know now that Amy was wrong. Carrie is not insane. I've had some firsthand experience with real live insanity in the past few days—and compared to our moms, Carrie is the most normal person in the whole world.

But you know what? All kidding aside, I'm a little worried. The more I hang out with Carrie, the less I hang out with my real friends. When Aimee made that crack on the bus today about my new "best buddy," I didn't give it a second thought. But now I can't _stop_ thinking about it. What if she wasn't joking? What if Amy and Aimee think that Carrie's lameness really _is_ rubbing off on me?

No. I know that's not true. Deep down, I know that I'm probably wigging out for no reason. But still, these kinds of thoughts have a way of creeping up on you and taking over your whole brain. . . .

Maybe that's why I also feel guilty. Because something else is bothering me, too. And it's something I can't admit to anyone—least of all Amy and Aimee.

I'm starting to think that Carrie isn't all that lame.

Like, she's really funny—in her own weird way, obviously. And when we staged that fight today . . . it was kind of like we were in on this private joke that nobody else in the world could possibly understand. We were united against our moms, but it was more than that. It was like there was this secret agreement between us. We _had_ to fight. That's because we can _never_ be friends. Our real friends would think we were both crazy.

And in this totally strange way, pretending that we hate each other makes us sort of like each other.

Well. _That_ makes no sense at all. I guess I already _am_ crazy. It wouldn't surprise me, though. Like mother, like daughter, right?

Eight

"Melissa . . . ?"

Mel shook her head. She was *not* going to answer. She was way too into *The Shining* right now to deal with her mom.

"Melissa? Are you up there?"

Mel doggedly clutched the book in front of her face. But she couldn't concentrate. Her mom's voice was like a needling, unscratchable itch. The whole reason she'd shut herself up in her room and buried herself in bed with this book was because she specifically wanted to *escape* from—

"Mel*issa!*"

"*What*, Mom?" Mel shouted, glaring at the closed door. She let the paperback fall to the pillow beside her. "I'm *reading*, okay?"

There was a pause.

"Oh." Her mom's voice suddenly sounded muted and faraway. "Never mind."

Mel sighed. She knew what *that* meant. It meant: *Get out of bed and come down here.* "What do you want?" she asked.

"No, don't worry—"

Thankfully the phone started ringing.

"I'll get it!" Mel cried. *That* would provide a convenient excuse to ignore her mom. She hopped out of bed, took three quick steps across her book-littered floor, then grabbed the phone off her desk. "Hello?"

"Hi. Is Mel there, please?"

Mel paused. It was a girl—but she couldn't place the voice. "This is Mel," she replied.

"Oh. Hey. It's Carrie."

Mel blinked. *Carrie?* A weird flutter passed through her stomach. Why was *she* calling? Hadn't they had enough of each other for one day?

"Is this a bad time?" Carrie asked in the silence.

"What do you want?" Mel whispered. She knew she sounded sort of harsh, but she couldn't help it. She was actually a little mad—not to mention nervous. Carrie shouldn't have called. This was wrong. If her mom knew that the two of them were talking, she might get all *sorts* of crazy ideas. . . .

"Look—you *are* a math whiz, right?" Carrie asked.

Mel frowned. That was a strange question. "Why?" she asked.

"Because I wanted to ask you a question about my geometry homework," Carrie said matter-of-factly. "I really *do* need help. I should have used you today when I had the chance."

"Oh." So this wasn't a social call. For some bizarre reason, Mel felt sort of let down. But why? It was only Carrie Mersel. Besides, her *friends* called her with math questions all the time. As a matter of fact, Amy needed help with her homework pretty much every single night.

Carrie sighed. "Look, if you're busy or something—"

"No, no," Mel interrupted.

"Are you sure?" Carrie asked.

"Yeah." Mel absently twirled the phone cord around her fingers. "Really. It's either help you with math or help my mom with some bogus chore, like rinsing out old mayonnaise jars for recycling."

Carrie chuckled. "You're on recycling detail, too, huh?"

"Don't get me started," Mel groaned. She eased herself down into her cushiony desk chair and shook her head. "That's the least of my problems."

"Do they make you take out the garbage?" Carrie asked.

Mel grinned slightly. "Let's just say that I'm the one who has to deal with all the foul substances in the Eng household."

"Me too. Whenever my dad finds something gross that was buried in the back of the fridge for years—like moldy cheese or something—my mom's like, 'Don't touch it, dear. Why do you think we have Carrie?'"

"Me too!" Mel said, laughing. "It's like my parents don't want to risk contamination, so they send me in to do all the hazardous stuff."

"Yeah, well, just wait till the garden club gets going full swing," Carrie muttered.

Mel stopped laughing. "What do you mean?" she asked.

"I bet we're gonna be forced to haul around sacks of horse manure," Carrie said. "They use that stuff for fertilizer, you know."

Mel grimaced. "You're kidding, right?"

"I wish I were." Carrie sighed. "You think it's bad right now. Come springtime, you and I are gonna be hanging out every single day. The only difference is that we're gonna be knee-deep in poop."

"Carrie, please . . . ," Mel protested, but she was giggling again. Even though Carrie was being disgusting, the whole thing *was* undeniably funny, in a twisted way. The thought of the two of *them* standing in a garden full of horse manure . . .

Mel was kind of surprised at herself. She *never* talked about really gross stuff like this. Of course, compared to Carrie, her friends were all a little prudish. So was she, for that matter.

"I'm just hoping my mom is gonna forget about gardening by then," Carrie added. "It isn't nearly high-tech enough for her. Plus, she's a total clean freak. She hates getting dirty."

"Mine too," Mel said dryly. "But that's why they need *us*. They're gonna sit back and watch while we do all the dirty work—"

"I thought you were reading, Melissa."

Mel glanced up with a start.

Her mom was standing in the doorway. She looked less than pleased, to say the least. Mel hadn't even heard her come in. Then again, her mom wasn't in the general habit of knocking.

"I'm on the phone, Mom," Mel hissed impatiently, cupping her hand over the mouthpiece.

"I *know.*" Mrs. Eng's eyebrows were tightly knit. "I can hear you chattering and laughing all the way downstairs." Then her face softened a little. "Look, just tell Amy you can talk to her tomorrow at school. I need you to help me with the garbage."

Mel smirked. So her mom had no idea that she was on the phone with Carrie. And that was good. What was bad was that her mom really *did* want her to do something nasty.

"What's up?" Carrie whispered at the other end.

Mrs. Eng stood in the door, waiting.

"I . . . uh, gotta go," Mel mumbled.

"Is your mom there?" Carrie asked.

Mel let out a deep breath. "Exactly."

"That's cool," Carrie said. "Look, uh—I'll just call someone else. I'll talk to you later."

"Bye," Mel murmured. She placed the phone down on the hook.

Mrs. Eng turned and headed back downstairs. "Let's go," she called. "It won't take long. When you're done with the garbage, you can clean your room."

"Gee—thanks, Mom," Mel muttered sarcastically.

Nag, nag, nag. Her gaze swept the floor. Her room wasn't *that* messy, was it? So there were a bunch of books on the floor. And Mr. Bubbles, her stuffed monkey, had fallen off the bed . . . but that was about it. She wondered for a moment if Carrie's mom nagged her as much. Probably not. Carrie's room wasn't very disorganized. There wasn't a whole lot of junk in Carrie's room left over from the second grade, like there was in here.

"Come on, Melissa," her mom called.

"In a minute." Mel shook her head. Maybe she *should* get rid of some of her model ponies and stuffed animals. Besides, if anyone besides Amy and Aimee ever found out she slept with a big fluffy monkey named Mr. Bubbles, her reputation as one of the hippest, coolest, most mature girls in the state of Washington would probably be shot. She could just imagine what Carrie would think.

Hold on, she said to herself angrily.

Why would she even *care* what Carrie thought? They *weren't* friends. Okay, talking to her on the phone was fun. She *was* easy to talk to. But that was just because Mel didn't have to act any kind of certain way around her. Carrie was just another loser. More importantly, she was one of Amy Anderson's worst enemies. And any enemy of Amy's was also an enemy of Mel's.

"Melissa!" her mom yelled.

"Coming!" Mel pushed herself to her feet and determinedly marched out the door. *I don't like Carrie Mersel*, she swore to herself. *I'm not becoming friends with her. . . .*

But even as she silently uttered the words, she had a horrible feeling that they weren't true.

Nine

When Carrie got off the bus in front of Sky's houseboat that Tuesday afternoon, it was like coming home after a long vacation. Finally everything was *right* again. Once again, she was hanging out with Alex and Sky after school. Once again, it was pouring rain.

The three of them scampered down the narrow rain-slicked dock and held their book bags over their heads in a lame attempt to keep dry—the way they always did.

Yup. Life was back to normal.

"Whew," Sky said breathlessly, shutting the door behind them. She tossed her book bag on the floor, then wiggled her long, damp, curly brown hair—just like a wet puppy dog. Water splattered all over the place.

"Hey!" Alex cried.

"What?" Sky rubbed her face with the sleeve of her brown sweater and grinned. "You're already wet."

Alex laughed. "Yeah, but I kind of want to start drying off. . . ."

All of a sudden, Carrie noticed something. Alex was decked out in her usual tomboy garb—baggy black pants, a soaked black T-shirt, sneakers—but one vital piece of her wardrobe was missing. It was the green Supersonics cap she had stolen from her older brother, Matt. She *always* wore that hat when it rained. But today, her shoulder-length brown hair was uncovered, dripping, and plastered to the sides of her head.

"Where's your hat?" Carrie asked.

Alex flashed her a puzzled glance. "I didn't tell you?"

Carrie shook her head.

"Oh, *man* . . . ," she groaned.

"What?" Carrie asked.

Alex shook her head. "It's at the bottom of the sound," she mumbled.

"The *sound?*" Carrie asked incredulously.

Alex looked at Sky—and the two of them started cracking up.

"What happened?" Carrie asked.

Alex took a deep breath. "It's all Jordan's fault," she mumbled, collapsing onto the brown sofa in the little main cabin.

"We should have never let him near the grill," Sky added, sitting beside her.

Carrie just stood there, feeling completely clueless. "What did he do?"

"It happened Friday—when you were with Mel," Sky explained. "He had the spatula, right? See, he was cooking the burgers because my dad doesn't even really know *how* to cook burgers. . . ."

"And he started waving the spatula around," Alex continued. "You know, acting like a total goof, as usual."

"He kept saying something, too," Sky said distractedly. She started laughing again. "It was like a rap. Something about 'The chef is cookin' and the burgers is smokin'—I'm the best and I ain't jokin'.'"

Alex rolled her eyes. "Something dorky."

Carrie was smiling along with them, but the more they talked, the more she began to feel an odd sort of emptiness inside. Her smile became strained. Whatever Jordan had done had obviously been really funny. And she had totally missed out on it.

"So anyway," Alex went on, "Jordan starts flipping burgers. But he's out of control. Finally one goes over the side of the boat and *plop*—right into the water. Everybody starts yelling, but Jordan doesn't stop. The next one goes into the air. I make a dive for it. But Jordan does, too. *With* the spatula. So we go slamming into each other, and the spatula catches the bill of my hat . . . and, well, you can guess the rest. The hat sunk like a stone when it hit the water. The burgers floated, but my hat sunk." She giggled. "Can you believe that?"

Carrie just shrugged.

"It was totally amazing," Sky said. "It was like one of those slow-motion replays you see at a football game. The hat goes flying, and the burger goes flying, and these two things are, like, hanging in the air, and everybody is freaking out. . . ."

Carrie swallowed. She couldn't smile anymore. And she was angry, too, because she couldn't figure out *why* she was so upset. So she had missed something funny. Big deal. It wasn't as if Jordan's dumb antics had changed anybody's life in any major way. But she felt . . . *outside* somehow. She wasn't a part of this. And there was nothing she could do to *become* a part of it. She couldn't change the past.

"Hey, Carrie—are you all right?" Alex asked.

"Huh?" Carrie glanced at the two of them.

They were both staring at her with these alarmed looks on their faces. She hadn't even noticed.

She shook her head, forcing herself to smile again. "Uh . . . yeah," she mumbled. "I was just thinking about how I'm going to have to hang out with Mel. *Again*."

Alex nodded thoughtfully. She scooted over into the middle of the couch and slapped the empty spot, moist now from her wet clothes.

Carrie sighed and slumped down beside her.

"You're really bummed, huh?" Alex murmured.

Carrie nodded. That was true—to some extent. She *was* bummed that she would have to miss another afternoon with Sky and Alex. Of course, she wasn't dreading this visit with Mel nearly as much as she had dreaded the last one.

"What happened yesterday, anyway?" Sky asked. "Did Mel throw another fit?"

Carrie hesitated for a moment. Her eyes

wandered out the window—through the rain to where Puget Sound met the sky in a seamless blur of dull gray. Once again, it was time to spin a tale about Mel. So why wasn't she psyched? Yesterday, she'd had the time of her life talking about Mel. But that was before last night's phone call and the fake fight.

"We got in a fight," she said finally.

"Lemme guess." Alex gave her a meaningful look. "Mel started it."

Carrie shrugged. "Actually, her mom kind of started it. See, I was just looking for an excuse to avoid hanging out with her, so I told everyone that I had to do math homework. Then Mrs. Eng was like, 'Oh— Mel's a math genius. She'll help you.'"

"And?" Sky prodded. She leaned forward, twirling her hair around her fingers.

"And . . . she came up to my room and made a point of calling me an idiot, like, a million times," Carrie lied. She smirked halfheartedly. "Of course, *she's* failing geography."

"She *is?*" Alex laughed once. "Now *there's* something I didn't know. I thought all The Amys were total brainiacs."

Carrie lowered her eyes, staring at the

worn knees of her black corduroys. "Not all of them," she said quietly.

Alex shook her head. "So did she help you?"

"Are you kidding? I wasn't about to let Mel Eng become my math tutor," she lied. "I'd rather fail the eighth grade."

"What other dirt did you find out?" Sky blurted impatiently.

Carrie paused. "Dirt?"

"The dirt on *Mel*. You must know some more juicy gossip about her, right?" Sky cocked her eyebrow. "Or at least about Amy Anderson or Aimee Stewart?"

"Oh . . ." Carrie looked at her lap again.

Yesterday, she wouldn't have hesitated to make up something about Mel on the spot.

But now . . . now she couldn't. The only juicy gossip was that she and Mel Eng got along. Of course, that *would* qualify as "dirt" as far as her friends were concerned. That was the dirtiest secret of all.

"Well?" Sky asked.

Carrie shook her head. "There's really nothing," she breathed.

"Mel wouldn't tell you anything,

anyway," Alex said. "Why would she? You guys hate each other."

Carrie winced. She suddenly wished she was far away from this boat. It was crazy. *These* were her friends. But Alex's words made her very, very uncomfortable. She'd never felt more confused in her life.

She thought that if she could just hang out with Alex and Sky and Jordan and Sam, everything would be fine. Life would be back to normal.

But life was *not* back to normal—not by a long shot.

Ten

Mel couldn't concentrate. It was a little scary. She *never* lost her focus when it came to planning the layout for the *Robert Lowell Observer*. In three whole years of staying after school every other Tuesday to work on the newspaper with Amy and Aimee, she had always been razor sharp. They *all* had. That was why Principal Cashen had named the three of them joint editors in chief at the beginning of the semester.

It was a perfect situation: The most popular girls in school now controlled the *Robert Lowell Observer* from start to finish. Mel knew that she couldn't have *dreamed* of anything better. She had the freedom to print pretty much whatever she wanted. So why couldn't she just shove her stupid personal problems aside and *enjoy* it?

"... Hello ... uh, Mel? Are you with us, Mel?"

Mel blinked and shook her head.

"Sorry," she murmured. "What was that?"

Amy and Aimee exchanged an annoyed glance. The three of them had been sitting cross-legged on the gray tile floor of the art studio for the past forty-five minutes, putting different parts of the paper together under the pale glow of fluorescent lights. But Mel hadn't been much help. She'd spent most of the time staring out the windows at the rain, trying to figure out how she would avoid going to the Mersels' house tomorrow afternoon.

"Where do you think the sports page should go?" Aimee asked.

Mel shrugged. "I'm sorry. I . . . uh, wasn't listening."

"No duh." Aimee sat up straight and peered at Mel closely. "Are you all right?"

Mel lowered her eyes. "I'm just a little out of it," she mumbled.

"She's got PCSD," Amy announced.

"I've got *what?*" Mel asked, frowning.

"Post-Carrie Stress Disorder," Amy explained casually. A thin smile appeared on her lips. "It comes from spending too much time with a certain . . . shall we say, *garden*-variety loser. Symptoms include depression, a tendency to wig out for no apparent reason, becoming a space cadet—"

"All right, all right," Mel grumbled. "Joke's over."

Amy raised her eyebrows, glancing at Aimee. "Touchy, aren't we?"

"Well, excuse me," Mel said. Her tone was flat. "I thought we had better things to do than talk about Carrie Mersel."

Amy's steely blue eyes met hers. She blinked a few times. "We do," she said calmly. "*We* aren't the ones who are spacing out."

"I'm *sorry*, all right?" Mel growled. "Jeez... how many times do I have to *say* it?" She forced herself to look at the big blank sheets of newsprint spread out in front of them.

"You know, I noticed something," Amy said in a toneless voice. "You haven't said one word all day about yesterday's date with the Mersels. Don't you have anything to tell us?"

Mel didn't look up. *Great.* She knew this was going to happen sooner or later. She'd avoided it at lunch, because Amy had spent the whole time babbling about some cute guy she'd seen in a movie the afternoon before. But now...

"Carrie?" Amy prodded.

"There's nothing to tell, really," Mel grumbled. "I went to Carrie's house—and it was even more lame the second time around. End of story."

"Come on, Mel," Aimee whined. "*Something* must have happened."

Carrie squeezed her eyes shut, then let out a deep breath. "I'm telling you, *nothing* happened. Carrie had to study for some math quiz. My mom—"

"Math quiz?" Amy interrupted. "That's impossible. Carrie and I both have Mr. Engel. *We* didn't have any quiz in *my* class."

Mel opened her eyes. She couldn't believe this. They actually thought she was lying. Now, of all times, when she was telling the truth.

"She was making it up," Mel explained. "You know—to avoid hanging out with me. So my mom was like, 'Mel will help you study.' Then Carrie had to admit she was lying, and we got into a fight, and I went home. My mom is making me go back there tomorrow. Satisfied?"

Neither of them said anything.

Mel breathed a secret sigh of relief. *Finally.*

"So," she said after a minute. "We were talking about the sports page. . . ."

"Right," Amy replied in a very businesslike manner. "The sports page." She tossed her head back and yanked a fuzzy hairband out of her jeans pocket—then in one single and amazingly graceful maneuver, she pulled her long blond locks into a perfect ponytail. "I think we should scrap it altogether."

Mel's eyes narrowed. *That* made no sense.

"Uh . . . scrap it?" Aimee asked.

Amy leaned over the paper again. "That's right. I want to run a full-page ad instead."

"A full-page ad," Mel repeated blankly. She turned to Aimee. But Aimee looked just as baffled as *she* did.

Amy looked up and flashed them both a wicked grin. "I've got a plan."

Uh-oh. Mel knew that look on Amy's face all too well. It usually appeared right before she suggested something totally outrageous.

"What is it?" Aimee whispered.

Amy took a deep breath. Mel couldn't remember the last time Amy had looked so pleased with herself. But in spite of her foul mood, Mel actually found herself smiling as well. A full-page ad? This was going to be crazy.

"Well, I was thinking," Amy began slowly. "We never run any personals. You know: 'Eighth-grade geek seeks beautiful sixth-grade girl to share a lifetime of crossword puzzles, zit medicine, and polyester Hawaiian shirts.'"

Aimee's brow became slightly furrowed. "You want to run personals for losers?"

"Aimee, please," Amy scolded jokingly. "I think it's about time we reached out to Robert Lowell's romantically challenged, don't you?" Her voice grew serious. "As editors in chief, we have a duty to serve the school community. That includes losers as well. We can't be prejudiced."

Mel smirked. "Right," she said. "And you really expect people to run personal ads? Do you know how *embarrassing* that would be?"

"You're absolutely right, Mel," Amy stated. "That's why *we* need to do it for them."

Mel stared at her. She started laughing. "Are you saying . . . ?"

"I'm saying that in the next issue of the *Robert Lowell Observer*, we're going to run a full-page personal ad that will feature a very special person making a very special request for love."

Aimee was giggling now, too. "Who?"

"Who do you think?" Amy raised her hands and looked Mel directly in the eye. "Mel's brand-new best friend. Carrie Mersel."

Eleven

Mel stopped laughing. "Carrie Mersel?" she repeated.

Amy didn't even blink. "Of course," she said simply. "Who else?"

Mel's stomach twisted queasily. She should have known. Whenever Amy had something up her sleeve these days, it was *always* directed at Carrie. After all, Carrie *was* Amy's biggest enemy. Mel had said those exact words to herself only yesterday. And she swore to herself that Carrie was *her* enemy, too. But pulling this kind of prank wouldn't do any good. Pranks like this only accomplished one thing in the long run: a full-fledged prank war. Amy and Carrie were almost at that stage already.

"Is there a problem?" Amy asked as innocently and politely as ever.

Mel hesitated. "Well, what are you planning to *say* in the ad, exactly?" she asked.

Amy chuckled. "I have it all planned out." She pointed to one of the big blank sheets of newsprint on the floor. "There's gonna be a huge photo of Carrie that takes up the entire page. Then there's going to be a caption that says, 'Hi! I'm Carrie Mersel, and I'm really, really desperate for a man. This is no joke. So if you are male, under the age of seventy, and have an IQ of more than ten, I'll take you. As you can tell from the picture, weight is not an issue."

Mel's mouth fell open. She was too horrified to respond. That was sick.

Aimee clapped her hands delightedly. "That is *awesome!* Do you have a picture?"

"Not yet," she replied. She raised her eyes to Mel. "That's where *you* come in."

Mel was already shaking her head.

"Don't look so *freaked*, Mel," Amy teased. "It'll be easy. You just have to do one simple thing. Do the Mersels have any photographs of Carrie on their walls or in frames or anything?"

"How should I know?" she muttered dismally. "I never bothered to look."

Amy sighed. "Well, when you go over there tomorrow, *look*, all right? Because you're gonna have to grab a picture of her and sneak it out of her house. And try to look for a black-and-white one that was taken in the last few months if you—"

"No," Mel interrupted, glowering. "I am not going to *steal* something from the Mersels. Do you have any idea how much trouble I'd get into if I got caught?"

"You're *not* going to get caught," Amy mumbled irritably. "You're too *smart* to get caught."

"Amy—that-that's not even the *point*," Mel stammered. "Stealing is *wrong*, all right? I've never stolen anything in my life."

But Amy just laughed. "You're not going to be *stealing*, Mel." She sounded as if she was talking to somebody incredibly stupid—like Jordan Sullivan or something. "You're gonna be *borrowing*. You're just gonna bring the photo in here so I can make a photocopy of it and blow it up for the paper. As soon as I'm done, you can take it back."

Mel didn't even answer. She was no longer nervous—she was *angry*. Did Amy really think she would "borrow" a picture of Carrie from the Mersels just so Amy could pull off the cruelest, most . . . *low* prank Mel had ever heard of? Well, she wasn't going to have any part in it. She didn't care *what* Amy thought.

"See, I knew these little get-togethers would come in handy," Amy continued. She had a smug and self-satisfied smile, as if nothing was wrong at all. "I actually got the idea yesterday at lunch, when you started telling me about what happened at that first visit. I mean, knowing that you were actually in Carrie's *house*, well, the possibilities—"

"Don't you think we're gonna get in trouble for putting a fake personal ad in the school paper?" Mel snapped.

Amy made a face. "Excuse me?"

"You heard me," Mel said. Her voice was quavering slightly.

"We're the editors in chief, Mel," she replied. Her voice was cold. "We can do whatever we want."

"Yeah, Mel—what's your problem?" Aimee demanded. "Why are you wigging out?"

"Wigging *out*?" Mel cried. "*You're* the ones who are wigging out. A prank is one thing, but this is too much. Pranks are supposed to be funny. This isn't funny at all. It's just plain *mean*. That's all it is."

Amy's lips twitched. Her blue eyes were blazing. "You've got some nerve," she hissed.

Mel swallowed. "What? I'm telling you—"

"What about what *Carrie* did?" Amy spat. "She pasted that horrible picture of me up on my locker for the whole world to see the first week of school. Do you even have the slightest idea how *embarrassing* that was? What's the difference between what Carrie did to me and what *we're* gonna do to her?"

Mel didn't answer. When Amy thought she was right, Mel knew that there was no point in arguing. But she was starting to get a little nervous. Amy was *mad*—probably more mad than Mel had ever seen her. Aimee was shaking her head in disappointment.

"What's wrong with you, Mel?" Amy's voice rose to a shout. "If you had any kind of backbone at all, you would—"

"It has nothing to *do* with backbone!" Mel yelled back.

Amy blinked once. Then she pushed herself to her feet. She jerked a finger toward the door. "I want you to leave," she stated quietly.

Mel just gaped at her.

"I'm serious."

Mel shook her head. How did this happen? Why were they fighting—over *this?* "Amy . . ."

"You know, I guess your mom's little scheme worked," Amy said with a cruel smile. "You *are* friends with Carrie Mersel."

The color drained from Mel's face. *No . . .*

She felt sick. She couldn't believe it. Her worst nightmare was coming true—right here, right before her eyes. Amy *did* think Carrie had rubbed off on her.

"That's what happened, isn't it?" Amy whispered.

"No," Mel said in a hollow voice. Her throat was dry. "That's not what—"

"Don't even try it, Mel," Amy said dismissively. "You've always been a total softy. But the fact that you became friends with Carrie isn't even the point. The point is, we're *going* to pull a prank on her—whether you like it or not." She shrugged. "And we can't exactly discuss it if one of her *friends* is around, can we?"

Mel shook her head again, desperately. "I'm not her *friend*," she insisted.

89

"Whatever, Mel," Amy said in a dull voice. She waved her hand at the door again. "But you still gotta beat it."

Mel gave Aimee one last despairing look. But she knew it was hopeless. Aimee wouldn't even return her gaze. Besides, Aimee would never side with Mel over Amy—not in a million years. Aimee wouldn't side with *herself* over Amy. She lived for Amy Anderson, plain and simple.

"We're waiting," Amy said.

"What about the newspaper?" Mel croaked. Her eyes were starting to moisten.

"We'll finish it," Amy stated tonelessly. "Don't worry about that. You weren't much help to us today, anyway."

Mel opened her mouth one last time, but no words would come.

What could she say? She stumbled to her feet, sniffing. *Why are you doing this to me?* she wondered. *Why . . .*

"Oh yeah—Mel?" Amy said.

Mel hesitated. There was silence. Rain pounded incessantly against the windows. Still, one last tiny flame of hope flickered inside her.

"Be sure to shut the door on your way out."

Mel

Dear Diary,

So it's pouring rain right now, and I'm sitting here at my desk, and I think I might start crying.

But you want to know the crazy thing? I can't stop thinking about this cheesy eighties movie I once saw. I can't even remember the name of it. All I remember is that I was flipping through the channels on a rainy afternoon just like this one, and I ended up watching this really bad movie.

One scene keeps flashing through my mind. A really beautiful girl is having a fight with a really good-looking guy. I think they were fighting about money. It must have been about money, because they were both throwing a lot of expensive china at each other.

Anyway, the scene ends with the girl saying: "When you've had money and lost it, it's a whole lot worse than not having had it at all."

That's <u>exactly</u> the way I feel about popularity.

Just substitute the word <u>popularity</u> for <u>money</u>, and I could have been the girl in that scene. The point is that in one incredibly stupid move, I lost my two best friends. I had it all—and now it's gone. Even the biggest losers at Robert Lowell are better off than I am. Everybody has <u>someone</u>. Everybody has at least one other person to talk to. But not me. I have nobody.

Okay, I still have Mr. Bubbles. But how pathetic is <u>that?</u>

I feel as though I should be angry at someone. I guess I <u>am</u> angry at my mom. If my mom hadn't met Mrs. Mersel, none of this would have happened. But the truth is that I'm too depressed to be angry. Besides, if there's one thing I've learned, it's that you can't say "what if." Those two words never get you anywhere.

So now I have a decision to make.

Either I beg Amy to forgive me and go along with her prank, or I tell Carrie.

Neither of those choices is very appealing.

The thing I want most is to be friends with Amy again, obviously. And it's not even like the idea of a prank on Carrie bothers me all that much. I don't have any loyalty to Carrie.

No, it's the prank itself. I don't think it's fair. Having your picture in the school newspaper with the words "I desperately need a man" is _much_ more embarrassing than anything that has happened to Amy — no matter what she says. It's the kind of thing that can really hurt someone. And I don't want to do that. Not to Carrie, not to anyone.

But one thing I do know is that I am _not_ going to give up my friendship with Amy. My friendship with Amy is the most important thing in the world.

So what am I going to do? How did I even get into this mess?

It doesn't matter. What matters is that Amy and I become friends again. And you know what? I'm pretty much prepared to do anything. That scares me.

It scares me because if things get worse, I might start thinking that Amy's prank isn't so bad.

Wednesday:

Decisions, Decisions . . .

8:27 A.M. Mel boards the bus. Aimee boards a few seconds later—but sits in Amy's seat, without a glance in Mel's direction.

8:31 A.M. Amy boards the bus and sits next to Aimee. She ignores Mel, too. For the first time ever, Mel is alone on Bus #4.

8:32 A.M. Carrie boards the bus, casts a sidelong glance at Mel, and hurries to the backseat.

8:35 A.M. Sky boards the bus, stares confusedly at Mel for several seconds, then hurries to the backseat.

8:36 A.M. Sky wants to know why Mel isn't sitting with Aimee. She pesters Carrie about it until they get to school.

8:45 A.M. Aimee informs Amy that she brought a Polaroid camera to school today to take a certain girl's picture for a certain personal ad. Amy is extremely pleased.

10:15 A.M. Mel leaves a note in Amy's locker:

I'm so sorry about
what happened yesterday.
I acted like a jerk. I
want to talk to you and
straighten this out before
I really wig out.
                              Mel

10:55 A.M. Amy finds Mel's note and stuffs it in her pocket.

11:03 A.M. Carrie listens in horror as Mr. Engel announces a "comprehensive" geometry exam this coming Friday.

11:41 A.M. Amy bumps into Aimee in the hall and shows her Mel's note. The two of them shake their heads. Doesn't Mel understand? She already *has* wigged out.

12:31 P.M. Sky wants to know if she can come over to Carrie's this afternoon and watch MTV. The cast members of *Friends* are going to be guest veejays. Carrie glumly informs her that she'll have to watch somewhere else. Carrie has plans—with the Engs.

12:32 P.M. Mel sits with Amy and Aimee. Neither of them says a word.

12:43 P.M. Carrie hangs her head in misery as Sky makes plans with Alex, Jordan, and Sam to watch MTV at Alex's house. Once again, she'll be missing out.

12:50 P.M. Amy and Aimee finish their lunches and leave the table without saying good-bye.

12:54 P.M. Sky instructs Carrie to use her visit with Mel to find out what's going on with The Amys. Carrie is briefly tempted to throw her applesauce in Sky's face.

1:35 P.M. Amy listens in horror as Mr. Engel announces a "comprehensive" geometry exam this coming Friday.

2:32 P.M. Mel goes to the girls' bathroom and flips a coin. Heads, she'll tell Carrie; tails, she'll go along with the prank. After five heads and five tails, she gives up.

3:14 P.M. Aimee wants to take Carrie's picture as soon as Carrie leaves the school building, but Amy can hardly think about the prank. She's *way* too freaked about the geometry exam.

3:15 P.M. Aimee snaps a bunch of photos, anyway, just as Carrie dashes down the front steps to Bus #4.

Twelve

"This is so totally weird," Sky kept whispering as the bus rattled up Pike's Way. Her gaze was locked on Mel, as if she were a moth and the back of Mel's head were a giant hundred-watt lightbulb. "Mel is sitting by herself again. I can't get over it—"

"Will you give it a *rest* already?" Carrie moaned.

Sky looked at her. Her eyes widened.

Carrie glanced around the backseat. Alex was looking at her, too. So were Sam and Jordan. Everyone was staring at her as if she were a lunatic. Great. Not only was she spending less and less time with her friends, but they all thought she was losing her mind.

"Sorry," she muttered. She managed a tired grin. "Look—maybe she's just embarrassed because she stained her shirt at lunch or something."

Jordan smiled. "Mel Eng's a slob?"

Carrie rolled her eyes.

"Listen, I'm sorry to keep harping on this Mel thing," Sky said, leaning back into the seat. Her eyes wandered up the aisle again. "But I'm totally fascinated by it. You have to admit, this is *epic* in the history of Robert Lowell. The Amys have never, ever turned on each other. *Ever.*"

For a moment, Carrie was half tempted to say: *So?* But the truth was that she couldn't stop thinking about the "Mel thing," either. She just didn't want to admit *why*—to herself or to anyone else.

Part of it was guilt, of course. She was positive that the other Amys were dissing Mel because of *her*. Amy probably thought that Mel's soul had been polluted from spending too much time with somebody who didn't have a J. Crew catalog. And even though Carrie knew she shouldn't have given a sack of horse poop about *what* The Amys thought, she didn't want to be responsible for ruining somebody's social life, either.

But the other reason—the *scarier* reason— was that she could see herself in Mel's position. She could see herself being shut out. What if Alex, Sky, Jordan, and Sam started to get suspicious of her? What if they thought

100

that her personality was changing because she was hanging out with Mel so much? Would they still want to cram into the backseat with her every morning and afternoon? Maybe they wouldn't. Maybe she and Mel would wind up sitting together.

"You know, now that Mel's out of the picture, I think *I'm* gonna become one of The Amys," Jordan stated. "They could use a guy, and I think—"

Sky slapped him on the arm.

"Ow!" he yelped, laughing. "What? It makes perfect sense. I've got dirty blond hair and green eyes, just like Aimee Stewart. And I'm smooth-talking and slick, just like Amy—"

"You're just saying that because you have a crush on both of them," Sky interrupted with a smirk.

Jordan started shaking his head, but his face had turned slightly pink.

"Aha!" Sky teased. She nudged Carrie. "See! He's blushing. . . ."

Carrie tried to smile, but she couldn't. For some reason, she was beginning to feel empty again—the way she'd felt yesterday on Sky's boat. It didn't make any sense. She was *here*, with her friends. But she felt awkward, removed from the action. She almost felt as if she were watching a home movie of the four of them. Somehow, *knowing* she was about to miss out was just as bad as missing out itself.

"Enough with this crush stuff," Sam said in a deadpan voice from the other end of the seat. A few tufts of his spiky black hair poked out from behind Jordan. "I think I might yack. I don't want to think about Jordan and Amy Anderson. It's too gross. I mean, imagine what their kids would be like."

"Eww!" Sky whispered.

Alex laughed once. "Yeah—they'd be really horrible saxophone players who spent all their time watching lame soap operas."

Jordan shook his head. "Man. You guys are so lost. If me and Amy Anderson had kids, they'd be the coolest kids on the block. They'd be sharp-dressed, sharp-witted, amazing-looking basketball stars who . . ." He stopped in midsentence.

A hush fell over the backseat.

Carrie looked up. She hadn't even noticed—but the bus was already turning onto Whidbey Road. Her face fell.

Home at last, she thought grimly.

"See you guys later," she murmured. She

slung her book bag over her shoulder and began the long march up the front aisle.

"Bye, Carrie," they called in unison.

Carrie shook her head. Even *that* was depressing. They sounded like four parts of the same being—not four separate people. She just wished she wouldn't have to say anything to Mel. But Mel leaped up and bolted out before Carrie was even halfway to the door.

"Have fun!" Aimee said brightly as Carrie walked past her.

Carrie paused on the stairs and flashed her a wide smile. "Drop dead!" she cried in the exact same voice.

"Hey," Brick protested. "That's not . . ."

But Carrie was already on her way up the driveway. Mel wouldn't even look at her as the two of them made their way to the front door. Of course, Carrie wasn't surprised that Mel wasn't so happy. *She* didn't have any friends anymore.

But Carrie was *not* going to let that happen to her. Because today she was going to do something so awful, so ill-mannered, so *offensive* that Mel and Mrs. Eng would never want to set foot in this house again.

She wasn't sure what yet—but she'd think of something. She didn't have a choice.

Thirteen

"Hi, you two!" Mrs. Mersel sang out from the kitchen. She strode into the front hall. "So what do you think . . . ?"

Carrie's jaw dropped. She didn't know whether to start laughing or to call the nearest mental institution. For a second, she even forgot about Mel. Her mom was decked out in a pair of jeans, a paint-splattered sweatshirt, and ridiculous rubber boots. A blue bandanna covered her head. Her long blond hair was actually pulled back into a *ponytail*.

"So?" Mrs. Mersel prodded hopefully. "Do I look like a real gardener? Give me your honest opinion."

"I'm . . . uh, speechless," Carrie muttered. She shot a quick glance at Mel. But Mel didn't seem to care. Then again, Mel had no idea that Elizabeth Mersel hadn't worn anything but the latest businesswear since the late seventies.

"I'll take that as a compliment," Mrs. Mersel said.

"Hi, girls," Mrs. Eng called from the living room.

Carrie wrenched her eyes away from her mother. Mel's mom looked bizarre, too. What was going on here? Mrs. Eng was wearing a grubby pair of sweatpants and a flannel shirt—and the same shiny and totally absurd rubber boots as Carrie's mom.

At least *now* Mel was shocked—or amused, anyway.

"Um, are you gardening in our backyard or something?" Carrie asked as Mrs. Eng joined them in the hall.

"As a matter of fact, we're on our way out the door," Mrs. Mersel said. She grabbed her purse off the glass end table in the front hall and slung it over her shoulder. "There's a—"

"Wait a minute," Carrie interrupted, totally bewildered. "You're *leaving*?"

"Yes, dear," her mom said matter-of-factly. "Today we're learning how to plant basil and other herbs. We're due at Celia Tucker's house in Tacoma in less than an hour."

"But—but I thought the garden club met on Thursdays," Carrie stammered. This was insane. They *couldn't* leave. How was Carrie supposed to offend Mrs. Eng and her own mom if they weren't even *here?*

Mrs. Mersel shrugged. "There's a chance it might rain tomorrow, so we all decided to have our lesson a day early—"

"You're going all the way to Tacoma?" Mel cried, finally opening her mouth for the first time. "What are *we* supposed to do?"

"Calm *down*, Melissa," her mom said firmly. "You two will be just fine."

"Don't you see? This is the best possible situation for all of us." Mrs. Mersel flashed both Carrie and Mel a brief smile. "You two can make a fresh start. You'll have the whole house to yourselves for the next few hours. Why don't you watch a video? Or you can surf the Net or . . ."

Carrie couldn't listen. One thought kept running through her mind: Her plan was ruined.

". . . And there's plenty of food in the fridge," Mrs. Mersel concluded. She pushed the door open, letting Mrs. Eng out first. "So have fun!"

"Fun?" Carrie croaked. Her mom sounded exactly like Aimee Stewart.

"I'll be back no later than eight o'clock, Melissa," Mrs. Eng said with a backward wave over her shoulder.

Mel shook her head. "But—"

The door swung shut.

Carrie took a deep breath. It had all happened so fast—too fast to fully grasp the reality of the situation.

She turned to Mel. Her eyes roved over Mel's entire body—over Mel's beige turtleneck sweater and matching beige pants. In a way, she almost expected to wake up in bed. She couldn't be standing here by herself with Mel Eng. It was too crazy.

This can't be happening. This has to be some terrible nightmare. . . .

But it wasn't.

Carrie was stuck with Mel for the rest of the afternoon and evening . . . and probably the rest of her life, too.

Fourteen

For a few long moments, the two of them stood in the silent peach-and-white-checkered hall and stared at each other.

Finally Carrie shook her head. "How could they do this?" she breathed.

Mel looked at the floor. "Well, there's nothing we can do about it now," she said quietly.

"I guess you have a point," Carrie replied in a strained voice. She slipped off of her book bag, then tossed it onto the stairs and forced herself to walk toward the kitchen. *You are not going to freak out*, she commanded herself. *You are just going to pretend like nothing is wrong.*

"Are you hungry at all?" she asked as politely as she could. "I think we have—"

"Carrie, wait."

She froze in her tracks. There was a harsh edge in Mel's voice. What was her problem? Provoking each other wouldn't do either of them any good. It was tense enough in here already. Besides, nobody would be around to witness a fight.

"What?" Carrie asked flatly.

"I . . . uh, I wanted to give you back *The Shining*," Mel said. She didn't sound mad, but she didn't sound overly friendly, either. "I think . . . you should have it back."

Carrie glanced over her shoulder. Mel was hunched over on the floor, going through her bag. After a few seconds, she pulled out the worn paperback and held it up in front of her.

"Here," she said.

Carrie didn't move at first. Why was Mel giving her back the book *now?* It didn't make much sense—considering the circumstances. If anything, Mel should have held on to it so she'd have something to do for the next few hours.

"Are you done with it?" Carrie asked.

Mel shook her head. "No."

Carrie frowned. "So why—"

"I just want you to *have* it, all right?" Mel stood up and shoved the book into Carrie's hands. "Do I have to explain every little thing that I do to *you?*"

Mel's face was now less than a foot from Carrie's own. And Carrie could tell right then that something *serious* was bothering her—something *way* more serious than the book . . . and maybe even something more serious than being stuck alone in this house. Mel's lips were twitching. Her forehead was creased. . . .

The Amys.

Of course. Carrie had been so rattled by her mom that she'd forgotten the obvious. Mel blamed *her* for all her problems. Mel blamed *her* for getting dumped by Amy and Aimee.

"Look, Mel," Carrie said carefully, taking the book. "I'm sorry if, you know . . . if this whole thing with our mothers has caused any problems between you and your friends." She lowered her eyes. "But you shouldn't blame me—"

Mel suddenly laughed.

Carrie made a face. "What?"

Mel didn't answer. She just sighed hopelessly, then marched into the living room. "You have no idea what you're even talking about," she muttered.

"What is *that* supposed to mean?" Carrie demanded.

Mel plopped herself down onto the peach couch and stared morosely at the carpet. "It's just that 'this whole thing'—as you call it—is much more complicated than you realize."

"Complicated?" Carrie stood in the hall, glaring at her. Mel wasn't making any sense at all.

"Just forget it," Mel said quietly. "It doesn't even matter."

"*What* doesn't matter?" Carrie cried. "Will you stop acting like a jerk and *tell* me?"

Mel glanced up at her and opened her mouth, then closed it. She chewed her lip. Then she took a deep breath and said, "Let me ask you something. What's the worst thing you would do to get somebody back for something bad they did to you?"

Carrie took a step back. *Whoa.* Where had *that* come from? The worst thing Carrie would do . . . What kind of a quesion was that? It sounded like the kind of thing a demented killer would say in a made-for-TV movie. This conversation was actually starting to give her the creeps.

"Well?" Mel asked.

"I didn't know we were playing 'Truth or Dare,'" Carrie mumbled.

Mel shook her head. She fidgeted restlessly on the couch—fiddling one moment with the hem of her turtleneck, the next with the crease in her pants—never keeping still for more than an instant. "Just answer the question," she insisted.

"I . . . I don't know," Carrie stammered clumsily. "It's not like I have a ready-made answer or anything. Why do you want to know?"

"Because it's *important*," Mel stated.

"Well, it's important to me to know why you're asking," Carrie replied. She tossed *The Shining* onto the glass end table in the hall—mostly to avoid looking Mel in the eye. "You're making me nervous."

"You *should* be nervous."

Carrie whirled to face her. "Why?" she cried.

"Because Amy and Aimee are pulling a prank on you in the next couple of days. And it's gonna be *bad*."

Fifteen

Carrie gasped. So *that's* what this was all about.

"Wait, hold on," she said, raising her hands. A sickening feeling gripped her insides. She needed a second to think. "How do you . . ." Her voice trailed off. "Are you sure?"

Mel's gaze fell to the carpet again. "Of *course* I'm sure." She shook her head. "But I didn't even know until right this second if I was going to tell you or not."

Carrie drew in her breath. She *did* have a reason to be nervous. She chewed on a black-painted fingernail. "Is that why you asked me what *I* would do to get somebody back?"

Mel nodded. "See—listen, you have to understand . . . it's got nothing to do with *you*."

"It doesn't?" Carrie asked, wrinkling her brow. "Then who *does* it have to do with?"

"No, no, I didn't mean it like that." She frowned. "It's just . . . they're planning on putting a picture of you in the school paper. They're gonna make it like a personal ad. There's gonna be a caption that says something like: 'I'm Carrie Mersel, and I'm ugly, and I'm totally desperate, and I'll take any man, no matter how gross. Please call.' And they're *definitely* gonna do it, too. Nobody can stop them."

Carrie swallowed.

"It's true," Mel said.

Oh, jeez. This was bad, all right. If what Mel was saying was true, Carrie would never be able to set foot in Robert Lowell again without being the laughingstock of the entire school. Nope, she'd have to get radical plastic surgery and go into hiding.

"Why are you even telling me?" she asked. "I mean, if there's nothing I can do . . ."

"Because I think it's mean," Mel said simply. "That's what I meant when I said it has nothing to do with *you*. To be honest, I don't care what happens to you. I just don't think something like this should happen to anyone—no matter how much of a loser she is."

Carrie pursed her lips. Well, well, well.

That was a really beautiful thing to say. "Thanks a lot," she murmured.

"You *should* thank me." Mel stood up and began pacing agitatedly around the living room. "Look, Carrie. The truth is that if they'd come up with something else, I would have gone along with it, all right? You *deserve* a good prank."

Carrie laughed once. In a weird way, she couldn't exactly blame Mel for saying that. She could almost see Mel's point of view. After all, there was no denying that Carrie *had* pulled a few stunts on Mel and her best friends. Good ones, too.

Mel paused in midstep. "What's so funny?" she demanded.

"Nothing," Carrie mumbled.

"Well, I'm really, really glad you think this is so amusing," Mel said sarcastically. "Thanks to you, I may have lost my best friends."

Carrie snorted. "That's not *my* fault. *I* didn't force you to do anything. You could have gone along with them. It was *your* choice."

Mel gaped at her. She blinked a few times very rapidly, then turned away. "Don't you understand?" she whispered.

Understand what? Carrie thought. *That you take pity on "losers"?* She didn't even bother to answer. But Mel was trembling now, standing with her back to the hall and her arms wrapped tightly around her sides. She sniffed once loudly.

Oh, brother.

As angry and fed up as Carrie was, she didn't want to make Mel *cry*. She supposed she *should* have been thankful for the fact that Mel hadn't gone along with the prank. But why? The Amys were still going to get her. And Mel hadn't acted out of any loyalty or goodwill. No, Mel had made her position on their relationship perfectly clear when she said: "I don't care what happens to you."

So much for the fledgling friendship. At this point, Carrie couldn't believe she had even considered the *possibility* that she could get along with Mel Eng.

"I gotta get out of here," Mel whispered. She started rubbing her eyes. "I can't be stuck here until eight o'clock."

"Well, why don't you just go to Amy's house?" Carrie said. "She only lives like two blocks away. Seriously. Just go there, and when your mom comes back, I'll tell

116

her that we got in a fight and you went to hang out with your real friends."

Mel turned around. "Are you *nuts?*"

"What?" Carrie shrugged. At first, she was only semijoking, but the more she thought about it, the more she realized that it really wasn't such a bad idea. She didn't want Mel to hang around any more than Mel did. "If you've got problems with Amy, now's a perfect time to patch things up. I won't stand in your way."

Mel sniffed again. "What about the prank?"

"What about it? If you can talk your friends out of it, great. If not, I'll deal with it." Carrie said. "I'm sure I'll think of something."

"I don't want to tell them I told you," Mel said quietly.

Carrie snickered. "Fine. You think *I* want to tell *my* friends about this conversation? Or *any* conversation we've had?" She shook her head. "This works both ways, Mel. I want our lives to go back to normal. I feel the exact same way *you* do. I wish this had never happened. So you can walk out the door, and we can just forget about all the visits and the phone call—"

"And how I borrowed *The Shining*," Mel interrupted.

Carrie rolled her eyes. "Sure. Whatever. The point is that nothing we ever talked about has to leave this house. I don't want to lose my friends any more than you want to lose *yours*."

Mel nodded. "You're right." She marched determinedly into the hall and gathered up her book bag. "I *don't* want to lose my friends." She paused. "Just tell my mom . . ."

"I'll take care of it," Carrie mumbled. "Don't worry."

Mel put her hand on the doorknob. For the briefest instant, their eyes locked. But this time there was no smile between them. Mel opened the door.

"Bye, Carrie," she said.

"Bye, Mel."

The next moment, she was gone—out of Carrie's house, and hopefully out of her life forever.

Sixteen

Mel stepped back and forth across the flat concrete stoop of Amy's huge white house for what must have been the hundredth time. She just hoped none of the neighbors were watching her. She must have looked like a major loony-toon. But she couldn't bring herself to even *peek* at the doorbell. What if she rang and Amy just slammed the door in her face? What if—

No. She was *not* going to say "what if."

Finally, she reached for the doorbell with a trembling finger—but at the last second, her hand fell back to her side. She *could* just go back to Carrie's place. . . .

What was she thinking? Of course she couldn't go crawling back *there*. She wouldn't be able to live with herself if she did. Besides, she knew she'd be saying "what if" for the rest of her life if she lost her nerve right now. She was here. She was going to face Amy.

Just get it over with! she commanded herself.

She lifted her finger again and jabbed the glowing orange button.

After a few seconds, there was a sound of pattering footsteps inside.

"Who is it?" Amy called.

Mel opened her mouth. But her heart was suddenly pounding too hard for her to speak. She licked her dry lips and forced herself to take a deep breath. "Mel," she answered feebly.

The door flew open.

"Amy, I . . ."

Mel left the sentence hanging. At first, she had been planning to apologize before she even set foot in the house. But she hadn't been expecting Amy to be so *friendly.* Amy was standing there, looking as happy as could be, with the afternoon sun glistening in her bright blue eyes and her lips curled in a big, toothy smile.

"Am I glad to see *you,*" Amy said.

Mel blinked. This had to be some kind of cruel joke. Amy had spent the entire day treating Mel like an annoying stain that needed to wiped off the face of Robert

Lowell Middle School. Now she was glad to see her? Amy hardly ever said anything that nice—even when she *wasn't* mad. Maybe Amy was just trying to lull Mel into thinking that everything was fine before she turned and walked away.

"Hello, Mel—are you there?" Amy teased. "Anybody home?"

Mel swallowed. "I don't understand," she breathed hoarsely.

Amy raised her eyebrows. "About what?"

"You wouldn't even talk to me today."

"Oh, *that*." Amy waved her hand dismissively. "Forget about it. You were right. The prank *is* too mean. Plus, we don't have a picture. We took these Polaroids of Carrie today when she was getting on the bus, and none of them came out."

Mel's eyes widened. Was that it? Amy had forgiven her and called off the prank— just like that? Was it really that simple? It couldn't be so easy. . . .

Amy squinted at her. "Are you all right?"

Mel nodded. A long trembling sigh escaped her lips. Then she started giggling.

"What's so funny?" Amy asked confusedly.

Mel shrugged. She knew she looked foolish—but couldn't stop. She'd never felt more relieved in her entire life. But she should have known Amy would forgive her. That was the great thing about Amy. She was the most fickle person Mel knew—in good ways *and* bad. And that meant she could never stay mad at one person for very long, least of all one of her best friends.

"Well," Amy said, stepping aside. "As soon as you're done laughing, you can catch the last five minutes of *Days of Our Lives*. My mom taped it for us."

Mel shook her head, managing to get a grip on herself. "Thanks," she murmured. She followed Amy through the hall and up the stairs. Her knees were still a little wobbly. She just hoped she wouldn't do anything majorly stupid—like start crying or something.

But there was still something she had to tell Amy—just to put an end to this whole stupid incident once and for all. She paused outside the closed door of the TV room at the end of the hall. "Amy . . ."

"What?" Amy asked.

Mel bit her lip. "Look . . . just so you

know, I'm *not* friends with Carrie, okay?"

Amy nodded. "I know you aren't," she said gently. "You're *here*, aren't you?" She pushed open the door.

Mel smiled. So that was that. Carrie Mersel was out of her life for good. *Now* she could relax. She followed Amy through the doorway.

Then she froze.

Aimee was here, too. She was sitting on the couch, staring at the jumbo television as the closing credits of *Days of Our Lives* rolled across the screen. For a moment, Mel felt another twitter of anxiety. Had Aimee also forgiven her? Probably—if Amy had. Still . . .

"Who rang the doorbell?" Aimee asked distractedly.

"See for yourself," Amy said.

Aimee glanced up. Her face twisted into a scowl. "What's *she*—"

"Aimee, we both agreed that the prank was too mean, *didn't* we?" Amy stated, cutting Aimee off in midsentence. "We both agreed that Mel was right."

Mel gulped. So Aimee *hadn't* forgiven her. No . . . for once in Aimee's life, it looked as if she didn't agree with Amy at all.

"The prank's out of the question, anyway," Amy went on. "The pictures you took were way too lame."

Aimee's cheeks reddened.

"Weren't they?" Amy pressed.

Aimee looked at the floor, but she nodded grudgingly. "I guess you're right," she said after a moment.

"Show Mel," Amy instructed.

Aimee sighed, then reached into the back pocket of her jeans and pulled out a few crumpled Polaroids. She shoved them in Mel's direction. "They're really bad," she mumbled. "So you don't need to say anything."

Mel took the photos and began flipping through them. Aimee was right. They *were* really bad. All she could see were a bunch of blurry human-shaped smudges. These were supposed to be pictures of Carrie? She couldn't even tell if Carrie was in any of them.

"Aimee, I know this is totally rude, but I'm gonna have to ask you to leave," Amy suddenly announced.

"What?" Aimee cried.

Mel glanced up from the pictures. What was going *on* here?

Amy smiled apologetically. "It's just that you know I have this dumb geometry exam on Friday," she said. She took the remote control off the couch and flicked off the TV. "And I'm, like, completely wigging out about it. My mom will *kill* me if I mess up." Her eyes wandered over to Mel. "So it's really kind of lucky that Mel showed up."

Mel felt a smile spreading across her face. Of course.

That's why Amy was so glad to see her.

But what did it matter? If anything, it showed that nothing had changed. Amy needed help with math—just like she always did. And if a little geometry exam was enough to make Amy forget about their fight, then that was fine with Mel.

"You don't mind helping me a little, do you?" Amy asked innocently.

Mel shook her head. She handed the photos back to Aimee. "Not one bit. You can always count on me. Always."

Amy smiled—that sweet, embracing smile that drew people to her like a magnet. "I *know* I can," she said. "That's why you're the only Mel who could ever be an Amy."

Heather's mother burst into the room. Her eyes glowed with a fiery, demonic light. Her bloodred lips were curled in a fiendish smile.

"What do you want?" Heather asked in a trembling voice.

"There's somebody I want you to meet," her mother whispered. "She's right here."

Heather shook her head. "No . . ."

"Oh yes," her mother replied. She took a step closer to the foot of Heather's bed. Her purplish nails were outstretched. "You're eighteen now. It's time you met somebody your age who has already been initiated."

Heather desperately backed away, pushing herself against the satin sheets, trying to somehow escape her mother. But there was nowhere to go. She was trapped.

"What do you mean . . . initiated?" Heather gasped.

"She's one of us. A witch . . ."

Seventeen

"Hi, Mel! Hi, Carrie! We're home!"

Carrie looked up from her typewriter.

Uh-oh.

"Where are you?" Mrs. Mersel called.

"I . . . uh, I'll be right down," Carrie stuttered quickly. She glanced at the clock. It was already seven forty-five. Wow. *That's* why it was so dark in here. She hadn't even thought about the time. And she definitely hadn't thought about how she was going to explain why Mel wasn't here anymore.

"What have you two been doing this whole time?" Mrs. Eng asked as cheerfully as ever.

Carrie leaped out of her chair. "Uh . . . I gotta tell you . . ." She ran a hand through her hair. Tell her *what*? Two pairs of heavy footsteps were pounding up the stairs. *Think!* she ordered herself. But her brain was taking a snooze. All she could think

127

about were those dumb shiny boots, getting closer and closer. . . .

"Melissa?" Mrs. Eng asked.

There was a loud knock on the door.

"Carrie?" Mrs. Mersel asked.

Carrie hung her head. It was hopeless. She'd have to make up something on the spot. "Come in," she mumbled.

The door creaked open.

"Carrie, what are you two *doing* in here?" her mother asked with a laugh. "I can't see three inches in front of my face." She snapped on the light.

Carrie squinted at the two of them. They were still dressed in the same silly outfits— only now they were filthy from head to toe. Carrie was actually a little annoyed. Her mom hated it when *she* tracked dirt around the house. She took a deep breath. "Mom, before you say anything, I just have to—"

"Melissa?" Mrs. Eng asked, stepping into Carrie's room. She peered around curiously, then looked at Carrie. "Where's Melissa?"

Carrie shrugged. A dozen possible answers flashed through her brain—but there was really only one she could give. And that was the truth. "Uh . . . she's at Amy Anderson's house."

Mrs. Eng flinched. *"What?"*

"Amy Anderson's house?" Mrs. Mersel cried. "What on *earth* is she doing there?"

"How should I know?" Carrie muttered, unable to think of any reasonable excuse. "She just took off. . . ."

Mrs. Eng was staring at Carrie now. Her bright black eyes were suddenly very cold. "I'm sorry, young lady," she snapped. "But my daughter would not just *take off.* So why don't you tell us what really happened."

"What really happened?" Carrie's voice rose slightly. "I just told you." She was starting to get a little angry herself. Who did Mrs. Eng think she was? She had no right to accuse Carrie of lying. Of course, Carrie *was* lying, but that wasn't the point. The point was that Mrs. Eng's precious daughter was just as much to blame as she was.

"Did you two get into another fight?" Mrs. Mersel asked. "What time did she leave?"

"What did you *do*, Carrie?" Mrs. Eng asked insistently.

Carrie's gaze shifted between the two of them. She felt as if she were being questioned by the police or something. It was ridiculous. They were treating Carrie like an archvillain, just because Mel had gone over to her friend's house. What was the big deal, anyway?

"Let me ask *you* something," she said. "Was this what you two had in mind when you wanted Mel and me to be friends?"

Mrs. Mersel threw her grimy hands in the air. "Of *course* not! What kind of a question—"

"Because you should have learned the very first time you put us together that this was *not* going to work out," Carrie interrupted. "We don't get along. Don't you get it? We've *never* gotten along. And we sure aren't gonna start now, just to please *you. That's* why Mel left."

For the first time all day, Carrie felt satisfied. She'd told the truth. And it was probably the first entirely honest thing she'd said about Mel since the whole thing started.

Mrs. Mersel's hands fell to her sides. She shook her head disgustedly. "I don't know what's gotten into you. . . ."

"You still haven't answered the question, Carrie," Mrs. Eng stated, folding her arms across her chest. "What did you *do?*"

"I didn't *do* anything!" Carrie yelled. "Mel said that she didn't want to be stuck here until

130

eight o'clock. So I told her to go hang out at Amy's house. Amy is her *friend*. I'm not. If you don't believe me, ask her yourself."

"Carrie, *please*," Mrs. Mersel pleaded. Her face was flushed. "Where are your manners?"

Carrie laughed shortly. "*My* manners!" She thrust a finger at Mel's mom. "What about *hers*?"

Mrs. Mersel clasped her grubby hands over her mouth. For a moment, Carrie wondered if she was going to keel over from shock. Well, *this* was a royal disaster. Then again, she'd succeeded at one thing. She'd definitely done a good job of offending them both. All she had to do was take one look at Mrs. Eng's sour smile to see that. But that *was* her original plan, anyway, wasn't it?

"You've obviously got a lot of growing up to do, young lady," Mrs. Eng breathed.

"Maybe you're right," Carrie said. She sighed tiredly. "But in that case, why would you want me to hang out with Mel in the first place? I mean, she's *obviously* much more grown-up than I am, right?"

Mrs. Mersel whimpered. Her hands were now covering her entire face.

"I'm not going to stand here and argue with a thirteen-year-old girl," Mrs. Eng growled. She turned to face Carrie's mom. "I'm sorry this didn't work out, Elizabeth. But I think it would be best if our daughters didn't spend any more time together."

"What do you think we've been trying to tell you for the past week? *Jeez!*" Carrie marched over to her bed and collapsed facedown on the mattress.

"I am so sorry," Mrs. Mersel murmured.

Carrie heard feet shuffling. Their footsteps began to fade. There was some hushed conversation on the stairs—but Carrie couldn't catch any of it. Of course, she didn't really care *what* they were saying. As long as Mel never came back.

The front door slammed.

Finally.

Carrie rolled over on her back. She laughed once. Well, she'd done it. She'd gotten Mel Eng out of her life. Now she just needed to get her friends back *in.* Sighing, she reached for the phone on her night table and dialed Alex's number.

The line rang twice, then somebody picked up.

"Hello?" Alex answered.

"Hey. It's me."

"Hey, what's up?" Alex asked eagerly. "How'd it go today? Are you all right?"

Carrie smiled. For the first time all week, she felt as if she was right where she belonged. For the first time all week, life *was* back to normal. The Amys were probably planning on getting her with some terrible prank, as always. Her mom was majorly angry, as always. And most importantly, nothing stood in the way of her and her friends.

Yup. Everything was just as it should be.

"Alex," Carrie said. "You'll never guess what happened. . . ."

Mel

Dear Diary,

What a day. My mom just finished grounding me for the next week. But honestly? I'm kind of relieved. I thought I was going to be grounded for a month. I don't think I'll ever forget the look on my mom's face when she pulled up in front of Amy's house tonight. She was one seriously unhappy woman.

But in this crazy way, I was happy she was so mad. Because at long last, she gave up on trying to make me be friends with Carrie. I guess Carrie said a bunch of really rude things to her. Of course, my mom blamed <u>me</u>.

It boggles the mind. Really. She said _I_ must have given Carrie a reason for wigging out. My mom always finds a way to make _me_ responsible for things I can't control.

Oh, well. Who cares? I have my best friends again. I'm one of The Amys again. I rule Robert Lowell again. And I'm never going to have to say another word to Carrie Mersel for the rest of my life.

Not too shabby, if I do say so myself.

I do have to make one little confession, though. I'm really glad that Amy didn't pull that prank on Carrie. I kind of hope she just forgets about Carrie completely. It's not that I _like_ Carrie. It's just that

I don't want to be mean to her. I don't want to be mean to anybody.

Maybe if life were a whole lot different, Carrie and I would be friends. Maybe if there were no one else on the planet except the two of us and Stephen King, Carrie and I would get along great. But thinking about something dumb like that is just another way of saying "what if."

And you know what? I <u>hate</u> saying "what if."

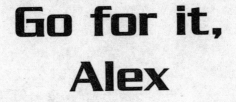

Go for it,
Alex

<u>Alex Wagner's Book of Deep Thoughts</u>

<u>Entry 10</u>

I hate to say it, but school has gotten really, really boring.

It's true. I'm not even sure why. I mean, looking back on the year so far, I know that a lot of crazy things have happened. But it doesn't feel that way. It's more like I'm locked into the same old dull routine. Sometimes I literally feel like a robot or something. I mean it. I could probably program my entire day from start to finish and let an android live my life for me.

<u>Instructions on How to Live My Life</u>

1. Wake up. Put skateboard in hall to make sure Matt trips over it on way to bathroom.
2. Eat cereal with Matt and Dad. Call Matt a dork at least twice.
3. Get into backseat of bus with Jordan and Sam. Get mushed against the window once Carrie and Sky get on.

4. Pray Ms. Tyler doesn't announce surprise biology quiz.
5. Blah, blah, blah . . .

Anyway.

The point is that I could fill this entire notebook with that kind of stuff. It's sort of depressing, in a way. I didn't expect my last year at Robert Lowell Middle School to be so . . . well, predictable. I expected it to be crazy and wacky and full of perfectly timed surprises, like a TV sitcom.

Well, maybe not a sitcom. That would be pretty silly.

The _real_ point is that I want to shake things up a little.

Of course, writing that down here is a lot easier than actually _doing_ something. Because if you really think about it, "shaking things up" is just a nice way of saying "doing something really dumb that will get you into big trouble." And I have a hard enough time avoiding things like that as it is.

Maybe _that's_ why they haven't made a TV sitcom of my life.

One

"Um . . . Alex?" Sam asked. "What's up with those pants?"

Alex paused in the crowded hallway and raised her eyebrows at Sam Wells, faking astonishment. "What do you mean?" she asked innocently.

Sam rolled his bright black eyes. "They have holes in them, Alex," he replied. "Holes the size of bowling balls. Not to mention the fact you were wearing a completely different pair of pants up until about two minutes ago."

"I *was?*" Alex exclaimed. She peered down at her grubby blue jeans. Both of her bony knees poked through huge tears in the cloth. She started laughing. "Hey, you're right. I don't know what happened."

Sam smirked. "Alex . . ."

"Shh," Alex whispered. She cast a furtive glance in either direction to make sure no teachers were around, then leaned close to Sam's ear. "See, I brought these pants to wear at recess. I want to try some new skateboarding tricks, and I don't want to mess up my good pants. As soon as recess is over, I'm gonna switch back." She lifted her shoulders. "No problem, right?"

He laughed once. "Right. Unless Principal Cashen sees you. Then you have a problem."

Alex sighed, shaking her head. "Sam, Sam, Sam. You worry too much." Her eyes roved over Sam's perfectly pressed outfit: his crisp blue jeans, his white T-shirt, and his gray sweater vest. She had to smile. Sam always looked as if he stepped out of a Gap ad or something. Even if Ocean's View were suddenly hit with a freak hurricane, every strand of his spiky black hair would probably stay in place. "You need to loosen up a bit," she added jokingly.

"Loosen up," he repeated dryly. "Yeah. I've seen what happens to people who loosen up." He grinned. "Don't you remember the look on Principal Cashen's face when Jordan wore that I Surf Naked shirt to—"

"This is totally different," Alex insisted. "I'm not wearing anything, like . . ." She snapped her fingers, racking her brains for the right word.

"Offensive?" Sam suggested.

Alex smiled broadly. "Exactly." She stole a peek at her reflection in the glass door that opened from the hall into the sunlit courtyard.

Okay, maybe the pants *had* seen better days. In fact, everything about her appearance right now was a little . . . well, disheveled. Her baggy black T-shirt was untucked, hanging sloppily past her waist. She hadn't had time to take a shower this morning, either, because her older brother, Matt, had hogged the bathroom. Just because he was a freshman in high school he thought his showers were more important than hers. She brushed a stringy clump of shoulder-length brown hair out of her eyes and frowned.

"Hey, *I* don't think you look offensive," Sam offered. "I'm just thinking about our big, bald principal. You heard that speech at the beginning of the year." He straightened his shoulders and pursed his lips, holding his skateboard in front of him as if it were a piece of paper. "Furthermore," he stated in an imitation of Principal Cashen's gruff voice, "I'd like certain students to think more seriously about their attire. Robert Lowell Middle School will not tolerate torn garments, no matter what the supposed fashion value—"

"Hey, keep it down." Alex giggled. *"You're the one who's gonna get in trouble, pal."*

"Nah—not me," he said confidently. He dropped his skateboard on the floor. It bounced once and rolled to a quick stop under one of his sneakers. "Me and Principal C. are tight."

"That's because he loves geeks," she teased.

Sam chuckled. "Call me what you want," he replied, hopping up onto the board. He flung out his arms to balance himself. "But you won't see *me* in detention. See, Alex, one of these days you're gonna learn that it pays to have friends in high places."

"Thanks for the brilliant advice," Alex said sarcastically. "I think I'm gonna go get my skateboard now." She turned and hurried toward her locker at the end of the hall. The last of the seventh- and eighth-graders were already filing out the glass door for recess. She shook her head. She and Sam had been jabbering for so long that they'd already wasted five minutes of valuable skating time.

"Hey, Alex," Sam called. His voice echoed across the rows of red lockers. "I bet you can't flip your board under your feet between where you're standing now and where I'm standing."

Alex turned her head, fixing him with a cocky smile. "You gotta be kidding me."

Sam shrugged. "Let's see it, then." A grin spread across his face. "You talk the talk, but can you walk the walk?"

"You *really* don't think that I can do a simple little trick that any third-grader could do?" She clucked her tongue dismissively, surveying the distance between them. What was it—thirty feet or so? She could flip the skateboard *twice* in that amount of space. "Sam, you're forgetting that I taught you everything you know."

Sam laughed again. "Whatever. I'm waiting."

"What'll you give me?" she prodded.

He scratched his head for a moment. "A new Supersonics cap," he replied.

"You're on." The Supersonics were Alex's favorite pro basketball team, and she would never miss a chance for free stuff.

Without another moment's hesitation Alex plucked her skateboard from her locker and swung the metal door shut with a loud clang. Good old Sam. He knew she lived for dares like this. In one graceful movement she tossed the skateboard onto the floor and leaped onto it, swiftly pushing off with one foot.

"There she goes!" he cried. "Just watch her fly, ladies and gentlemen!"

Now this is what school is all about, she thought. Her hair whipped back as she hurtled toward Sam. *Skateboarding in the halls, showing off . . .*

Holding her breath, she tucked the tip of her right sneaker under the board, then bounced and hopped—straight up. The board flipped neatly under her feet. Her hair fell in her eyes as she landed, but with a toss of her head her line of sight was clear. She shifted her weight and skidded to a stop in front of Sam with a screech.

Perfect, she said to herself. She stepped off the board, not even out of breath.

"One Seattle Supersonics cap, please," she said as nonchalantly as possible. "And make sure it has—"

"*Alexandra Wagner!*" a furious voice boomed from behind her.

Uh-oh.

Alex swallowed.

"Ms. *Wagner!*"

She couldn't see who was yelling—but judging from the sudden queasy look on Sam's face, she could just guess.

"Look at what you've done to the hall!" the voice barked. Angry footsteps clattered toward them. "Just *look* at it!"

Yup, Alex thought miserably. *Principal Cashen.*

Her gaze fell to the floor. *Oh, jeez.* Several ugly black streaks marred the white tile directly beneath her feet. What had she been thinking with that skid? She *hadn't* been thinking. That was the problem. . . .

"What do you have to say for yourself?" Principal Cashen demanded.

Alex chewed her lip, wishing she could just rewind the last thirty seconds and erase them. She forced herself to raise her eyes. Her stomach lurched. Principal

Cashen was *not* a happy man. Nope. His pudgy face was creased, and the bald spot on his head had turned slightly pink. He folded his arms in front of his necktie, glaring at her over the rim of his glasses.

"Well?" he growled.

Alex shook her head. "I . . . I . . . ," she sputtered hopelessly.

His beady brown eyes shifted to Sam. "Mr. Wells? Perhaps *you* can explain why you two are skateboarding in the halls during recess on a perfectly beautiful day."

Sam didn't even reply.

Alex hung her head. This was just great. Perfect . . .

"I see," Principal Cashen stated dryly. He sighed. "Ms. Wagner, I'm not even going to *bother* asking why you're wearing those . . . those tattered remnants of what I suppose were once jeans. . . ."

A small crowd of kids had now formed by the door, staring at Alex. Blood rushed to her face. How much more *humiliating* could this get?

"I'm afraid I'm going to have to call your father," Principal Cashen continued. "I'm going to ask him to come in this afternoon.

The two of you can meet with Ms. Tyler."

Alex's head jerked up, her eyes bulging. *"What?"* she cried.

"You leave me no choice," he stated evenly. "Alex—your behavior was grossly inappropriate. And the state of your wardrobe leads me to believe that you require something above and beyond the call of normal disciplinary action."

Alex started shaking her head. This was crazy. People only went to see Ms. Tyler if they were literally insane. The last person who went to see her was this kid Chad Henderson, and he'd tried to take a cast off some other kid's broken leg with his bare hands. Well, that was the rumor, anyway. . . .

"No, wait, it's my fault," Sam piped up. "Really, I—"

"Spare me, Mr. Wells," Principal Cashen interrupted, but his tone had softened. "I appreciate the virtue, but I've been principal long enough to know that when a student says, 'It's my fault', it means he's taking the blame for someone else."

For a second Alex almost felt as if she might yak. She'd *never* gotten into this much trouble before. Not even close. What was the

151

big deal? So she'd marked up the floor a little. So her jeans were a little worn. She opened her mouth to protest, but all that came out was a pathetic little gasp. Principal Cashen didn't even hear her. He was already marching back toward his office.

"Sam, you can spend the afternoon clapping erasers," he called over his shoulder. "Come see me after the final bell."

He disappeared around the corner.

Alex couldn't move. She couldn't even think.

"I don't believe it," Sam muttered. He put his hand on her shoulder. "Alex, I am so sorry. . . ."

"It's—it's not your fault," she finally managed.

He gazed at her somberly. "Look, if there's anything I can do . . ."

She shook her head. The truth hit her then—as powerfully as a smack in the face. "I don't think there's anything anybody *can* do. Because at this point I'm already a goner."

Two

Alex squirmed and fidgeted on the slick vinyl couch. She felt as if she might slide off any second. She wished she *could* slide off, actually—slide off and roll under the door and get as far from Ms. Tyler's office as possible. This place gave her the creeps. It wasn't only because she was about to get eighty years' worth of detention, either. The room was cramped and stuffy and totally quiet.

"Your father is due here any minute," Ms. Tyler said distractedly, squinting at some papers on her desk.

Alex just nodded. She had no idea what to say.

Tick, tick, tick went the clock over the couch.

"I spoke with him on the phone," Ms. Tyler added without looking up.

"Oh," Alex replied lamely.

Ms. Tyler shuffled the papers.

Alex sighed. Usually she got along pretty well with Ms. Tyler. But that was in biology class. She'd never had to deal with Ms. Tyler when Ms. Tyler was doing her other job, namely, acting as the assistant principal. It was as if she had transformed into an entirely different person. Her blue eyes were cold. Her tone was flat. She'd let her hair down, and the brown waves shadowed her high cheekbones. She normally smiled a lot, too. But now her lips seemed to be frozen in a permanent scowl.

Alex shook her head. *That is the last time I'm ever going to let Sam talk me into doing something stupid,* she swore to herself. *From now on I'm going to shape up, fly right—*

There was a loud knock on the door.

A *familiar* knock.

Alex groaned inwardly.

"Come in," Ms. Tyler called, pushing herself away from the desk.

The door creaked open. Alex blinked. It was her dad, all right. But he looked so formal. True, she was used to seeing him slouch around the house in a sweat suit and socks, but still—he'd actually combed

154

his graying brown hair. He was wearing a tweed jacket. His button-down shirt was tucked into a nicely ironed pair of pants. He was even wearing a belt. . . .

This is serious. Really, really serious.

"Thank you for coming," Ms. Tyler said quietly, stepping out in front of the desk to shake his hand. A brief smile crossed her face. "Rebecca Tyler."

"Tom Wagner," he replied, gripping her hand firmly.

Alex stared at the two of them. The clock ticked loudly. Their hands remained clasped together. She frowned. Why did grown-ups always feel as if they had to shake hands for at least an hour to be polite? A high five was much easier.

Finally Ms. Tyler withdrew her hand and waved it toward the couch. "Please, make yourself comfortable," she said, easing back into her own chair.

"Thank you." The couch squeaked loudly as Mr. Wagner slid beside Alex.

"I appreciate your coming in to talk to me," Ms. Tyler continued. "I know how difficult it can be for some people to get time off from work on such short notice."

Mr. Wagner shook his head. "It's no problem. I work at home. I set my own hours. Besides, Thursdays are always pretty slow for me."

"You work at home?" A curious smile curled on her lips. "Do you mind if I ask what you do?"

Mr. Wagner laughed. "Not at all. I'm a freelance adman."

"Is that so?" Ms. Tyler's face brightened. "That must be fascinating."

He shrugged. "In theory," he said wryly.

Ms. Tyler raised her eyebrows. "That sounds like something I might say about being a teacher."

The two of them chuckled.

Alex's eyes narrowed a little. Okay . . . what was going on here? Weren't they supposed to be talking about *her*? They sounded as if they were at a dinner party or something.

"Actually, I decided to work at home to be closer to the kids," Mr. Wagner went on. He leaned forward in the seat and lowered his gaze a moment. "You see . . . Alex's mother died when she was very young. So I've had to be father *and* mother. To both

Alex and her brother, Matt. It can be difficult sometimes."

Alex swallowed. All at once her face felt hot. That was a pretty personal thing to say. *Very* personal, in fact. And none of it had anything to do with ripped jeans or skid marks in the hall, either.

Ms. Tyler nodded, peering at Alex's father closely. "I'm sorry."

"Don't be." He looked up at her with a reassuring smile. "I don't mean to sound as if I'm fishing for sympathy. It's just that . . . sometimes when you're juggling several responsibilities at once, it's hard to provide guidance all the time. Unfortunately, Alex may act a little wild sometimes as a result."

Alex's jaw dropped. Now she was starting to get majorly ticked off. Her father was acting as if she weren't even in the same room. It would be one thing if he dissed Alex in the privacy of their own home. But he was telling a total stranger their entire life story. And insulting her in the process.

"I understand perfectly," Ms. Tyler murmured. "It's so hard for a young girl to grow up without a mother. My own brother's wife died when their daughter was seven. . . ."

Oh no. Please don't. Please just shut up.

Alex squeezed her eyes shut. Now Ms. Tyler was getting into all kinds of deep, dark personal stuff, too—blabbing about her poor, motherless niece. This was nuts! Couldn't they see how awkward this was for all of them? Alex didn't even *think* about her mother. Well, not much, anyway. Besides, her mother had nothing to do with anything. Why couldn't they just punish her and get it over with?

"Alex?" Her father's voice broke into her thoughts. "What's the matter, honey?"

"The matter?" she echoed loudly. She laughed. Her eyes opened. "I'll tell you. I'm in trouble, right? So let's just get it over with. I'll start clapping erasers right away. I'm ready."

Ms. Tyler and her father exchanged a brief, knowing glance.

"*What?*" Alex demanded, totally fed up.

"I'm afraid it's not that simple," Ms. Tyler said, sighing. "There are some issues we need to discuss first. I'm not simply a disciplinarian, Alex. I'm also here to counsel you. Is there anything you want to talk to us about?"

Alex flopped back against the cushions. "Like *what?*" She groaned.

"Like the extra pair of pants you brought to school—in flagrant violation of the dress code." Ms. Tyler's voice grew stern. "I mentioned it to your father on the phone. Apparently he had no idea."

Mr. Wagner shifted in the seat. The couch squeaked again. "That's right, Alex," he breathed concernedly. "Why did you do it? Why did you change your pants?"

Alex gaped at her father, then at Ms. Tyler.

Then she started cracking up.

She couldn't help it. They were looking at her as if she were a dangerous criminal. Because of a pair of pants. Well, one thing was for sure—her life was finally starting to feel like a TV sitcom. A really bad one, too.

Her father's brow furrowed. "What's . . . so funny?" he asked apprehensively.

"Dad—I brought a lousy pair of pants to school!" she cried, sitting up again. "It has nothing to do with any deep psychological problems! I didn't want to mess up my other pants when I went

159

skateboarding at recess." She shot Ms. Tyler a pleading, matter-of-fact look. "That's *it*. I know it was wrong. I broke the rules. I'm sorry, okay?"

But Ms. Tyler just shook her head sadly. "Alex, it's not that simple," she said for the second time.

Alex just stared at her. She felt as if she were talking to a brick wall.

"I think your father and I should talk about your friends, too," Ms. Tyler continued in a firm but gentle tone. "Sometimes they can influence you to do things you might not otherwise want to do. Did Carrie Mersel or Jordan Sullivan put you up to this? I know that Jordan in particular can let his sense of humor get the best of him. . . ."

That's it, Alex said to herself. She was not going to sit around and let Ms. Tyler bad-mouth her friends. Carrie and Jordan had nothing to do with any of this. They weren't even *there*. She abruptly stood.

"I'll tell you what," she announced. "I'll make it easy on you. If you two want to talk about me and my friends, go ahead. *I'll* go outside, and then *you* can discuss all

160

the incredibly complicated things that need to be done with *my* life."

Her father started shaking his head. "Alex, wait—"

"I'll be in the car," she finished. And with that she slammed the office door behind her.

<u>Alex Wagner's Book of Deep Thoughts</u>

<u>Entry 11</u>

Did I say I was bored? I take it all back.
I'm serious. I will never, ever complain about
being bored again. Really. I like being bored. I will
never try to shake things up. Give me the
same old dull routine, and I'll be just fine. . . .
   Whew.
   You know that old saying: Be careful what
you wish for, because it might come true?
It's a really great piece of advice. I never
understood that until now. All I did was wish
for excitement, and what I got was Principal
Cashen freaking out on me.
   Still, I shouldn't complain. For some bizarre
reason I didn't get into nearly as much
trouble as I thought I would. I thought I
was going to get suspended or something. But
I only have detention for a week—starting
tomorrow. And the only really bad part is
that since I have to stay late after school
every day, I can't ride the bus home. My dad
has to pick me up. I feel kind of guilty about

that. But hey — he agreed to it, right?

What I can't figure out is why it took so long for him to agree to it.

I mean, he was in that office with Ms. Tyler for like an hour, at least. I sat on the front steps of school the whole time. Alone. And believe me, there's nothing worse than sitting by yourself while your dad and your teacher are talking about all your problems and all your friends behind your back. That pretty much wins the grand prize for lame situations.

But like I said, I shouldn't complain.

Because after that meeting my dad wasn't even mad. Not at all. It was really weird, actually. The whole drive home, he just kept talking about how great Robert Lowell Middle School is, and how the faculty really cares about the students, and a bunch of other stuff that I didn't understand. He didn't even mention the skateboard.

Now, if he thinks I'm strange because I bring an extra pair of pants to school . . .

But after all, he's a grown-up, right? So obviously nothing he does ever makes any sense. I gave up trying to understand grown-ups a long time ago. Especially my dad.

Three

Skyler Foley wrapped her arms around herself, shivering as she watched Taylor Haven's Bus roll slowly down Pike's Way. Sometimes she hated the fact that little Taylor Haven was all the way out at the end of the peninsula. Ocean's View, where she went to school, wasn't even that far away, but somehow it always seemed warmer there.

She couldn't *believe* how cold it was. Hadn't it been, like, ninety degrees only two weeks ago? She was totally freezing. Goose bumps rose on her skin every time the frigid breeze blew off Puget Sound.

"Why don't I live in Florida?" she mumbled.

She really should have worn a sweater. But she didn't have any sweaters that went with this particular blue dress. And she wasn't about to sacrifice fashion for comfort. Nope. No way. It didn't help that her long brown curls were still wet from the icy shower she'd taken this morning, either. In typical space cadet fashion her father had used all the hot water in the houseboat washing last night's dishes.

Not that it was *that* big of a deal. Compared to the problems Alex was probably having with *her* dad . . . using up the hot water seemed pretty unimportant.

Poor Alex.

Sky still hadn't heard any word about how Alex's meeting with Ms. Tyler went. But she could just imagine. This was major. Especially considering the fact that Alex's father had been there, too. At least Mr. Wagner was a pretty mellow and laid-back kind of guy. . . .

The bus roared to a stop.

"Hi, Brick!" she called to the bus driver, dashing up the stairs. She made a beeline for the backseat. Carrie, Jordan, and Sam were all hunched over, listening to Alex.

"Hold it right there!" Sky commanded, squeezing into her spot between Jordan and Carrie. "Start from the top, all right?"

Carrie brushed a lone strand of dyed

black hair out of her hazel eyes and smirked. "Don't worry, Sky. Alex was waiting for you."

"Really." Alex grinned. "I know better than to start a story without you."

Jordan patted her on the shoulder. His green eyes sparkled impishly under his messy blond bangs. "Besides, once *you* hear something, we can be sure that everyone at Robert Lowell will find out in the next two hours."

"That's funny, Jor-*dumb*," Sky replied flatly. She stared at Alex. Okay, something *weird* was going on here. Alex seemed to be in a pretty good mood for somebody who had just gotten into major trouble. A *really* good mood, actually.

Alex's smile widened. "What?"

"Nothing," Sky replied slowly. "It's just . . . I was kind of expecting you to be bummed."

Alex shrugged. "To tell you the truth, I was expecting to be bummed myself."

"So what *did* happen?" Sam piped up from the other side of the seat. "You can start now. We're all here. The suspense is killing us." His voice fell. "Not to mention the fact that I still feel guilty about the whole thing."

"Don't," Alex replied. She raised her eyebrows. "I only got detention for a week."

"Only a week!" Sam exclaimed. "I mean, that's awesome . . . but Principal C. looked like he was going to have a heart attack. I've never seen him that mad."

Alex shrugged again. "I know. But I guess he left the decision up to Ms. Tyler. It's a good thing *he* wasn't at the meeting."

"So what happened at the meeting, anyway?" Sky pressed eagerly.

Alex sighed, leaning into the seat as the bus bounced along Pike's Way. "Well, at first I thought I was gonna die. I'm not even joking. I've never been so embarrassed in my entire life. As soon as my dad walked into the office they started talking about all this dumb stuff that had *nothing* to do with why I was in trouble. . . ." She made a face.

"Like what?" Sky asked.

Alex shook her head. "Never mind," she said with a moan. "I don't even want to *think* about it."

Sky exchanged a quick, confused look with Carrie. Carrie just shook her head.

"Anyway," Alex continued, "I was just

like, 'Can't you please punish me and get it over with?' But Ms. Tyler kept on saying, 'It's not that simple, Alex.' It was *ridiculous*."

Jordan frowned. "I don't get it. What wasn't that simple? Was she trying to come up with some really complicated way of torturing you or something?"

"No!" Alex cried, giggling. "That was the really strange thing. I didn't understand any of it. So finally I was just like, 'I'm outta here. *You* guys talk about what needs to be done. I'll wait for you outside.' And I took off."

Nobody said anything for a few seconds. Sky kept waiting for Alex to add the next part of the story—like how her father and Ms. Tyler chased her down the hall, or how they blocked all the exits . . . but there was nothing.

"*And?*" Sky finally prompted.

Alex raised her hands. "And that was pretty much it," she said simply. "They were in there for, like, an hour. I just sat on the front steps."

"That's *it?*" Jordan exclaimed incredulously. "They didn't even want to *talk* to you?"

Alex started smiling again. "I guess not."

"Do you know what they talked

about?" Carrie asked, absently flattening a wrinkle on her long black dress.

"Nope." Alex shook her head. "But whatever they talked about was fine by me. Ever since he got out of that meeting, my dad has been . . . I don't know." She laughed nervously—as if she were suddenly embarrassed.

"What do you mean?" Sky prodded.

Alex took a deep breath and glanced at all of them. "It's like Ms. Tyler slipped him some kind of happy pill or something," she mumbled, blushing slightly. "Like, last night . . . he was acting really giddy. He kept on telling all these corny jokes. And then when I went to sleep, I heard him talking on the phone and laughing really hard. My dad *never* talks on the phone late at night."

"You're lucky," Sky joked. "My dad talks on the phone at, like, four A.M. all the time. Sounds like your dad is turning into *my* dad. Next thing you know, he'll be growing dreadlocks."

Alex shook her head. "You know—at this point it wouldn't surprise me. I'm serious. Because that's not even the weirdest thing." She lowered her voice to a whisper and leaned forward, looking around to make sure nobody else on the bus was listening. "This morning when I woke up, I heard my dad singing in the shower."

Sky bit her lip to keep from giggling—but she lost it. She exploded in a fit of laughter. She could just picture Mr. Wagner standing in the shower with his eyes closed, lathering up his hair like one of those shampoo commercials and belting out opera at the top of his lungs: *"Figaro, Figaro, Figaro . . ."*

"Shh!" Alex hissed, but she was laughing, too. "It's not funny. It was horrible! Matt and I just stood there in the hall. We didn't know whether to crack up or call a mental institution or something. My dad *never* sings. He doesn't even sing the national anthem at Supersonics games."

Finally Sky managed to get a grip on herself. She drew in her breath.

"That does sound crazy," Jordan agreed. "What do you think the deal is?"

Alex shook her head. "I don't know. All I know is, if any of you guys ever get in trouble, make sure your parents meet with Ms. Tyler." She leaned back into the seat again. "It'll solve *all* your problems."

Skyler Foley's
Theory about Why Mr. Wagner
Has Gone Bananas

You know what? I'm pretty sure I know what's going on with Alex's dad. After thinking about it all day, it came to me in a flash. It's simple, really.

Mr. Wagner has a crush on Ms. Tyler.

I know, I know—it sounds as if I'm just trying to start some really heinous rumor or something. But I'm not. Honestly. It's just that if you look at all the evidence in a totally scientific way, everything makes sense. Allow me to explain.

First of all, they were alone together for like an hour. Then, all of a sudden, Alex's father was in a great mood. Everybody knows that being in love with someone puts you in a great mood, right? Not that I have any firsthand experience or anything, but I've seen enough cheesy movies to figure it out.

The most crucial piece of evidence is

that he was singing in the shower. That's the clincher. No doubt about it. Any man who sings in the shower is obviously in love. It's a classic symptom. Again, all you have to do is watch any cheesy movie — like Splash, the one where Tom Hanks falls in love with a mermaid.

So it seems pretty obvious to me: Mr. Wagner is in love with Ms. Tyler. But for once in my life I'm going to keep my theory to myself until I have absolute proof. I am not going to gossip. For one thing, I know Alex would kill me if I was wrong. Not that I would blame her. This is serious stuff. Not to mention kind of gross . . . but in a sweet way, of course.

My dad always tells me I'll understand these things when I get older. Then again, he tells me that I'll end up liking the Grateful Dead, too—and I know that's not going to happen. Maybe I should just forget about it altogether. . . .

Nah. It's way too juicy.

Four

Ever since Alex could remember, her father had spent Saturday morning working in the study. It was kind of a Wagner family tradition—like taking the boat out in the summer or having cookouts at the beginning of the fall. It was just one of those normal parts of life.

But not today. He'd been gone since before Alex woke up.

Now it was almost three. All he'd left was a note that said: *Out shopping. Be back early this afternoon. Love, Dad.*

What was *that* all about?

"Do you really think he's out shopping?" Matt asked, dribbling a basketball absently.

Alex shrugged, teetering back and forth on her skateboard. The two of them had been hanging out in the driveway of their small wood frame house for the past forty-five minutes even though the sky was a sunless gray and a cold wind was coming off the sound. Neither of them had said much. There wasn't much to say, Alex realized. The truth of the matter was that they were both starting to get freaked out.

"Maybe he's gonna surprise us with something," Alex finally mumbled, even though she knew she sounded totally unconvincing.

"Maybe," Matt muttered. He brushed a hand through his straight brown hair, then tossed up a halfhearted shot. The ball slammed off the backboard, missing the basket completely.

"Maybe . . ." Alex's voice trailed off. She heard a sound: the familiar sound of a car motor.

She whirled on her skateboard. Her father's blue sedan lurched onto Yesler Street. It jerked to a stop in front of the driveway.

"Hey!" Mr. Wagner called cheerfully, stepping out of the car. "How're you guys doing?"

Alex blinked at Matt. *How're you guys doing?* Her father never called them "guys."

"Where have you *been*, Dad?" Matt demanded.

"Out shopping," he said, still smiling. He closed the car door. "Like it said in my note." He glanced between the two of them. "You weren't worried or anything, were you?"

"Nah," Alex said quickly. Now that he was home, she didn't want to make a big deal out of it. She pushed off on her foot and glided over to the car, then hopped off the board. "So did you get anything . . . ?" She didn't finish the question. She was going to ask him if he'd gotten anything good, but something about him caught her eye. He looked so . . . *nice.* Even in the wind she could tell that he'd combed his hair again. He was also wearing those same shiny shoes he'd worn at the meeting with Ms. Tyler and a really nice pair of khaki pants.

"I got a lot of stuff," he babbled excitedly, seemingly oblivious to Alex's puzzled stare. He stepped around to the trunk and popped it open. "I went ahead and bought a few things for you at the mall, Alex. Give me a hand, all right?"

For a second Alex was too flabbergasted to even move. She suddenly felt as if she had stepped into an *X-Files* episode or something. This was too weird. Since when had her father gone ahead and bought her things at the mall? Actually she knew the answer to that question: never. The only times he'd ever bought her stuff at the mall was when the two of them had gone together.

"Alex?" he asked, grinning at her. "Are you all right?"

"Yeah, yeah—fine," she stammered, shaking her head. She reached into the trunk and distractedly grabbed a couple of shopping bags, then followed her dad up the front walk and into the house. With a grunt she set the bags down on the small table in the cozy little kitchen, then frowned. One of the packages was labeled Nancy's Boutique. She knew that place. It was really trendy—not to mention, well . . . kind of horrible.

"What's the matter?" her father asked worriedly, setting his own bags down on the floor.

Alex shook her head. "Uh, nothing," she mumbled.

He gestured toward the bag. "Go ahead," he announced proudly. "Open it."

Alex hesitated for a second, then peered into the bag. She stifled a gasp.

Inside was a T-shirt. A bright pink baby-doll T-shirt. The kind of T-shirt she would never wear in a million years . . .

"What do you think?" he asked.

She didn't reply. Instead she pulled it out and held it up in front of her face. This thing looked too small for a rabbit. What had gotten into him?

"I got some other stuff, too," he added, shuffling through the bags on the floor. "Some CDs. The Spice Girls—"

"Whoa, whoa, wait a second," Alex interrupted. She lowered the T-shirt and stared uncomprehendingly at her father. "You got me the *Spice Girls'* CD?"

He nodded, beaming. "Yeah."

Alex swallowed. She forced a feeble smile to match his. Sure, the Spice Girls were funny; she liked some of their songs . . . but she'd never *once* expressed any interest in owning their CD. The last CD she'd asked for had been the newest album by Soundgarden. She'd never gotten it. But that wasn't even the point. The point was that she preferred the hard stuff—and he knew it. She wanted Soundgarden pumping through her Walkman headphones when she was on her skateboard. *Not* the Spice Girls.

"The guy at the record store said it was a hit with girls your age," her father explained. "So I figured, what the heck?"

"What the heck," Alex echoed hollowly.

But at the same time another part of her brain was exclaiming: *Aha!* First the shirt, then the Spice Girls. A definite pattern was forming here. A *girly* pattern. What would be next—lipstick?

"There's some perfume, too," he mumbled absently, stooping over to fish through another bag.

I've got to get out of here, she said to herself. She tossed the T-shirt onto the table and backpedaled toward the door. *This is way too freaky. I've gotta call Sky or Carrie—or somebody. Anybody. I need help.*

"Uh . . . thanks a lot for all the stuff, Dad," she offered. Her voice sounded squeaky. "I'm just gonna go to my room. . . ."

Alex turned on her heel and bolted. She had no idea what had gotten into her dad. But she was going to find out—somehow.

Five

Carrie Mersel hung up the phone and stared out the window at the rapidly gathering clouds. She couldn't believe what Alex had just told her. Why would Mr. Wagner ever even *think* of buying Alex a pink T-shirt? Maybe he had eaten some bad fish or something. Maybe he'd been kidnapped by aliens and replaced by a brainless pod. Hey! Maybe there was a story in that idea. Carrie glanced longingly at her typewriter.

But she didn't have time to concentrate on writing. Alex had sounded totally freaked out. She was even cleaning out all the junk from under her bed so that she could *hide* from her father if he tried to spray her with some weird perfume he had bought. Carrie had to figure out a way to help her friend before she did something drastic—like agreeing to wear the T-shirt and listen to the Spice Girls just so her father would leave her alone. Carrie shuddered at the thought.

She grabbed the phone again and immediately dialed Sky's number. If anybody could understand a bizarre parental crisis, it was Sky. After all, Sky's dad and Alex's dad were a lot alike. They both worked at home, they both . . .

Well, okay, maybe they weren't *that* much alike. But they were both cool. And that was much more than Carrie could say for her own father.

"Hello?" Sky answered.

"Hey," Carrie said. "Have you talked to Alex today?"

"No. Why? Did she tell you something?"

"Just that her father went out and bought her the Spice Girls' CD and a pink T-shirt," Carrie replied matter-of-factly.

Sky didn't say anything for a few seconds. "You're kidding, right?" she finally asked.

"Nope." Carrie smirked. "But that was *my* reaction, too."

"Wow." Sky took a deep breath. "Did Alex say *why*?"

"No, she's just as clueless as we are," Carrie said. "Not to mention a little freaked out. She said it was totally out of the blue. He disappeared this morning, then came back with all these weird un-Alex-like gifts."

There was another pause. "Did she, uh ... mention anything about Ms. Tyler?" Sky asked tentatively.

"Actually I did," Carrie said. She sat up in bed again and stared out the window at the dark gray sky. "I told her that maybe Ms. Tyler had given Alex's dad some kind of advice during that meeting. You know, since Alex is so much of a tomboy, maybe she told Mr. Wagner to buy things that were untomboyish."

"Maybe," Sky said slowly. "But I think ..." She didn't finish.

"You think what?" Carrie prodded.

"Nothing, nothing. Forget it." Sky cleared her throat. "You know what?" she suddenly announced. "I think there's only one thing we can do to get to the bottom of this."

Carrie grinned. "What's that?"

"Spy on Mr. Wagner."

Carrie rolled her eyes. "Seriously, what?"

"I *am* being serious," Sky stated very casually.

Oh boy, Carrie thought. "Yeah, that's just what Alex needs right now," she said dryly. "Her two best friends spying on her own father behind her back."

Sky laughed. "Who said anything about doing it behind her back? I'm talking about all *three* of us."

Carrie started shaking her head. If there was anything in the world that Alex Wagner would not go for, it would be spying on her dad. Or spying on anyone, for that matter. Alex hated doing things like that. . . .

Of course, Sky could be pretty persuasive. And weirder things had happened. After all, Carrie would have never expected in a million years that Mr. Wagner would buy Alex the Spice Girls' CD. According to Alex, her father usually enjoyed shopping for girl stuff about as much as he enjoyed a trip to the dentist. Besides, Alex was desperate. Yup, that much was clear from her phone call.

"Trust me, Carrie," Sky said confidently. "Alex will go for it."

Sunday:
Sky's Spying Failure

9:45 A.M. Alex awakens to the sound of her father singing in the shower, belting out some weird song that goes: "Ain't no woman like the one I got," over and over. He sounds like a cat being strangled. Alex promptly buries her head under the pillow.

10:11 A.M. The phone rings, but somebody in the house answers right away.

10:13 A.M. Alex walks downstairs—just in time to see her father heading out the door. When she asks him where he is going, he cheerfully replies, "Shopping at the mall."

10:17 A.M. Alex informs Matt that Dad has gone "shopping" again. Amazingly

183

enough, Matt just shrugs. "Maybe Dad will get something for *me* today," he says with a strange smile. He grabs his basketball and leaves the house.

10:18 A.M. Alex calls Carrie and asks if she can move in with the Mersels. Now both her dad *and* her brother have gone insane. Carrie gently tells her to relax. Sky has a plan. They should meet at Sky's house at noon.

EARLY AFTERNOON

12:04 P.M. Alex rolls up to Sky's dock on her skateboard with her backpack stuffed full of her father's presents. She gives them all to Sky. After all, Sky is the only one of them who can truly appreciate the Spice Girls, the color pink, *and* perfume that smells like strawberry yogurt.

12:30 P.M. Sky outlines her plan: The three of them will report directly to Ocean's Edge Mall—in a very sneaky way, of course—and discreetly follow Alex's dad until they find out the truth.

12:31 P.M. Alex can't believe it. Spy on her dad? Now her *friends* have lost their minds. Maybe all of Taylor Haven is being possessed by some weird evil being or something. . . .

1:03 P.M. Alex finally agrees to go to the mall—mostly because she's too tired to argue anymore.

1:45 P.M. Skyler's dad drops the three of them at the mall. Much to Alex's relief, her father is nowhere in sight.

2:03 P.M. The three of them have sat down to a plate of french fries when Ms. Tyler suddenly appears in the food court. Alex tries to escape, but it's too late. Ms. Tyler gives them all a big friendly wave, then pulls up a chair.

2:04 P.M. Alex sits in shock as Ms. Tyler bombards her with all sorts of strange questions, none of which have anything to do with school or biology or ripped pants. When did Alex start skateboarding? Has she always been athletic? How was Matt doing? And on and on . . .

2:16 P.M. Thankfully Carrie announces that they all have to leave, making up some excuse about catching a ride home. The three of them bolt.

2:17 P.M. Alex vows never to follow one of Sky's plans again.

LATE AFTERNOON

4:30 P.M. Alex returns home to find her father puttering around the kitchen and humming to himself. He's making spaghetti with tomato and basil sauce—Alex's favorite. Finally Alex breaks down and asks him what on earth is going on. He says he's happy. He's got a wonderful daughter and a wonderful son. Doesn't a man have a right to be happy about that?

4:32 P.M. Alex calls Sky and repeats the bizarre dialogue for Sky's benefit. Sky seems on the verge of telling her something—then changes her mind at the last second. She claims she has to go before Alex can ask anything more.

4:45 P.M. Mr. Wagner knocks on Alex's door. Apparently he just wants "to chat." Alex mentions that she ran into Ms. Tyler at the mall. "Isn't she wonderful?" Mr. Wagner asks. "Yeah," Alex replies dismally. "Sure. Whatever."

Six

I

"No change of pants today?" Sam teased.

"Very funny." Alex groaned. The two of them pushed through the glass door and joined the rest of the mob in the courtyard. Just being *near* this door made Alex's stomach twist. She felt as if she were standing at the scene of some terrible crime or something. A few faint traces of the skid marks still streaked the floor. "Believe me, I don't want to do anything that will get Ms. Tyler's attention."

Sam tossed his skateboard onto the smooth white flagstones and immediately hopped on board, snaking his way through a few students. "Has she been on your case today?" he asked, squinting at Alex in the early afternoon sunshine.

"I wouldn't say *that*," Alex mumbled. She slouched down on the one remaining empty bench, resting her own skateboard on her lap. The truth of it was that she didn't know *what* to make of Ms. Tyler. All during biology class that morning Ms. Tyler kept sneaking these weird little smiles at her. And when Alex knew the answer to some dumb question about photosynthesis, Ms. Tyler acted like it was the Fourth of July.

"What's the problem, then?" Sam asked, gliding to a stop in front of her.

Alex shrugged. "Beats me. All I know is that every single person in my life, except for you, has gone totally—"

"Alex Wagner!" Jordan's sarcastic voice boomed across the courtyard. "My favorite person in the whole wide world!"

Alex shook her head. "See what I mean?"

Jordan pushed through the crowd, clutching his sketch pad under his arm. He flashed Alex and Sam a broad, goofy grin. "Sorry if I embarrassed you," he murmured, plopping down beside her on the bench. "I just want your dad to think that you're really popular—you know, in case he's listening."

Alex smirked. *Listening?* That was a totally bizarre thing to say—even for Jordan. "And how could my dad possibly be listening?" she asked, staring into his bright green eyes. "Did he rig up a hidden microphone or something?"

"It's always best to play it safe," Jordan said solemnly. He nodded toward the skateboard on her lap. "Good thinking, by the way. Stay off your board till he's gone. Then you can start terrorizing the halls again—"

"Wait a second," Alex interrupted. "What do you mean, 'till he's gone'?"

Jordan frowned confusedly. "When he's done meeting with Ms. Tyler."

Alex's heart bounced violently in her chest. *"What?"* she gasped.

"He's in her office." Jordan exchanged a quick glance with Sam. "I mean, I just saw him walk in there, like, five minutes ago. . . ."

II

Carrie didn't like the courtyard much. Nope. At recess she liked to just roam the halls aimlessly. Even though the fifth- and sixth-graders ate lunch while the older kids were outside, the courtyard was *way* too small for every single seventh- and eighth-grader. It was kind of like a prison yard. Plus everybody was always messing about, screaming at the top of their lungs about something. And if you didn't ride a skateboard or play soccer, you had to sit on a bench and pray you didn't get hit by flying balls.

Whoopee.

Of course, the other reason Carrie liked being inside during recess was that you weren't *supposed* to be inside. Not that you could get in that much trouble . . . well, not unless you were doing wild skateboard tricks, like Alex. But still, it was kind of *bad*. And being a little bad was always fun. Occasionally she even managed to convince Sky to stay inside with her. Of course, Sky usually got pretty nervous about it. Like today, in fact . . .

"Eww!" Sky hissed, suddenly grabbing Carrie's arm.

"What?" Carrie whispered, glancing around anxiously. They were right outside the main offices—but the halls were clear, as far as she could see.

Sky yanked her over to the wall. "Alex's dad is in there," she mouthed, pointing toward the open door. "In Ms. Tyler's office."

Carrie grinned. "Get out of here."

"I'm serious," Sky breathed, feverishly twirling her hair around her finger—the way she always did when she was really stressed out. "Take a look."

For a moment Carrie hesitated. But Sky didn't look as if she was kidding around. No, as a matter of fact, she looked majorly freaked.

As carefully and quietly as she could, Carrie tiptoed over to the door frame. Holding her breath, she peeked around the corner with one eye. . . .

Oh, my gosh!

III

Alex buried her face in her hands. *This can't be happening. This can't be happening. Tell me this is a joke. . . .*

"Uh-oh," Jordan mumbled. "I thought you knew."

Alex shook her head. She drew in a deep breath, then let her hands drop. Okay.

Enough was enough. Her father had taken things way too far. Showering her with freakish gifts was one thing. But meeting with Ms. Tyler behind her back . . . no, *that* was intolerable. She was doing her time in detention. What more did they have to talk about? Her eyes smoldered. Something had to be done about it. Immediately. She thrust her skateboard aside and stood up, clenching her fists at her sides.

"Um . . . Alex?" Jordan asked anxiously. Both he and Sam were staring at her. "Where are you going?"

"To say hi to my dad," she growled.

"Alex?" Sam called after her. "I don't know if that's such a great idea. . . ."

But Alex was already halfway to the door.

IV

Carrie blinked a few times, not trusting the totally bizarre sight that greeted her eyes.

Mr. Wagner was in there, all right. He wasn't more than five feet away, sitting on that ugly vinyl couch. And Ms. Tyler was sitting right next to him.

Holding his hand.

Carrie bit the side of her cheek. She wasn't sure whether to laugh or gag.

Well, well, well.

Now, she might be wrong, but she was pretty sure that holding hands was *not* part of normal school policy. Especially when it came to the parents of a kid who had just gotten in big trouble. Then again, neither was staring deeply into a parent's eyes. Or smiling that totally corny smile.

Which meant that there was only one explanation.

But still . . . Ms. Tyler and Mr. Wagner? A *couple?* It was totally, completely, utterly insane.

Of course, it would explain a lot of things. . . .

Without any warning, Mr. Wagner stood up.

Carrie jerked her head back from the doorway.

"What?" Sky hissed.

"We gotta motor," Carrie whispered. She grasped Sky by the elbow and tugged her down the hall. *"Now."*

Sky stumbled along beside her. "What's going on?" she murmured nervously, glancing over her shoulder.

"Mr. Wagner's on his way out," Carrie replied. She kept her head down as she rounded the corner. "If he sees us . . ."

"Uh-oh," Sky moaned, freezing in her tracks.

Carrie glanced up—and gasped.

Uh-oh was right. Because Alex was marching down the hall. Straight toward them.

V

Of all the slimy, underhanded things he could do, Alex grumbled to herself, stomping loudly on the tiles. *Meeting with a teacher in private without even telling me . . .*

"Alex?"

Alex raised her head. Her eyes narrowed.

Sky and Carrie were standing right in front of her. Both of them had these really guilty, wide-eyed expressions—as if they'd just been caught stealing or something.

"What are you guys doing here?" she whispered.

"You know . . . uh, you know how I like to stay inside during recess sometimes?" Carrie stammered awkwardly.

Alex rolled her eyes. "Look, you guys—I know my dad's in Ms. Tyler's office. Jordan told me. They're having some secret parent-teacher conference."

Sky and Carrie looked at each other. Sky started fiddling with her hair.

"What?" Alex demanded impatiently.

Carrie licked her lips. "Uh . . . parent-teacher conference?"

"Yeah," Alex stated. "And I'm going to find out why." She stepped around them—but Carrie reached out and clamped a hand down on her shoulder.

"Wait!" Carrie yelped.

Alex sighed. "Don't worry," she said, gently removing Carrie's hand. "I'm already in trouble. A little more trouble isn't gonna kill me."

"No, no, it's not—it's not that," Carrie stuttered. "It's . . . see, he's already left. . . ."

Alex peered at Carrie closely. *Hmmm.* Carrie was *not* somebody who usually got all flustered like this. She was hiding something. Maybe she'd overheard what Ms. Tyler and Alex's dad were talking about.

Before either Sky or Carrie could say another word, Alex dashed around the corner and sprinted toward Ms. Tyler's office. But sure enough, when she burst through the door, the office was empty.

Alex shook her head, panting. Well, her father had escaped this time. But she wasn't going to let him off the hook. No . . . she wasn't going to rest until she had gotten to the bottom of this weirdness.

Once and for all.

Skyler Foley
Is Right Again

I knew I was right. Yes, siree. Like I said,
all the classic symptoms of romance were
there. And as if witnessing that little
rendezvous in Ms. Tyler's office wasn't
enough, my mom just gave me the final
piece of evidence. She bumped into Ms.
Tyler this afternoon at the Taylor Haven
food co-op.

And guess what?

Ms. Tyler told my mom she "just started
seeing somebody." You know who.

What can I say? It helps to have a mom
who's friendly with all the teachers—
not to mention one who's as big a gossip
as I am.

So now comes the tricky part. Alex still
doesn't know about the romance. But
after she freaked out in the hall, Carrie
and I told her she should just come out
and ask her dad what's going on. It's only

fair that she should hear the bad news from him, right? I know I couldn't tell her. I mean, having your parent dating a teacher at your school ... that's like serious nightmare material.

I guess the best thing to do is act like it isn't a big deal. We should remind Alex of all the possible benefits, too. I mean, there's no <u>way</u> she's going to get a bad grade in biology now. That's a good thing, because Alex hates biology. Plus, she can come to school wearing whatever she wants. She can dress like a total slob. What's the worst that can happen? If she gets in trouble, she'll just have to meet with her dad's girlfriend.

Now that I think about it ...

Maybe Alex's situation <u>isn't</u> nightmare material.

On the other hand, I'd probably feel a whole lot different if I were in her shoes.

Seven

Sky decided to wait until precisely six P.M. that same Monday evening to call Alex.

There was no reason for that, really. She just wanted to give Alex a few hours to think things over. Talking to her dad must have been really, really harsh.

But hopefully by now Alex would have calmed down enough to actually talk about it.

Sky stretched out on her narrow bed and reached for the phone on her desk. After punching in Alex's number, she stared out the porthole at the sound as the other end rang and rang and rang. . . .

"Hello?" Alex finally answered.

"Hey," Sky said carefully. "It's me. How's it going?"

Alex laughed. "I've had better days," she mumbled. "How's it going with you?"

"Not bad," she replied. She was actually

a little surprised. Alex sounded much more upbeat than Sky would have expected. She took a deep breath. "Alex—I know this is the last thing you probably want to hear right now, but look at it this way. You have a totally major connection on the inside now. I mean, in a way, I'm kind of jealous. Seriously. If *my* dad were going out with the assistant principal, I'd totally—"

"*What* did you just say?" Alex shrieked.

Sky flinched. *Oops.* Maybe the part about an inside connection was a little over the top. "What I meant was—"

"You said if your dad were going out with the assistant principal," Alex stated. Sky could hear her breathing heavily. "What is *that* supposed to mean?"

Sky blinked. Maybe she should have waited a little longer to call. Alex was obviously in a serious state of denial right now. "Come on, Alex," she murmured shakily. "You talked to your dad, didn't you?"

"No. He's not here. I haven't seen him since this morning. *You've* seen him more recently than *I* have."

Sky started shaking her head. Suddenly she felt vaguely sick. "So—so he hasn't told

201

you about . . ." She couldn't bring herself to complete the question.

"Told me about *what*?" Alex cried.

The color drained from Sky's face. This couldn't be happening. It wasn't possible. . . .

"What about my father and Ms. Tyler?" Alex demanded.

Sky squeezed her eyes shut. Why couldn't she have waited for Alex to call *her*? She should have known. But it was too late now.

"Sky . . ."

"Listen, Alex," she managed to choke out. "I don't know how to tell you this, but see, uh, my mom . . . my mom ran into Ms. Tyler just now." The words seemed to pour out of her mouth in a nonsensical jumble. "And they started talking. Um, see—she told my mom that she's, well . . . she's kind of dating your dad."

She let out a deep breath.

Alex didn't respond. Sky couldn't even hear her breathing anymore.

"Alex?" she murmured cautiously, opening her eyes.

"*Dating* my dad?" Alex shrieked. "This is *crazy*!"

Sky sat up in bed and ran a clammy hand over her curls. "Listen, Alex, I am so sorry. I thought you knew—"

"Hold up a second," Alex interrupted. "Are you *sure?* I mean really positive? Maybe your mom got my dad confused with somebody else."

Sky hesitated. "I don't think so, Alex," she whispered. "See . . . today when Carrie and I ran into you in the hall, we saw your father and Ms. Tyler, and—and . . ." She couldn't bring herself to finish.

"And?" Alex prompted.

Sky hung her head. "And they were holding hands," she finished miserably.

"Are you serious?" Alex cried. "That is so *gross!*" She moaned. "And right in front of my own friends . . ."

"They didn't know we were there," Sky offered—as if that would help at all.

"I really should have known," Alex muttered. She sounded as if she were talking to herself. "That song he was singing in the shower yesterday . . . I should have known. *That's* why he's been disappearing. *That's* who he's spending all his time with."

"So what are you going to do?" Sky asked anxiously.

"What *can* I do?" Alex barked. "It's *nuts!*"

Sky winced. "Look, Alex, what I said was true," she offered lamely. "I mean, it's not necessarily a bad thing. Ms. Tyler is a really nice woman and—"

"Spare me, Sky," Alex cut in. "I'm sorry. I mean, I appreciate what you're trying to do. Honestly. But right at this moment I gotta tell you . . . whatever you say is probably just gonna make me feel worse."

Oh, man. Sky blushed, desperately wishing she could just hang up the phone and forget about the whole thing. "I guess you probably want to go now, huh?" she asked, feeling like a complete fool.

"Yeah," Alex mumbled. "I guess so."

"Hey, Alex?" she quickly piped up. "I know this isn't the best time to ask any favors—but would you mind not telling your dad that I was the one who told you?"

Alex sighed. "Of course I won't. Listen,

Sky—I'm not mad at you. I promise. I'm just kind of . . . I don't even know."

"I hear you," Sky murmured. "So what *are* you going to say to your dad?"

Alex moaned again. "I have no idea. Maybe I'll start by telling him that he can stop buying me all those stupid presents."

Eight

The moment Alex hung up the phone, she heard the sound of the front door opening. *Perfect timing,* she thought grimly. She hopped over the dirty laundry on her floor and marched to the top of the stairs.

Oh, brother.

It was only Matt coming home from basketball practice. His hair was still damp from the shower.

"It's you," she grumbled.

Matt glanced up the stairwell. "Nice to see you, too, Alex," he said flatly. He immediately headed for the kitchen.

"Wait!" Alex called. Now that she thought about it, Matt had been acting kind of strange, too. He probably knew all about their father. He'd probably known all along. She bounded down the stairs and followed him all the way to the refrigerator.

"What do you want?" he muttered, sounding bored.

"Do you know about Dad?" she demanded.

He snickered, then opened the refrigerator door. "What about him?" he asked casually. He didn't even bother to look at her. His eyes roved over the food in the fridge.

"What do you think?" she hissed through tightly clenched teeth. She was starting to get even more mad—a pretty major feat, considering her already foul mood. What was Matt's problem? Why was he acting like this was some kind of joke?

Matt sighed. "I assume you're talking about Dad's romantic entanglement," he said. He reached for a carton of orange juice and closed the door as calmly as if they were talking about the weather.

Alex's face darkened. "You can skip the vocabulary lesson, Dork Boy," she growled. "You're not impressing me."

"Whatever." Matt shrugged, grabbed a glass from the cupboard, and poured himself some juice. Then he slouched down at the table. "Why are you freaking out?" he asked, finally meeting her gaze.

"Freaking out?" Alex yelled. "What do you expect me to do?"

Matt shrugged again, eyeing her as he took a huge gulp of juice. "Maybe you should be happy for him," he said after a moment.

"Wait a second; wait a second." She sneered. "Why should I be *happy* for him? I didn't even *know* until five minutes ago! Sky told me! He didn't even tell me himself!"

Matt raised his eyebrows. "You could have asked him what was going on, you know."

"I *did!*" Alex threw her hands in the air. "He just said some garbage about how he was happy to have a wonderful daughter and a wonderful son."

"Look, Alex," Matt stated firmly. "I'm sure he'll tell you when he's ready. It's probably hard for him. Think about it from *his* point of view. He's dating one of your teachers."

Alex made a face. "Thank you, Mr. Genius. I didn't know."

Matt shook his head, mumbling something under his breath. He took another sip of juice.

"Why did he tell *you,* anyway?" she demanded.

He fixed her with a condescending stare. "Well, Alex, as you so brilliantly suggested, it didn't take a genius to figure it out. I mean, he was singing 'Ain't No Woman Like the One I've Got' in the shower. *Obviously* he met somebody." He downed the juice in a final, noisy slurp. "So I just went and asked him who."

Alex just stood there, too overwrought to even *speak*. How was it supposed to be obvious to her? She didn't know the first thing about how you were supposed to act when you "met somebody."

"Why don't you chill out, all right?" he added quietly.

"Chill out," she repeated. She was seething now. "Why should I?"

Matt scowled. "Because you're being *selfish*, Alex. I mean, can't you see that Dad is really, really happy? Have you ever even *seen* him this happy?" His voice rose. "Have you?"

Alex folded her arms in front of her, struggling to remain calm. "*I'm* the one who's being selfish," she stated. "What about Dad? Huh? Of all the women on the entire planet, he had to pick the assistant principal at *my* school. Do you have any idea—"

"Hi, kids, I'm home!"

The front door slammed.

Finally, Alex said to herself. She'd been yelling so loud, she hadn't even heard her father come in. But that was all right. Because now she was going to have a chance to speak her mind. Oh yes. She was going to ask a *lot* of questions.

"So what do you think?" Mr. Wagner asked, cheerfully sauntering into the kitchen. He patted his hair—or what was left of it. Alex couldn't believe her eyes. His wild curls were gone. His hair hadn't been this short since . . . well, probably since before Alex was born. It was as if the rumpled-looking man she'd known all her life had disappeared. He'd become an entirely different person. A total stranger.

Alex forced a brittle smile. "Real nice, Dad. Real nice."

Her father glanced confusedly at Matt, then back at Alex. "What's wrong?"

"You tell us," she spat.

His brown eyes softened. "Oh," he said quietly. He sat down beside Matt. "I guess you heard the news."

She swallowed. "Yeah." Her voice became strained. "No thanks to you."

He shook his head. "I'm sorry, Alex. I was going to wait for the right moment to tell you, but—"

"But *what?*" she shouted, unable to control herself.

A pained look crossed her father's face. "Alex, please . . ."

"You know what? I'm happy for you. I really am. Congratulations." She sniffed loudly, then stormed out of the kitchen.

Without another word she clambered up the stairs and slammed her bedroom door behind her. She couldn't let her father see her so upset. Besides, she knew that all the questions in the world wouldn't do a bit of good.

No . . . it didn't matter *why* her father and Ms. Tyler were going out.

All that mattered was that they *stopped* going out.

As soon as possible.

Alex Wagner's Book of Deep Thoughts

Entry 12

Okay, now that I've totally embarrassed myself in front of my father and Matt, I think I'm finally calm enough to think straight. I don't even know why I got so upset. Maybe it was the haircut. Ha, ha.

No, actually, I do know the reason. For the first time ever, my dad was dishonest with me. In a way, he lied. Everybody else found out the truth way before I did. It's like I can't even trust him anymore. I feel . . . what's that word when somebody stabs you in the back? Betrayed. Yeah. That's it. That's exactly how I feel.

I know that sounds harsh. It sounds like I'm overreacting. But I'm not. He not only committed the most heinous possible act in the world, but he kept it a secret. I mean, how could he go out with somebody from my school? Doesn't he know what this will do to me?

If anybody besides Carrie, Jordan, Sky, and Sam finds out about this, I'm dead. I'm not kidding. I'm going to be the butt of every stupid joke at Robert Lowell for the rest of the year.

But that's not even the worst of it.

No. That's just the school part.

See, now Ms. Tyler is a part of my nonschool life, too. My _real_ life. And she's taking up all my dad's time. I don't even _See_ him anymore. And when I do, it's like hanging out with a mental patient or something.

I just know Ms. Tyler is going to try to act like my mom. My lousy assistant principal. I can already tell. I bet she's going to force me to get rid of my skateboard. I mean, it's completely obvious that she hates tomboys. Why else would my dad buy all those stupid presents? She doesn't think I'm girly enough.

So. Something needs to be done. Pronto. If my dad really thinks that I'm going to just sit back and take this, he's got another think coming. Because I'm not going to act all nice and sweet and pretend like everything's groovy. No way. I hereby declare that it is my life's mission to break the two of them up. I'm going to make Ms. Tyler wish she'd never even <u>heard</u> of the Wagner family. If she thought that the ripped jeans and skid marks were bad, she ain't seen nothing yet.

I'm going to become her worst nightmare. Starting now.

Nine

Ms. Tyler tossed her wavy brown hair over her shoulder and pointed to the crude diagram of a leaf on the chalkboard. "So plants breathe, too," she said. "Only, they breathe *in* carbon dioxide and breathe *out* oxygen. . . ."

Alex rolled her eyes dramatically, trying to look as bored as possible. Not that looking bored was very hard. She could barely listen to this stuff under *normal* circumstances. She twirled her pencil around her finger, slouching back in the cramped wooden desk.

". . . Which leads us back to our original topic," Ms. Tyler continued. Her eyes scanned the classroom. "Bobby, do you have a question?"

Alex grimaced. Ms. Tyler was still ignoring her. She'd deliberately sat in the front of the classroom to annoy Ms. Tyler.

But it didn't seem to be working. And something drastic needed to be done. Soon. Class was almost over.

"That's right," Ms. Tyler said. "So plants can replenish the earth's atmosphere—"

Alex yawned loudly.

Ms. Tyler raised her eyebrows. "Alex?" she asked, sounding vaguely irritated. "Do you want to share something with the class?"

"I thought I just did," Alex muttered.

A few kids giggled.

Ms. Tyler frowned. "Settle down," she commanded. She fixed Alex with an even stare.

Alex's eyes narrowed. Was it her imagination, or was Ms. Tyler more dressed up than usual? She was wearing a sleek blue dress. Teachers almost *never* wore dresses. Also, her hair was down again. Maybe she was meeting Alex's dad today for another secret visit.

Yuck.

"Perhaps you can answer the question I posed earlier," Ms. Tyler stated.

"What question was that?" Alex asked dully.

Ms. Tyler folded her arms across her chest. "You weren't listening?"

"Just ask me the question," Alex insisted. Every pair of eyes in the class was suddenly focused on her. Now *this* was more like it.

"Fine." Ms. Tyler sighed. "Name a member of the plant kingdom that can move."

Alex batted her eyelashes. "I don't know. *You?*"

The classroom erupted with laughter.

"Quiet!" Ms. Tyler barked. "Alex, I will *not* tolerate—"

The bell rang, drowning out the rest of her words. The room filled with chattering voices and chairs screeching and books slamming shut. Ms. Tyler shook her head hopelessly.

Alex smirked.

"Don't forget—problem set four is due tomorrow," Ms. Tyler called as everyone shuffled out of the classroom. She thrust a finger at Alex. "I'd like *you* to stay a minute."

Alex shrugged. *I thought you'd never ask,* she said to herself. She put her hands behind her head, grinning contentedly.

Ms. Tyler closed the door once they were alone. "What was that all about?" she asked.

"What?" Alex replied with as much innocence as she could muster.

"Your new attitude." Ms. Tyler's forehead grew creased. "I'm concerned. You aren't acting like yourself."

Alex sneered. "How would *you* know?"

"Because you're my student," Ms. Tyler replied matter-of-factly. "And you're usually attentive and considerate." Her face softened. "Alex, listen, I know this new situation must be confusing for you—"

"Oh, *please*," Alex moaned, lowering her eyes.

Ms. Tyler didn't say anything for a few moments. Finally she let out a deep breath. "Your father must have talked to you, right?"

"A little," Alex admitted grudgingly.

"I think I know your father pretty well. Not as well as you do, of course, but from what I've seen . . ."

Blah, blah, blah, Alex thought. Why did

grown-ups always feel the need to talk so much? Why couldn't they just shut up every now and then? Besides, Ms. Tyler was way wrong. She *didn't* know Alex's dad. So she had no business talking about him.

Wait a second.

Ms. Tyler hardly knew him at all, in fact. They had just met. For all she knew, he could be some kind of crazed, ax-murderer maniac. Or a womanizer. Or have multiple personalities. He could act one way in front of Ms. Tyler—and a totally different way at home alone with his family. Ms. Tyler would have no way of knowing the truth. Unless, of course, Alex spilled the beans about Tom Wagner's terrible dark side . . .

"Don't you agree?" Ms. Tyler asked.

"Huh?" Alex shook her head, snapping back into reality. "Sorry. What?"

Ms. Tyler sighed. "Did you hear a word of what I just said?" she asked.

"Uh . . . no." Alex rubbed her eyes. *No better time than the present.* "I'm sorry—it's just that I'm a little tired." She added just the right amount of scratchiness to her voice. "I didn't really sleep all that well last night."

Ms. Tyler bent forward, studying Alex's face closely. "You didn't?"

"No," Alex lied. "You see, my dad was up kind of late and . . ." Her voice trailed off. She shot a quick glance at Ms. Tyler, then looked away. "Never mind."

"Did your father keep you up?" Ms. Tyler asked incredulously.

Alex scratched her head, mussing her hair in a discreet effort to look as worn-out and haggard as possible. "It wasn't really *him* so much as his friend. . . ."

The second bell rang, signaling the start of the next class.

"Whoa!" Alex cried, hopping out of her chair. "I gotta go." She snatched her book bag off the floor, then scrambled past Ms. Tyler. *Please ask me to come to your office this afternoon,* she prayed silently. *Please, please, please . . .*

"Wait," Ms. Tyler called just as Alex reached the door.

Alex cast a forlorn look over her shoulder. "Yeah?" she croaked.

"I think we should finish this conversation," Ms. Tyler stated slowly. "Come to my office after class this afternoon in lieu of detention."

Alex nodded, doing her best to look miserable. "Okay. I'll be there."

And I'll make sure you never, ever want to see my dad again, she added silently.

Ten

By the time Alex flopped down onto Ms. Tyler's slippery couch at three-fifteen that afternoon, she really *was* exhausted. But that was good. It made everything more realistic. She'd spent the last five minutes in the girls' bathroom with Sky and Carrie, trying to make herself look as run-down and waiflike as possible. Her hair was a tangled mess. Carrie had used some gray eye shadow to paint circles under Alex's eyes—barely noticeable, but just enough so that she looked really unhealthy.

It was perfect.

"Hi, Ms. Tyler," she mumbled.

Ms. Tyler squinted at her from across the desk. "Alex—are you all right?"

Alex pretended to be trying really hard to smile. Her lips twitched. "Yeah, fine," she breathed. "Like I told you this morning, I didn't get a whole lot of sleep. . . ."

"Do you want a glass of water or something?" Ms. Tyler asked worriedly. "I could open the curtains a little, let a little more light in here."

"No, no, really," Alex murmured. "But, uh, do you mind if I just stretch out on this couch?"

Ms. Tyler shook her head. "No, not at all. Make yourself comfortable."

"Thanks." Alex shifted on the cushions, propping her feet up on one armrest and laying her head on the other. She was half tempted to smile. This was going even better than she'd expected. "Just wake me if I pass out," she whispered, closing her eyes.

Ms. Tyler cleared her throat. "Alex, if you don't mind my asking . . . what exactly happened last night?"

Alex opened her eyes. "Nothing out of the ordinary or anything," she muttered, staring at the ceiling. "See, my dad sent me to my room after dinner because he was having company, and he—"

"I'm sorry," Ms. Tyler interrupted. "He did *what?*"

Alex turned her head, meeting Ms. Tyler's concerned gaze. "He sent me to my room," she explained simply. "That's what he always does when he has friends over."

Ms. Tyler's eyes widened. "He *does?*" She sounded absolutely aghast.

"Mm-hmm," Alex said, yawning. "Anyway, last night it was this big blond woman . . . um . . ." She paused for a minute, as if trying to remember the woman's name. "Rebecca!" she exclaimed.

"Rebecca?" Ms. Tyler frowned. "That's my name, too."

"Oh." Alex blinked. "Maybe it wasn't Rebecca. Roberta? Ronda? I'm pretty sure the name started with an *R.* Anyway, I've seen her before."

Ms. Tyler began drumming her fingers on the desktop. "Who was this woman?" she asked. A nervous, high-pitched laugh escaped her lips, but then her expression flattened. "I mean, you said she was a friend of your father's. . . ."

Alex lifted her shoulders slightly. "I guess so. Like I said, I've seen her before. I don't think she's involved with his job or anything, though. She only comes over when it's late at night. I wouldn't mind so much, but she has this really loud laugh. That's what kept me up."

"I see." Ms. Tyler's jaw tightened. "How late . . . did she stay? I mean, did you keep track of the time?"

Alex nodded. "I think it was around four or something." She sighed. "Hey, Ms. Tyler? I'm really sorry about the way I acted in class today. It's just that sometimes I can get a little grouchy when I don't get enough sleep."

Ms. Tyler shook her head. "Well . . . I, uh—there's no excuse for being rude, of course," she stammered. "But I appreciate the apology. And I understand. Everybody gets a little out of sorts when they don't have proper rest."

Just like you are now, Alex thought delightedly. Ms. Tyler couldn't keep still. She kept fidgeting in her chair—crossing her legs, uncrossing them, playing with her hands. She was getting majorly worked up.

"So does your father have late-night company often?" Ms. Tyler suddenly asked. "Because if it's affecting your performance in school, maybe I should call him in for another meeting—"

"No!" Alex blurted, sitting up straight. Another meeting was *not* an option. Alex would be *so* busted if he heard about this little get-together. "I mean—he'd, uh, he'd get really mad at me if he knew I was telling you all this stuff. He's real big on privacy."

Ms. Tyler raised her eyebrows. "I would imagine he is," she muttered.

"Listen, Ms. Tyler—you have to promise me you won't tell him about this," she pleaded. "He'd kill me if he found out."

Ms. Tyler leaned across the table. "Alex, are you afraid of your father?" she asked. Her tone was deadly serious.

Alex swallowed. Okay, maybe this had gone a little too far. Telling lies about made-up women was one thing, but she couldn't go around pretending like she was scared of her own dad. "Uh . . . not really," she choked out. "It's just . . ."

"It's just that you want to keep this as our little secret," Ms. Tyler finished with an understanding smile.

Alex breathed a huge sigh of relief. "Exactly."

"I understand." Ms. Tyler stood up and

walked over to the window, absently peering through the crack in the curtains. "Maybe you should come in tomorrow at this time," she suggested in a very businesslike fashion. "We can continue this conversation when you're not so tired. I think that's only fair."

Alex allowed herself a little grin. "Wow," she murmured gratefully. "That would be really nice. Thanks so much."

Ms. Tyler flashed a brief smile over her shoulder. "No problem. I'll see you in biology tomorrow." She paused. "Oh—and Alex? No more outbursts, okay?"

Alex nodded solemnly. "No more," she lied. She couldn't help thinking that Sam had been right that day in the hall: It really *did* help to have friends in high places.

Skyler Foley's Confession

So we all agreed to help Alex ruin her father's budding love affair with Ms. Tyler. And I'm going to do whatever she wants me to do. I mean, she practically begged me to help. She really seems upset, and I wouldn't feel like a true friend if I let her down. Besides, maybe I'd feel the exact same way if I were her. But there's this part of me that thinks this is a really, really bad idea.

I mean, from what she's told me, it sounds like her father has totally flipped for this woman. Totally. He's more psyched on life than he's been in a really long time. So isn't that good for Alex?

I know that when my parents are psyched on life, I can't help but feel pretty psyched, too. Obviously, they drive me crazy with their goofy baby talk and their hippie songs and all the rest of that

cheesy stuff. But it's a _good_ kind of crazy.
That may sound corny, but it's true. It
sure beats the way I feel when I hear
them fighting. Luckily that happens about
as often as Carrie wears white spandex.

So I bet that deep down, Alex is kind of
psyched, too. Not that she would ever
admit it, even to herself.

See, I know Alex. A lot of times she
pretends to be a lot tougher than she is.
Usually the tougher she acts, the more
scared and unsure she is about something.
And she's _really_ scared about this—for a
million different reasons. They're all good
reasons, too.

That's why this is such a weird and
touchy situation. There really isn't a right
or wrong. We all just have to wait and see
what happens.

I _hate_ stuff like that.

Oh, well. I just hope Alex doesn't get
hurt. I hope her father doesn't get hurt,
either. That's not too much to ask, is it?

Countdown to Splitsville

TEN...
WEDNESDAY MORNING

Alex pretends to snooze during biology class, snoring softly. When questioned about her exhaustion after the bell, she informs Ms. Tyler that one of her father's friends kept her up again. This time it was some woman named Georgette. At least . . . she *thinks* it was Georgette. She's too tired to remember.

NINE...
WEDNESDAY AFTERNOON

As Alex sprawls across the vinyl couch, Ms. Tyler asks her if she minds having a bunch of strange women in and out of the house at all hours. Not really, Alex says. The only thing she worries about is the way her father sleeps until noon after they leave. His employers have been leaving a lot of angry messages on the machine. He's kind of behind in his work.

WEDNESDAY, EARLY EVENING

Alex calls Sky and Carrie. She asks them to approach Ms. Tyler privately and explain that they are worried about her: She's been tense, short-tempered, and generally crazy. Sky takes a lot of convincing because she doesn't like to be dishonest, but Alex reminds her that she really *has* been tense lately. Reluctantly Sky agrees, but not before telling Alex she *really* doesn't think Alex should mess with her dad's love life. Carrie's an easier sell. When Alex reminds her of the pink T-shirt and perfume, Carrie agrees that Alex's plan is all for a good cause.

SEVEN...
WEDNESDAY NIGHT

Sky secretly calls Carrie. She's not sure if she wants to go along with Alex's plan. Carrie tells her to relax. It's not like they can get in *trouble* or anything.

SIX...
THURSDAY MORNING

Sky and Carrie report to Ms. Tyler's office before first period to tell her that they're really concerned about Alex. Ms. Tyler nods grimly. They aren't the only ones.

FIVE...
THURSDAY, EARLY AFTERNOON

Much to Sky's dismay, Alex throws a temper tantrum in Ms. Lloyd's English class. Alex is promptly sent to the principal's office. Principal Cashen tells her that she will have to meet with Ms. Tyler again this afternoon.

FOUR...
THURSDAY, LATE AFTERNOON

Alex anxiously tells Ms. Tyler that her father slept through an important meeting yesterday. It looks likes he might lose his most important account. She's starting to get seriously freaked. All the late nights are finally catching up with him.

THREE...
THURSDAY NIGHT

The phone rings just before Alex gets into bed. It's Ms. Tyler. She wants to speak to Alex's dad. He isn't around, Alex says, but she'll pass along the message that she called. She thinks he's out with one of his woman friends. As soon as she hangs up, Alex's dad walks in to kiss her good night. Who was that on the phone? he asks. Carrie, Alex replies without blinking an eye.

TWO...
FRIDAY MORNING

Alex stays late after biology class to inform Ms. Tyler that her father didn't get in until seven o'clock this morning. Ms. Tyler instructs Alex to meet with her one more time after school today.

ONE...
FRIDAY AFTERNOON

In the privacy of her office Ms. Tyler promises Alex that no matter what happens, she'll always be available to talk. Alex should feel free to come by anytime . . . even if the situation between Ms. Tyler and her father should ever change. Alex suppresses the urge to jump for joy.

Eleven

When Alex awoke on Saturday, her ears were greeted by the most welcome sound in the world: silence. The house was as quiet as a classroom at exam time. Nobody was singing in the shower. Nobody was laughing hysterically. Nobody was bursting into her room and yelling, "Hi, honey! Rise and shine! It's another beautiful morning!"

Which could mean only one thing.

Everything was back to normal.

Unless, of course, her father was out "shopping" with Ms. Tyler. But Alex had a hunch that wasn't the case.

She stretched and stumbled out of bed, nearly tripping over her book bag on her way out the door. The smell of coffee wafted through the air. That was definitely a good sign. It meant her father was working. "Dad?" she called hoarsely. She rubbed her puffy eyes with a flannel pajama sleeve as she trudged down the stairs. "Dad . . . are you home?"

"In here," came the faint reply from the study.

A smile spread across her face. She picked up her pace a little as she rounded the corner. Sure enough, there he was: sitting at his computer in his socks and coffee-stained sweat suit. His hair was rumpled (okay, it was still way too short, but it would grow back). His face was covered with a day's worth of stubble. He looked just the way he should look on a Saturday morning. Just like nothing had ever happened.

She paused in the doorway. "Working?" she asked cheerfully.

"Uh . . . yeah," he mumbled. He didn't look up from the computer screen. He was obviously deep into some big ad campaign.

Alex stepped into the room. "I'm gonna get some orange juice. You want me to—" She broke off, frowning.

The computer wasn't even *on*.

"Uh, Dad?" she asked, baffled.

He didn't reply. He simply gazed straight forward, as if the blank screen were the most fascinating thing he'd ever seen in his life.

"Dad?" she repeated.

Suddenly he stood. "I think I'm gonna make some coffee," he said distractedly.

Alex sniffed the air, growing more puzzled by the second. "It smells like you already did."

"Oh yeah." He dropped back into the seat. "I must have forgotten to bring it in here."

Alex bit her lip. She placed her hand on his shoulder. He didn't budge.

"Hey," she murmured. "Are you all right?"

He nodded once. "Fine," he replied. "Just a little tired." But his tone was totally flat and emotionless, as if he were speaking with one of those computerized phone voices.

"You want me to get you some coffee?" she suggested.

"Coffee," he echoed. "Good idea."

Alex forced a smile and hurried from the room. *Whoa.* She shook her head. Well, at least he wasn't acting like a circus clown anymore, right? But now he was acting like a complete zombie. She couldn't exactly call it much of an improvement. When would he just act like *himself?*

Matt was in the kitchen, sitting at the table in a T-shirt and boxers, groggily drinking orange juice. He barely looked up when Alex walked in. "Talk to Dad yet?" he asked.

"Sort of," she muttered. She reached for a mug from the kitchen cupboard, then pulled the coffeepot out from the coffeemaker. It was full, just as she'd suspected. Her father had probably made it no more than five minutes ago—and then forgotten about it. He was *never* that absentminded.

Matt made a face. "Since when do *you* drink coffee?"

"I don't," she said simply. She poured a cup. "It's for Dad. He really needs it, too. He's, ah . . ." She hesitated, thinking of an apt description. "Let's just say he's out of it." She stuck the pot back into the coffee-maker.

Matt shrugged. "What do you expect? He got dumped."

Alex lowered her eyes. "Oh," she said after a moment. Somehow hearing the truth wasn't nearly as sweet as she'd expected. Maybe it was Matt's choice of words. *Dumped* sounded kind of ugly. And something about his tone was so . . . well, *harsh*. But she wanted this, right? This was *good* news.

"Aren't you going to give him his coffee?" Matt asked.

"In a second," she answered. A hot, unpleasant sensation began to tug at her stomach. Her dad was a little more bummed out than she would have expected. But he couldn't be *that* heartbroken, right? After all, he and Ms. Tyler hadn't been going out for *that* long. Just a week . . .

"You want me to bring it to him?" Matt asked.

"Uh . . . no." Alex paced restlessly across the floor. "I'm just thinking. What can we do? We have to do *something*. I've never seen him like this."

Matt shrugged, his face somber. "We're just gonna have to wait it out."

"Wait—wait it out?" Alex stuttered. Her voice rose. "But how long do you think it's going to take?"

Matt shook his head. "You know what, Alex?" His face darkened. "Let me put it this way. You better get used to the way Dad's acting right now. It might not change for a long, long time."

<u>Alex</u> Wagner's <u>Book</u> of <u>Deep</u> <u>Thoughts</u>

<u>Entry</u> 13

Boy. Matt wasn't kidding around when he
said that Dad isn't going to be feeling better
anytime soon. It's been four days now, and
he still hasn't smiled once. From what I've
seen, he barely works, either. He just stares
at his computer. Most of the time the screen
is blank.

I promised myself that I wouldn't start
freaking out until Friday, but I can't help it.
I'm scared. I also feel like the most spoiled,
selfish brat in the world. I guess Matt was
right about that, too. (Not that I'm going
to tell him or anything.) But I mean, the
word <u>guilt</u> doesn't even come <u>close</u> to
describing what I'm going through right now.
If I could take back all that stupid stuff I
did last week . . .

Anyway.

I realized something. I just figured it out
today. I had no idea why I was even messing
with my father's love life. I thought it was

because I was scared of being the laughingstock of Robert Lowell or because I was worried Ms. Tyler would start bugging me to clean my room. But it wasn't. Not entirely. I mean, those were all parts of it, of course. But they weren't the main reasons.

The main reason was that I was jealous of Ms. Tyler.

I know that sounds completely insane. I couldn't even admit it to my/self. I was too ashamed. But it was like . . . when my dad kept disappearing all the time, I felt sort of abandoned. I mean, for the first time since I can remember, there was another person in his life besides Matt and me. Somebody who obviously made him feel really good. And that kind of made me feel bad.

But enough with the sob story. It's hard enough thinking all that stuff, much less writing it down. (I've already made up my mind to throw this notebook in Puget Sound as soon as I'm done with it.) The point is that I can't take it anymore.

That's right.

I'm going to get them back together, if it's the very last thing I ever do.

I know now that dealing with Ms.

Tyler —even if she _does_ try to make me
clean my room or study all the time —is a
million times better than feeling this miserable.
Besides, I was wrong about her. She
doesn't hate tomboys. She's actually really
cool. I mean, I've gotten to know her
pretty well this last week, what with going
into her office almost every single afternoon.
I can't believe some of those lies I told.

So now I just have to come up with a
plan.

Great.

That'll be about as easy as getting my dad
to laugh right now.

Twelve

Carrie couldn't remember the last time all five of them had piled into her room. There wasn't really enough space—especially with all the books on the floor. Not that she was going to complain. Alex had insisted on everybody's presence. And they couldn't exactly meet at *Alex's* house. So Jordan and Sam crammed onto the edge of the bed while Alex and Sky sat on the floor—right beneath the drawn velvet drapes. Carrie pulled out her desk chair and turned it around.

"All right," Alex announced once everybody had settled in. "We've gotta think. How can I possibly get my dad back together with Ms. Tyler?"

Nobody said a word.

Oh, brother, Carrie thought. She'd known this was going to happen. Unfortunately breaking up a couple seemed to be a lot easier than getting them back together.

"Um . . . Alex?" Sky asked, playing with one of her curls. "I know this probably isn't the best time to ask—but what *exactly* did you tell Ms. Tyler about your dad?"

"You don't want to know." Alex groaned miserably. She stared at the floor. Her hair fell in her face. "A lot of really, really bad stuff."

"But we *should* know," Sam said in a quiet voice. "It's important if we really want to come up with something that'll work."

Carrie nodded. She agreed—but she didn't really expect that from Sam. He had never been known to pry. Then again, he probably still felt vaguely responsible because of the whole skateboarding dare.

"Basically I told her that my dad stayed up all night with all kinds of different women," Alex muttered, sighing. "And that he was messing up his work, and that . . ." She hesitated. "And that he was sometimes mean to me."

Carrie cringed. *Wow.* She'd known that Alex had said a lot of bad things—but she'd had no idea they were *this* bad. "How did

243

you say he was mean to you?" she asked cautiously.

"It wasn't anything really bad," Alex mumbled, brushing her hair out of her eyes. She leaned back against the curtain. "Just that he made me stay in my room when he had dates over and stuff like that . . . nothing too serious."

"And Ms. Tyler *believed* it?" Jordan asked, amazed.

Alex shrugged. "I guess I was pretty convincing."

"Well, the important thing is to make her forget about all that stuff," Sky said matter-of-factly. "We gotta make her see who your dad really is. I mean, that's the guy she fell for. She liked the real Mr. Wagner, not the one you made up."

Carrie bit her lip. That was true, of course. But that didn't really help matters. She drew in her breath. "There's really no way we can do that without admitting Alex lied."

Alex hung her head again. "I know," she moaned. "I've thought of that."

Carrie frowned, wishing for once in her life that she'd read more romance novels than horror novels. What did guys do when they wanted to get girls back? Buy flowers? Nah, that was too cliché. Besides, flowers probably wouldn't cut it in this case. This was serious. So what else? They wrote love letters. . . .

Love letters.

"Uh-oh," Jordan said. "Look out. Carrie has that look in her eye."

Carrie laughed. "No, I was just thinking . . . what if your dad wrote Ms. Tyler a love letter?"

Alex's nose wrinkled. "A love letter? How would we get him to do that?"

Carrie reached behind her and patted her typewriter. "We'd do it for him," she replied, smiling conspiratorially.

Sam started shaking his head. "I don't know—"

"No, that's totally it!" Sky exclaimed. "We could make it seem like he used to do all these horrible things, but after he started getting really serious about Ms. Tyler, he totally changed his ways." She waved her hands excitedly. "He made a promise. No more late nights. No more women. We could make it really romantic. When I was

over at Alex's once, I saw this episode of
Melrose where—"

"We get the point, Sky." Jordan groaned.

"I don't know if this is such a great
idea," Sam muttered.

"Oh, come on." Carrie chuckled. "I think
it's an awesome idea."

"But how would we make it seem real
enough?" Alex protested. "I mean, Ms.
Tyler is really smart, you know? She'd
probably see right through it."

"Not if it was in your father's
handwriting," Jordan interjected.

Alex grinned dubiously. "And how
could it possibly be in my father's
handwriting?"

Jordan shrugged. "Hey—I'm an artist,"
he said with a cocky smile. "You don't
think I only draw cartoons, do you?"

Sam rolled his eyes. "Are you honestly
saying that you can *forge* Alex's dad's
handwriting?"

Jordan pointed a finger at him. "Bingo."

"I don't know, Jordan," Alex mumbled,
shaking her head. "It would have to be
perfect."

"It will be," he insisted confidently. "Just

bring something with your dad's handwriting to school tomorrow—like a scrap of paper. Anything. If I take a look at it, I'll be able to copy it. I promise."

Carrie glanced at Alex. "It's worth a shot, right?"

Alex stroked her chin. She still didn't look entirely convinced. And Sam was shaking his head. . . .

"Well, let's just write the letter," Sky said impatiently. "We can worry about that stuff tomorrow."

Carrie nodded. Writing the letter was the thing to do. Before Alex or Sam had a chance to express any more doubts, she turned her chair around and snatched a piece of paper out of her desk drawer. "Let's go," she said, rolling the paper up into the typewriter. "How should it start?"

Sky cleared her throat. "'Dear . . .'" She giggled suddenly. "What's Ms. Tyler's first name?"

"Rebecca," Alex answered.

"Right." Sky took a deep breath. "So. Here goes. 'Dear Rebecca . . .'"

Dear Rebecca,

The days since we last spoke have been among the longest in my life. I haven't been able to eat, or sleep, or even properly care for Alex and Matt. It's difficult for me to write these words . . . but I haven't felt this way about anyone since my wife passed away all those years ago.

Rebecca, I miss that feeling. More than I can say. I can't take floating from one meaningless relationship to the next anymore. In the brief time we spent together, you provided more fulfillment than I ever dreamed possible. I realize now how immature and irresponsible I've been. _You_ made me realize that. And even if we never speak again, I want you to know how much that means to me.

I'm not sure what Alex told you about the women who came to see me recently, but I swear to you, Rebecca—nothing happened. I couldn't even _imagine_ seeing

another woman. Not after you.
You're everything to me.

That's all I have to say. I can't
blame you if you never want to
speak to me again. But I do want
you to know that I'll never forget
you. You'll be in my last thoughts.

                    All my love,
                    Tom

Thirteen

Alex had to admit it: Jordan did a pretty amazing job with her father's handwriting. He'd copied the letter onto a piece of her father's stationery that she'd taken—using an old grocery list as a guide. He'd almost looked as if he were drawing a portrait or something. And the result was perfect. Even Alex couldn't tell the difference between the letter and the grocery list, penmanshipwise.

But now she was starting to get nervous.

Ms. Tyler's office loomed ahead of her. Her knees wobbled as she marched past all the kids rushing in the opposite direction, hurrying out of school. Her hands were clammy. She hadn't really talked to Ms. Tyler since the breakup, except in biology class. And she couldn't shake the nagging voice in her mind: *Is this really going to work?* She could still just turn around and hop on the bus home. . . .

No. I'm here. I'm going to do it.

Of course it was going to work. She shook her head, shoving her doubts aside. The letter looked authentic. The stationery was even imprinted with the words *From the Desk of Thomas Wagner.* And she'd sealed it in a matching envelope. What could go wrong? She just had to march in there and give another brilliant performance. Besides, she wouldn't even be lying this time. Well, not much, anyway. But she was going to apologize. She *wanted* to apologize.

Summoning her courage, she strode down the hall and paused outside Ms. Tyler's closed door. After a few deep breaths she knocked.

"Who is it?" Ms. Tyler called.

"Alex," she replied as calmly as she could manage.

"Alex!" Ms. Tyler cried. "What a nice surprise. Come in, come in."

Alex hadn't expected her to sound so friendly. She hadn't known *what* to expect, actually. But a friendly mood never hurt. She pushed open the door.

"Well, well," Ms. Tyler said, looking up from the papers on her desk and flashing Alex a wry smile. Her hair was back in its usual bun. She hadn't worn it down all week, in fact. "I think this may be the first time you've come to see me of your own volition," she added.

Alex hesitated. "Volition?"

"It means 'free will,'" she explained gently. She gestured toward the couch. "Please. Have a seat. What can I do for you?"

Alex tossed her book bag on the floor and sank into the familiar vinyl cushions. Somehow they didn't seem quite as heinous or ugly as they once had. But she was still far from feeling comfortable. Very far. She glanced anxiously around the room, unable to bring herself to look Ms. Tyler in the face.

"What's on your mind?" Ms. Tyler prodded.

"Well, uh, you know how you said that I should feel free to come see you anytime?"

Ms. Tyler smiled. "Of course."

"See . . . um . . . I just wanted to thank you for listening to me all last week," Alex said clumsily. Her eyes fell to her lap. "I really appreciated it."

"You don't have to thank me," Ms. Tyler murmured. "It was my pleasure."

Alex nodded vigorously. "I also wanted to tell you . . . that you were right about my being confused. You know, about you and my dad. I guess I kind of took out my anger on you sometimes."

Ms. Tyler chuckled reassuringly. "Perfectly understandable, under the circumstances."

"So, anyway . . ." At last Alex forced herself to look directly at Ms. Tyler. "I also wanted to get something off my chest. I wanted to tell you that . . . you know, given my state of mind and all . . . I might not have been completely one hundred percent honest about some stuff."

Ms. Tyler's eyes narrowed. "What do you mean?"

Alex swallowed. "Like, you know how I said that my dad didn't come home till seven that morning?" Her voice faltered. She immediately stared at her lap again. "Actually he got home at eleven, when I was asleep. He was home all night. See, he was just coming in from taking the garbage out in the morning."

Ms. Tyler didn't say anything for a long while. Finally she took a deep breath. "Alex, did your father tell you to come see me?"

"No!" Alex cried. Her head snapped up. "No way. I just feel bad that I stretched the truth a little. I swear. It was like I was taking advantage of you or something. And you were really nice to me."

Ms. Tyler raised her eyebrows doubtfully. "Alex, I don't know—"

"I *swear*," Alex repeated. Okay, this was not good. Maybe it was time to bring out the letter. She leaned over and frantically tugged at the zipper on the front pocket of her book bag. "He did want me to give you something, though. . . ."

"He did?" she asked with just a hint of disdain.

Alex yanked out the envelope and held it in front of her. Her fingers were trembling. "I think it's a note or something." She pushed herself to her feet and dropped the letter onto Ms. Tyler's desk.

"I see," Ms. Tyler muttered. She drummed her fingers together, eyeing the envelope warily.

"He wasn't sure whether he wanted to give it to you or not," Alex added.

Sighing, Ms. Tyler snatched up the letter and tore it open.

Alex sank back into the seat, licking her dry lips. She couldn't watch Ms. Tyler read. It was way too stressful. She gazed at her sneakers, rubbing her moist palms on her baggy jeans. Maybe she should just bolt. The clock above her seemed to tick extra slowly, as if it had run out of batteries or something. She could barely even hear it over the rattling of her own heart. *Please work*, she prayed. *Please work. Please work. Please* . . .

There was a loud sniff.

Alex glanced up.

She nearly fell off the couch

Ms. Tyler's eyes were misty. She clutched the letter with one hand, dabbing her eyes with the other.

It was unbelievable.

She'd fallen for it. She'd actually fallen for it. . . .

"Are you all right?" Alex asked tentatively.

Ms. Tyler nodded and took a deep breath. "I'm sorry, Alex," she said quietly. "It's just so beautiful. It's the most beautiful thing I've ever read."

Fourteen

Half an hour later Alex glided down the length of Sky's narrow dock on her skateboard, triumphantly pumping her fists in the air. She literally felt as if she had won the lottery. Sky, Carrie, Jordan, and Sam were eagerly leaning over the rail of the houseboat's front deck, squinting in the afternoon sunlight.

"Well?" Jordan called.

"It was *incredible!*" Alex shouted. "We practically made her cry!" She jumped off her skateboard and flipped it up into her hands, then climbed on board the boat. Her hair fluttered in the cold, salty ocean wind. "I wish you guys could have been there. It was *awesome.*"

Jordan laughed. "What did I tell you?" he said coolly. "I'm the master."

Sky cocked her eyebrow. "Please, Jordumb. *I'm* the one who made Ms. Tyler all emotional. I came up with all the juiciest lines."

Give me a break, Alex thought, grinning. It figured they would start bickering now, of all times. "Hey, you guys, I thank *all* of you. Really. Besides, it was a total group effort."

"Totally," Jordan concurred. "Let's start celebrating."

Carrie wrapped her black wool sweater around her, shivering once in the breeze. "So what's gonna happen now?" she asked.

Alex shrugged. "I don't know," she replied happily. "I mean, I guess they're going to get back together, right?" She giggled. "You should have seen the look on her face. . . ."

"Hey, that reminds me," Sam piped up. "I have something for you." He dashed into the main cabin, then reemerged holding a small paper shopping bag. "I owe you, remember?"

Alex blushed. "Sam, if that has anything to do with the dare we made . . ."

"Just *take* it, all right?" he insisted. "Anyway, it's not what you think."

Sighing, Alex put down her skateboard. She took the bag from his hands. Her eyes widened as she peered inside. There was a really cool-looking brown wool cap inside. "This is for *me?*" she exclaimed.

Sam raised his hands apologetically. "It's impossible to find any Supersonics gear before the basketball season starts."

"Forget about that. This is totally awesome." She pulled the hat from the bag and put it on her head. "Thank you so much."

"Hey, look!" Sky teased. "Alex's face is getting red!"

Alex grimaced. "Sky . . ."

"You look like you belong in a rap group now," Jordan stated approvingly.

"Thanks a lot," Alex muttered, smirking. "I'm sure my dad will be psyched."

Sam pointed at the hat. "I wanted to wait to give it to you until I knew that everything worked out as planned," he explained. "You know, just to kind of symbolize that the whole thing is over."

Alex nodded gratefully. It really was

over. And everything had worked out for the best. Ms. Tyler and her dad would be getting back together, obviously. And then her dad would snap out of his bad mood. And then life would return to normal. . . .

"Speaking of which, how are you going to explain about the letter?" Sam asked.

Alex paused. "What do you mean?"

He blinked. "I mean, have you thought about what you're going to tell your dad? Ms. Tyler's going to tell him about the letter, don't you think?"

Uh-oh.

The laughter on the deck faded. Alex glanced at the others nervously. She hadn't even thought about that. She'd only thought about writing the stupid letter. But Sam was absolutely right. It was obvious.

"Oh, man," she mumbled.

Sam shook his head. "I was worried about something like this. Maybe we better hold off on the celebration. Maybe you better go home."

"I'll get my dad," Sky said, hurrying

toward the door. "He'll give you a ride."

Before she knew it, Alex was racing back down the length of the dock toward the Foleys' beat-up old van. She'd left her book bag and skateboard lying on the front deck. But it didn't matter.

All that mattered was that she get home in time.

Fifteen

"Dad!" Alex yelled, bursting through the front door. "Dad are you—"

She immediately clamped her mouth shut.

Oh, jeez. Her father was home, all right—right there in the front hall. He wasn't alone, either. Ms. Tyler was standing right next to him, looking totally embarrassed. Her face was pink. She stared at the floor.

Her dad's face, on the other hand, was flaming red. He held the letter in his trembling fingers, his eyes wide.

"Alex!" he barked, thrusting the paper at her. "What on *earth* is the meaning of this?"

Alex winced. Why couldn't Sam have mentioned the possibility of such a disaster *before* they wrote the letter? Alex had never seen her father come even close to being so mad. The veins in his neck and forehead bulged. His eyes were blazing.

"I think I'll leave the two of you alone," Ms. Tyler mumbled. She quickly shuffled out the door. "You probably have a lot of talking to do."

"No, wait!" Mr. Wagner protested, tearing his eyes from Alex.

"I think it's for the best, Tom," Ms. Tyler breathed. "I'll speak . . . I'll speak to you later." She closed the door behind her.

Alex swallowed.

"I don't believe it," he croaked, blinking several times rapidly. His eyes were bloodshot. "I just don't believe it."

"Dad, please," Alex whispered. "If you let me explain . . ."

"You'd *better* explain." He looked ill—as if he'd just eaten too many nachos or something. He clutched his stomach with one hand, waving the letter wildly with the other. "Alex, why did you *do* this? What's *happening* to you? This is . . . this is . . . I don't even know where to *begin!*"

Alex shook her head. "I had to—"

"Had to *what?*" he sputtered. He began pacing back and forth in front of the staircase as he ranted at her. "You had to forge a letter? And meet with Ms. Tyler? And tell outrageous lies?"

Blood rushed to Alex's face. She hung her head. She should have known better than to try to fool two grown-ups. "Ms. Tyler told you about that?" she whispered.

"Of *course* she did!" he cried. "I'm your *father*, Alex. Apparently some of the things you said about me were pretty serious. What *should* she have done?"

Alex tried to swallow again, but a painful lump had formed in her throat. She hadn't wanted to *hurt* him. But she'd been so caught up in her own lame schemes that she hadn't stopped to consider any consequences. "I'm sorry, Dad," she murmured hoarsely. "I really am."

Finally he took a long, shaky breath. "Alex, I've never known you to lie before. You're usually so honest. But now you've told so many lies that—"

"Because I was *scared*," Alex blurted. "I felt like I didn't have a choice."

Her father froze. His lips parted slightly. He looked completely bewildered.

"Scared? What do you mean by that? Scared of *what*?"

"Scared that things would change," she muttered, unable to stop herself. "I mean, when I found out you were dating Ms. Tyler, I was worried that you were gonna start spending more and more time with *her* . . . and less time with *me*. I know that sounds selfish, but I couldn't help it."

For a moment her father didn't say anything. Then he sat on the stairs. His brow furrowed. "But why would you think that?"

"Well, part of it was because you were acting so *weird*." A brief, sad smile curled on her lips. "You kept disappearing and stuff. And I had no idea why." She shook her head again. "Why didn't you tell me right away?"

He sighed. "I should have, Alex," he said, his face softening. "I know that now. But I was scared too. I was scared you'd be upset."

"Yeah, well, you were right about that," she muttered, staring absently at her sneakers.

"Alex, look at me," he said. "No matter

what happens, I will *always* be there for you. Okay?"

"I know," she mumbled. Her gaze flashed up to him for a moment, then fell back to her feet. She just couldn't bring herself to look at him right now. It was too awkward, too painful. She was worried she'd start bawling or something really stupid. "It's just that . . . nothing like this has ever happened before," she added. "I didn't know if I could deal with it."

"Is that why you started acting out in class and making up stories about me?" he asked quietly.

She shrugged. "I guess. But I never thought it would get this bad. And then when I saw how sad you were, I realized what a mistake I made. I mean, I acted like a spoiled brat. I was only thinking of *me*." She jerked a finger toward the letter. "That's why I ended up doing *that*. I just thought if I could get you two back together . . ." Her voice trickled out, mostly because she was too ashamed to continue.

Amazingly enough, he laughed. "How *did* you do this, anyway? I didn't know you could forge my handwriting so well."

She grinned sheepishly. "It wasn't me. It was Jordan. But everybody helped write it."

"I see," he said. "Well, for what it's worth—it's not bad."

Finally Alex managed to raise her eyes. He was clutching the paper in front of his face, shaking his head slowly as if he still didn't quite believe what he was seeing.

"Dad, I didn't mean to embarrass you," she whispered. "I just want you to know that."

He raised his eyebrows, then promptly folded the paper and shoved it into the pocket of his sweatpants. "I know. But imagine the way I felt. I mean, here I am, working at home, looking like a complete slob . . . and then all of a sudden Rebecca— er, Ms. Tyler—shows up at the front door, going on about how she'd never gotten a love letter before."

Alex felt her face getting hot, for what seemed like the hundredth time in the past hour. "I'm really sorry about that," she mumbled.

"Well." He laughed again. "It did accomplish something, though, I guess.

She finally told me what *you* told her. She figured out pretty fast that all those things about late nights and women were just as much of a shock to me as they were to her. I guess she also talked to Skyler's mom. Mrs. Foley put in a good word for me."

Alex nodded. *Thank heavens for the Foley family*, was all she could think. "I swear I'll never do anything like that again," she promised, meeting her father's gaze.

He nodded. "I know. But why didn't you even give Ms. Tyler a chance? It's not like you."

Alex bit her lip. "Because I thought she was going to try to act like a mom," she admitted after a moment.

"Oh, Alex . . ." Her father stood, stepped over, and embraced her, running a hand through her hair.

After a moment Alex stepped away. She knew if she let him hug her any more, she definitely *would* start crying. "I know I was wrong, though. Ms. Tyler is really cool."

He smiled. "I'm glad you think so."

"Look, I've got a great idea," Alex suddenly cried. It was time to fix things once and for all. "Why don't we just start over, okay? We'll invite Ms. Tyler over for dinner—just the four of us. It'll be like a peace offering. We'll just get to know each other all over again."

Mr. Wagner shrugged. "I don't know if she'll go for it," he murmured. "She's pretty embarrassed right now."

Alex shook her head. "That's okay," she insisted confidently. "Leave everything to me."

Sixteen

Burgers, Wagner style, Alex said to herself contentedly. *The key to peace on earth.* Cookouts *always* put people in a good mood. Except maybe Sky, of course. But vegetarians didn't count. Besides, they were peaceful enough, anyway.

Not that the evening had been *totally* snag-free. At first it looked as if Ms. Tyler wouldn't even come. But after Alex hung out in her office and pushed for what seemed like hours, she finally agreed. Still, it *was* a little chilly for a barbecue. Alex huddled around the grill with Matt and Ms. Tyler, shivering in the night air as her dad cooked up the last batch of burgers.

"Maybe we should eat these inside," Matt suggested. His teeth chattered. He rubbed his hands together and held them over the coals.

"Good idea," Alex agreed. She grabbed the paper plates and napkins and hurried back into the kitchen through the screen door on the porch.

Ms. Tyler followed close on her heels. "Where should I put these?" she asked, waving the ketchup and mustard.

"Right here on the table is great," Alex replied.

She still couldn't get over how *easy* it was to hang out with Ms. Tyler in a nonschool situation. Not only was she really funny and easygoing, but she knew about a lot of stuff that Alex's dad didn't—like bands that actually had members under the age of thirty.

"Hey, Ms. Tyler?" Matt asked cheerfully as he pushed through the door. "Now that I'm not your student anymore, can you give me some dirt about Robert Lowell?"

Alex rolled her eyes. "Leave her alone, you dork," she said with a groan, sitting at the table. "You're being rude."

Ms. Tyler grinned slightly. "No, that's all right. I don't mind." She pulled up a chair beside Alex. "And please, both of you, call me Rebecca—at least when we're outside school."

Alex exchanged a smile with Ms. Tyler. It was cool that she wanted them to call her by her first name, but Alex had a feeling it would take her a while to get used to it.

"What would you like to know, Matt?" Rebecca asked.

Matt immediately sat across from them. "What I really want to know is what the administration thinks of hoodlums like Jordan Sullivan and Carrie Mersel." He raised his eyebrows at Alex. "I mean, do they make you nervous?"

Ms. Tyler leaned back in her chair with a thoughtful expression. "You know, that's a good question, Matt."

"*What?*" Alex exclaimed. Ms. Tyler couldn't be serious.

Matt snickered delightedly. "So?"

Alex put her face in her hands. She could just picture what would happen for the rest of the year. Matt would bug Ms. Tyler for dirt on Alex's friends, and Alex wouldn't be able to do a thing about it. . . .

"I'm afraid I can't answer it, though,"

Ms. Tyler replied.

Alex's hands dropped. "You *can't?*" she asked hopefully.

Ms. Tyler shook her head. "No." Her own smile widened. "You see, I'm no longer part of the Robert Lowell administration."

Alex and Matt exchanged a blank stare.

"You aren't?" he asked, frowning.

"No, Matt. . . . I have some news, actually." She glanced over her shoulder. "I was going to wait to tell your father, but—"

"Hold on," Mr. Wagner called from outside. "I can hear you. Coming!"

A moment later he appeared with the last servings from the grill. He set the burgers down in the middle of the table, then pulled up the last empty chair. "So?" he prodded.

Alex held her breath. She was a little nervous, actually. Ms. Tyler wasn't going to say anything totally crazy, was she? Like she was quitting, or she got fired, or . . .

"I got a promotion," she announced, beaming.

"Congratulations!" Mr. Wagner cried.

He threw his arms around her.

"So what are you going to be doing now?" Matt inquired.

She flashed him a sly smile. "Getting reacquainted with you, as a matter of fact. I got transferred to the high school."

Matt's face fell.

"I'm going to be your principal, Matt," she said. "Isn't that great?"

Alex Wagner's Book of Deep Thoughts
Final Entry

I don't think I've ever been happier than when I saw the look on Matt's face the moment Ms. Tyler —Rebecca, I mean— dropped the bomb on us. I mean, how crazy is that? Principal! I didn't even believe it at first. But it's true.

I've got just one thing to say to Matt: Ha!

So now <u>he</u> has to deal with his dad's girlfriend in an "academic setting." (Those are his words, not mine.) Then again, I will, too —as soon as this year's over. Not that I'm worried or anything. In fact, I'm kind of psyched to drop by the principal's office and chat about Nine Inch Nails. I'm going to miss having Ms. Tyler around this year.

Wow. I never thought I'd say <u>that</u>.

I just hope the high school buys her a new couch. That thing has got to go.

Anyway, this whole strange experience did

teach me something. If I ever need my homework forged, I should just go to Jordan. . . .

No, seriously. I learned that having a dad who sings corny songs in the shower is much better than having a dad who mopes around all day. And I'll never, ever do anything to change that. That's a promise I know I'll keep.

Tough luck, Carrie

One

I know I'm going to end up at the mall this afternoon, Carrie Mersel thought, slumping in her chair. She stared at a plate of lukewarm meat loaf, listening to Skyler Foley jabber on and on about some end-of-the-fall blowout sale. *Yup. I just know it.*

Carrie wasn't a huge fan of hanging out at the mall. As a matter of fact, she wasn't a huge fan of shopping, period. But Sky had that insane look in her big brown eyes. It was almost as if there were a glowing billboard inside her head flashing: Prices Slashed! 50% Off! Everything Must Go!

"You *have* to come with me," Sky was complaining to Alex Wagner. She twirled her long brown curls around her fingers. "You can skateboard in the parking lot."

Alex shot a glance across the round cafeteria table at Sam Wells. "Sky, I hate to tell you this, but skateboarding at the mall ... well ..."

"Stinks?" Sam finished for her, raising his black eyebrows.

Alex laughed. "To put it nicely." She reached into her baggy jeans' pocket and grabbed her wool hat, then pulled it over her tousled, shoulder-length dark blond hair. "Come on, Sky. The parking lot there is totally flat and boring. Even *you* know that. And you don't skate."

Sky shrugged. "So you'll just have to come shopping with me," she said brightly.

Carrie had to smile. Poor Sky. She could never bring herself to go to the mall alone. She always figured she might miss out on something. Sky *hated* missing out. So she usually ended up trying to convince everyone else to do whatever she was doing. Of course, more often than not, that meant going to the mall.

"Carrie—you'll come, right?" Sky pressed.

"Sure," Carrie replied grudgingly. She knew it was pointless to fight Sky on this. Besides, Sky *was* the only person on the planet who could actually make the mall semitolerable. She always knew exactly where Carrie could find really good cheap black hair dye. And cheap black shoes. And cheap black dresses. Sky was the master bargain hunter.

"Well, personally *I* would *love* to join all of you in the wonderful world of shop-o-rama," Jordan Sullivan announced sarcastically as he used his fork to create a bizarre sculpture with his mashed potatoes. "But I can't."

Carrie rolled her eyes. She wondered for a moment how Jordan could even see what he was doing. His messy blond bangs practically hung to his nose.

"Why not?" Sky asked, smirking.

Jordan raised his head and brushed aside his hair. "Because I have basketball practice," he stated evenly.

Carrie hesitated, waiting for the punch line. Obviously this was some sort of goofy joke. She exchanged a quick, puzzled glance with Alex and Sam. But they looked just as confused as she did.

Jordan started grinning.

Finally Sky cleared her throat. "Uh . . . I hate to break it to you, Jor-*dumb*, but you aren't on the basketball team, remember?"

"Yeah, I am," he said in a perfectly natural voice. "I went to tryouts yesterday. They posted the roster outside Principal

Cashen's office this morning. You're looking at one of the Robert Lowell Panthers. It's official. You can check it out yourself."

Carrie frowned. Could he actually be telling the *truth?* No way. Jordan vowed long ago that he would never join any sports team. Joining a team meant following in the footsteps of his jock brothers. And as his best friend—or one of them, anyway—Carrie knew that Jordan would rather wear a bright pink polka-dot dress than do something his brothers would approve of.

"So what are you *really* doing?" Sky prodded, sounding impatient.

Jordan shrugged. "I told you."

Sam shook his head. His dark eyes narrowed. "Okay, man," he said, smiling dubiously. "Joke's over."

Jordan laughed again. "You guys—I'm *serious.*" He stopped sculpting the blob of mashed potatoes and looked Sam straight in the face. "Coach Powell told me I should give it a shot, so I did."

He is *serious*, Carrie suddenly realized. If he weren't, he wouldn't have been able to stare at Sam like that. He always avoided people's eyes when he was joking around.

"Look, I was going to tell you guys about it earlier," Jordan went on. "But it just never came up. Anyway—"

"You're really on the basketball team?" Carrie blurted.

He lifted his shoulders and smiled broadly. "Guilty as charged."

Carrie's brow grew furrowed. This was crazy. Everybody knew what kind of people played basketball at Robert Lowell Middle School—namely self-centered, stuck-up jerks. She just couldn't buy that Jordan wanted to be like *them*. "But *why*?" she demanded.

Jordan cocked an eyebrow. "Jeez," he mumbled jokingly. "You make it seem like I'm joining a motorcycle gang or something."

"It's *worse* than joining a motorcycle gang!" Carrie exclaimed. "It's . . . it's—"

"Hey, Jordan—you told me once that you would *never* join the team," Alex piped up. "Remember? You said you wanted to keep your hoop skills a secret from your family. Those were your exact words."

"I know." Jordan put down his fork and flashed her a cocky grin. "But Alex, when you got skills like mine, you *can't* keep them a secret."

285

Alex groaned. "Give me a break."

"I don't get it, though," Carrie said urgently, leaning forward and resting her elbows on the edge of the table. "What made you change your mind? I mean, I thought you wanted to avoid being like your brothers at all costs."

Jordan smiled crookedly. "Hey—just because I like playing hoops doesn't mean I'm gonna wind up like *them*. Not unless I get a brain transplant with a chimpanzee. Anyway, I would have joined the team last year if my brother hadn't been around. I just didn't want anybody to compare him to me. But now that Mark is gone, there's no reason to pretend that I don't play basketball anymore."

Carrie just shook her head. She was kind of annoyed, actually. This whole thing was so *un*-Jordan. It was almost as if he were selling out or something. Was he really going to waste his afternoons bouncing a dumb ball with meatheads like Johnny Bates and Chris Tanzell? When would he have time do all the other stuff he did—like draw cartoons? Or produce hideous screeching noises with his saxophone? Or hang out with his friends . . .

"So I guess we should congratulate you," Sky mumbled grudgingly. "Right?"

Jordan's smile widened. "I guess."

Sam nodded. "Definitely. Way to go, my man. I'm psyched to watch you go out there and kick some butt."

Carrie rolled her eyes.

"Or get your butt kicked," Alex teased. She quickly patted Jordan's shoulder. "Just kidding, pal."

"You probably won't see very much of either," Jordan admitted. "I won't be getting a lot of playing time. I mean, I'm not gonna be first-string or anything. . . ."

If you aren't going to be first-string, then why did you even bother joining the team? Carrie found herself wondering. Her gaze drifted through the big glass windows out to the courtyard. She caught a glimpse of a bunch of fifth and sixth graders with a basketball. They looked amazingly stupid. Jordan was giving up his free time for *that?*

"You can actually come watch me in three days," Jordan added. "Our first game is here on Friday, against Shepherd. You know, that school in Seattle? They beat us in the championship last year. They're our archrivals.

It'll be a great game." He glanced at Carrie. "What do you say? Will you be there?"

Carrie shrugged. "If I'm not going to the mall with Sky," she muttered.

"Oh, come on," Jordan protested with a good-natured smirk. "You guys can miss one day of shopping for this."

Sky shook her head. "I don't know, Jordan," she said matter-of-factly. "The sale *ends* on Friday."

Jordan glared at her. "Sky—"

"We'll be there," Carrie interrupted. "But will we get to see you play at all? I mean, if you're just going to be sitting on the bench . . ."

"Coach Powell always puts everyone on the team in at least once during a game," Jordan stated confidently. "Don't worry. You'll get to see me play."

Carrie forced herself to smile. But deep down she didn't really *want* to see Jordan play. Unless he wasn't going to play well. As mean as it made her feel, she wanted to see Jordan make a fool of himself on the court. That way he would get embarrassed. Then he would quit the team and give up basketball forever. Then everything would be back to normal. He'd *never* end up like his brothers. He wouldn't end up like the stuck-up jock dolts on the team, either.

He wouldn't change at all.

And that's what he really wanted, right?

Two

"Let's go, Panthers—let's go! Let's go, Panthers. . . ."

Jordan swallowed. The gym was packed. It was louder than a rock concert in here. Who would have thought that the entire school would stay after classes to watch a lousy basketball game? Okay—so the Panthers *were* playing their archrivals. But still . . . didn't people have better things to do with their Friday afternoons?

"Let's go, Panthers. . . ."

He couldn't bring himself to turn and look at the bleachers. If he saw how many people were back there, he'd freak. He should have never opened his big mouth to his friends about this. Joining the team had been a huge mistake—

"Sullivan!" Coach Powell barked from the opposite end of the bench.

Uh-oh. Jordan's stomach lurched. He wasn't going to have to play *now*, was he?

The game was almost over. He'd deliberately sat at this end in hopes that Coach Powell would just forget about him. He couldn't go out there. Not in front of so many people. . . .

"*Sullivan!*" Coach Powell shouted. His voice sliced through the chanting crowd. "Get over here!"

Jordan nodded. Okay, okay. So he was going to play. No big deal. Just as long as he didn't pass out or yack all over the place, it would be fine, right? Chances were that nobody would even pass him the ball. He wiped his moist palms on his thighs and forced himself to march the length of the bench.

"How ya feelin', Sullivan?" Coach Powell demanded.

"Fine," Jordan lied. He *had* to say that. Coach Powell wasn't exactly the most understanding guy in the world. He sort of reminded Jordan of a talking fist. His face was really craggy and square and hairless. He had no neck, either. His head looked as if it had been jammed onto the top of his body. Jordan just hoped the old man couldn't see his knees wobbling.

"I'm gonna put you in for Tanzell."

Coach Powell grunted. "I would have put you in earlier, but I decided to save you. I didn't want Shepherd to know about your outside shot." His thick lips curled in a grin. "They're gonna be surprised."

Jordan managed a nod. *They are?* Was that what Coach Powell really thought? It was flattering—but the awful queasiness in Jordan's stomach was now about a million times worse. He glanced at the scoreboard.

Oh no.

The score was tied at thirty-eight points apiece. There were only twenty seconds left. That meant Coach Powell was putting the fate of the entire game in Jordan's hands.

"Time out, Robert Lowell," the referee called, blowing his whistle.

"Let's go, Panthers!" the crowd kept chanting—except now they were stamping their feet and clapping as well. *"Let's go, Panthers!"*

Jordan forced a weak smile as his teammates jogged off the court and huddled around Coach Powell. "Great game," he mumbled.

None of them smiled back. None of them even said anything. Then again, Jordan hadn't really expected them to respond. When Jordan had first made the team, he'd been psyched to make friends with the rest of the Panthers. But guys like Chris Tanzell and Johnny Bates had made it clear all week long that they thought Jordan was the biggest loser in the state of Washington.

"All right, guys, listen up," the coach announced. "We're gonna have a substitution. . . ."

Why is he doing this to me? Jordan wondered miserably. Nobody wanted him to play. Jordan didn't fit in with this team, plain and simple. He even *looked* different from the rest of his teammates. Everybody else looked as if they were related or something. They all had dark hair and mean eyes and muscles that would probably be normal on an eighteen-year-old. Not Jordan. He knew his pale arms and legs looked ridiculously scrawny in this baggy black uniform.

"You're putting *Sullivan* in for *me?*" Chris Tanzell cried. "But Coach—"

"No 'buts,' Tanzell," Coach Powell growled. "Take a seat."

For a moment Chris looked as if he were going to say something else. Then he snorted. After glaring at Jordan, he stormed to the end of the bench.

"Hey, Tanzell!" Coach Powell yelled after him. "I can do without the attitude, all right? There's no *i* in *team*, remember?"

Jordan hung his head. This was just perfect. Now his teammates hated him even more than they had before. He could just picture what they'd do to him if he missed this shot. They'd probably stuff him down one of the toilets in the boys' locker room.

"Okay, guys," Coach Powell stated. "Go do your thing."

Right, Jordan said to himself. *Do your thing. Translation: Make a fool of yourself.*

"Number twenty-three, Jordan Sullivan, is entering the game," a voice bellowed over the gym's loudspeaker. "He replaces Chris Tanzell."

Oh, jeez. Jordan gulped. But there was no turning back. The substitution was official now.

"You better not blow this, Sullivan," Johnny Bates hissed. "You'll regret it."

"Thanks a lot, man," Jordan muttered sarcastically. He wished he could either punch Johnny in the nose or bolt from the gym—or both. But as much as he hated to admit it, he knew Johnny was absolutely right.

If Jordan blew this shot, he'd be regretting it for a long, long time.

Three

"Go, Jordan!" somebody yelled as Jordan walked out onto the court.

A cheer erupted from the crowd.

Jordan paused. Was that cheering for *him?* He summoned enough courage to look at the bleachers. Sure enough, Carrie, Sam, Alex, and Sky were on their feet, clapping and hollering for him—and everyone else in the stands had joined in.

"Go get 'em!" Sam shouted above the din.

A little half grin passed over Jordan's lips. *Wow.* Nobody had ever applauded for him before.

The whistle blew.

Jordan's knees buckled as the brief moment of confidence passed. Everyone on the basketball court scrambled to get into position.

Somebody passed the ball inbounds to Johnny.

Okay, Jordan thought, fighting back nausea and dizziness. *Just relax.*

Luckily he found himself being guarded by some little pipsqueak who came up to Jordan's chin. He couldn't help but smile. Shooting over this guy wouldn't be any problem. He felt a surge of hope. He just had to get open for the pass in time to make the shot.

The clock was ticking down. There were only fifteen seconds left.

"Move!" Coach Powell commanded from the sidelines.

Jordan faked to his left, then dashed to his right across the court—leaving the pipsqueak behind. Suddenly he was wide open. Johnny hurled the ball at him.

Jordan caught it and started dribbling. The pipsqueak was guarding him again, but Jordan could tell that the kid was tired—sweaty and out of breath. Not Jordan. Now that he was moving, he was pumped. More pumped than he'd ever been. Electric energy coursed through his veins.

All at once the crowd began counting down with the clock: *"Ten . . . nine . . . eight . . ."*

Jordan's smiled widened. The ringing of

voices filled his ears. Any last traces of anxiety melted away. He *should* be freaking out right now. But he wasn't. He was right where he wanted to be—about fifteen feet from the basket. He'd made this exact same shot a thousand times in the driveway at Alex's house.

"Five ... four ... three—"

"Shoot it, you yutz!" Coach Powell shrieked.

Slowly, calmly, Jordan lifted the ball and let it fly from his fingertips—just over the outstretched hands of the pipsqueak. Silence filled the gym. The ball looked as if it were traveling in slow motion as it floated through the air . . . then plopped into the basket with a *swish*.

The buzzer sounded.

The entire gym exploded with a single word: *"Yesss!"*

Jordan's eyes bulged. The next thing he knew, he found himself being mauled by his teammates. . . . People were crowding around him, patting him on the back, shouting. . . . But he was in a complete daze. He'd known he could make the shot, but still . . .

"Way to go, man!" Johnny Bates cried, clapping him on the shoulder.

"Nice one, Sullivan!" Chris Tanzell called, giving him a thumbs-up.

In the all the shock and chaos Jordan just grinned. He couldn't think of a word to say. Gradually he became aware of a chant from the stands: *"Sul-li-van, Sul-li-van, Sul-li-van . . ."*

Wait a second. The entire gym was shouting his name. He started laughing. This was wild. *His* name.

He'd done it.

He'd *won* the game for Robert Lowell.

People started pouring out of the bleachers and onto the gym floor. Jordan hopped up on his tiptoes, scanning the sea of faces for Carrie and the others. . . .

"Jordan?" a girl's voice asked from behind him.

Jordan whirled around. He found himself face-to-face with . . . *Aimee Stewart?*

She'd never even talked to him before. But why would she? She was one of the Amys—one of the three most popular, coolest, best-looking girls at Robert Lowell. The Amys didn't have time for guys like Jordan. He paused, half expecting her to ask him to get out of the way or something. But she didn't. She stood right in front of him, smiling shyly, her blue eyes glittering under her blond curls.

"I just wanted to congratulate you," she said over the noise. "That was an awesome shot."

Jordan's jaw dropped. *Congratulate me?* His heart pounded. "Uh . . . thanks," he finally mumbled.

"I want to talk to you about it later," she went on. "I'm going to write an article about it in the school paper."

"Schoo-school paper?" Jordan stuttered, totally overwhelmed. She laughed once. "Is that okay?"

"Yeah!" he exclaimed. "I mean . . . sure."

"Good. I'll give you a call later."

Jordan just nodded, unable to keep from staring into her eyes. He couldn't believe it. Aimee Stewart was going to write about him. Not Chris Tanzell, not Johnny Bates—but *him.*

He realized something at that moment.

He should have joined the basketball team a *long* time ago.

*   *   *

"Jordan!" Carrie yelled, struggling to climb down the bleachers onto the crowded gym floor with Alex, Sky, and Sam trailing behind her. She couldn't believe that Jordan had won the game. It was awesome. Well, not *that* awesome. She didn't want him to get full of himself or anything. But she *was* proud of him. Now if she could only make it through all these screaming people, then she could actually congratulate him for making the shot. . . .

"Jordan!" Alex shouted from behind her.

He was barely twenty feet away, in the middle of all the commotion, grinning and trying to answer a million questions at once. But he didn't even so much as glance in their direction. Nope. For some bizarre reason his eyes seemed to be glued to Aimee Stewart.

"Jordan!" Carrie called a second time.

For a split second his gaze seemed to flicker up into the stands. But then he turned right back to Aimee, as if his head were being yanked with an invisible string.

Carrie abruptly stopped.

"Jordan!" Alex shouted again breathlessly. "Over here!"

But Jordan just kept staring at Aimee. Carrie frowned. What was his problem? Why was he ignoring them?

Before Carrie could open her mouth again, the mob surrounding Jordan suddenly began to move. Once again people started chanting: *"Sul-li-van, Sul-li-van, Sul-li-van . . ."*

Carrie slowly folded her arms across her chest. Now *this* was absurd. Jordan didn't even know those people.

She couldn't believe it. Jordan Sullivan—*her* friend—was being treated like a full-fledged jock. Not only that, he was *acting* like one, too. He was wearing the same slimy, self-satisfied look on his face that all jocks wore. Yup, Carrie knew the look well. She saw it every single day on the faces of guys like Chris Tanzell and Johnny Bates.

He's becoming just like them, Carrie said to herself grimly. She shook her head as the crowd swept out of the gym, looking like some kind of giant alien creature with dozens of heads and arms and legs. *One lousy shot, and he's becoming just like them.*

She was *not* prepared to let that happen.

Carrie nodded, feeling as if she had a mission.

Yes, sir. She was going to have a little chat with Robert Lowell's newest hero. She was going to give him a piece of her mind. And after that, Jordan would think twice about letting his ego get in the way of his friends again.

Four

Carrie stood at the end of her driveway on Monday morning, waiting for the bus to pick her up. A light drizzle was falling. Unfortunately she didn't own a raincoat. Well, she *did* own a hideous yellow thing that made her look like a bumblebee. But she would never wear that in a billion years. Besides, she could care less about foul weather right now. She had more important things on her mind.

She still had to figure out what she was going to say to Jordan.

Maybe she would let *him* do the talking at first. Yeah. She would give him a chance to apologize for blowing her off on Friday. He deserved that much. After all, everyone had swarmed on him after the game like he was some kind of NBA superstar or something. He obviously didn't know how to deal with all that attention. So in a way his behavior was forgivable. Lame, but forgivable. Now he'd had the entire weekend to think about what a jerk he'd been—so he would say that he was sorry. Naturally.

Then she would congratulate him.

And she would definitely not overreact, either. Nope. After all, he'd only played for about twenty seconds.

She shook her head. This was so stupid. If he'd only messed up like he was supposed to, then she wouldn't have to think about what she was going to say. . . .

Bus number four swerved around the corner onto Whidbey Road. It jerked to a stop in a huge puddle at the end of the driveway—instantly soaking Carrie's black dress, her socks, and her combat boots.

Carrie frowned. How nice.

Brick, the bus driver, opened the door. "Sorry, Carrie," he croaked. His eyes were puffy, as if he hadn't slept in days. Of course, knowing Brick, he probably hadn't. He was quite the partier. "I didn't mean to get you wet."

"That's okay, Brick," Carrie mumbled, sighing. She lumbered up the steps.

"That's the great thing about black. It looks just as good wet as it does dry."

His haggard face brightened. "Hey, you're right!" he exclaimed. "I never noticed that!"

Carrie had to smile. What a guy. Brick had a brain the size of a pea and a heart the size of a watermelon. She turned down the aisle. "Maybe I should hose myself down every day—" Suddenly she froze.

What the . . .

Jordan was sitting in the first seat.

With Amy Anderson.

But that wasn't all. He was draped over the back of the seat, chatting it up with Aimee Stewart and Mel Eng, who were sitting behind him. They looked as if they were all lifelong buddies or something. Carrie's mouth hung open. For a second she literally felt as if she were witnessing a scene in one of her own horror stories. What on *earth* was going on here? *Nobody* ever sat with the Amys. Least of all her best friend . . .

"Did you go for a swim this morning?" Amy Anderson asked Carrie dryly, glancing at her sopping dress.

A few kids on the other side of the aisle giggled. But for once Carrie was *way* too freaked to acknowledge some lame wisecrack.

"Jordan?" she gasped.

He glanced up at her. "Hey!" he cried enthusiastically. He smiled as if absolutely nothing were wrong. "Guess what? I'm getting interviewed for the school paper. Aimee says it's going to be on the front page."

Carrie could only gape at him, horrified.

"Hey, Carrie?" Brick murmured. "You gotta have a seat."

Carrie shifted her stunned eyes to Mel and Aimee. Both of them were scowling. Their expressions clearly stated: *Beat it.*

Fine. Carrie shook her head—then stormed down the aisle to the backseat, where Alex and Sam were waiting. She slumped between them, folding her arms across her chest.

The bus bounced forward.

"I don't believe it," she grumbled, staring at the rain-splattered floor. "What's gotten into him? What does he think he's *doing?*"

"He's getting interviewed for the paper," Sam offered cautiously.

"So I heard," Carrie growled. She glanced up for a moment. Once again Jordan was yammering away happily, staring into the eyes of Aimee Stewart. It was completely disgusting. "'Aimee says it's going to be on the front page,'" she mocked in a high-pitched voice.

Alex laughed once. "What's the matter? Don't you think it's cool?"

"*Cool?*" Carrie cried. She turned and looked Alex straight in the face. "He's sitting up there with the Amys instead of back here where he belongs—and you think it's *cool?*"

Alex lowered her eyes. She reached for her damp brown wool cap and began to fidget with it. "I just think it's cool that there's gonna be an article about Jordan in the *Robert Lowell Observer*," she mumbled. "That's all I meant."

"Article, huh?" Carrie muttered. She shifted her gaze back to Jordan. Rage burned inside her. "I'll show him an article. . . ."

Hold on.

A wicked smile spread across Carrie's face.

Of course. She *would* show Jordan an article. She'd show everyone else at Robert Lowell an article, too. Aimee could write her dumb piece—but Carrie would write one, too. She would write an editorial. The Amys might have control of the newspaper, but they had no say over the editorials. Those went straight through Principal Cashen.

So if Carrie wrote a brilliant editorial that made fools out of all the incredibly stupid, conceited, and arrogant jocks at Robert Lowell . . . well, then Principal Cashen would be sure to print it. Even better, Jordan Sullivan would be sure to read it.

Ha!

And how would Robert Lowell's newest basketball star feel after *that?*

Five

I

By the time Carrie slumped down beside Alex at the lunch table, her editorial was nearly finished. But she was starting to have second thoughts about turning it in. It was pretty harsh. *Really* harsh, actually. She'd spent all morning in a total frenzy, writing the piece during her classes instead of listening or taking notes. Maybe she'd let her anger get the best of her. Besides, it was pretty clear that Alex, Sam, and Sky didn't think that Jordan had done anything wrong by sitting with the Amys on the bus that morning.

"Isn't it awesome about Jordan?" Alex suddenly asked, as if reading Carrie's mind. "Everybody's been talking about him all day. He's become like a . . . like a . . ." She snapped her fingers, searching for the right word.

"Jerk?" Carrie suggested dryly.

Alex smirked. "No, Carrie. I was

thinking more along the lines of like . . . like *legend* or something."

"Legend?" Carrie snorted. "Yeah—in his own mind."

"Oh, come on." Alex laughed. "You have to admit, this is a pretty big deal. . . ." Her voice trailed off as Sam and Sky sat down at the table.

"What's up?" Sam asked. "What are you guys talking about?"

"What else?" Carrie grumbled. "Robert Lowell's latest sports sensation."

Sam grinned at Carrie. "You aren't still mad about what happened on the bus, are you?"

Carrie bit her lip. Of course she was still mad. But nobody here knew just how mad. She hadn't told anyone about her editorial yet.

"Well, I think it's great that Aimee Stewart is writing an article about Jordan," Sam said quietly.

"What?" Carrie yelled.

Sam shrugged. "Hey, I'm not saying I *like* her. I'm just saying that a lot of people listen to what she says. Like ninety-nine percent of the school. And if she says good things about Jordan, well . . . then that's a good thing. Right?"

Carrie just grunted. Okay. So she kind of saw Sam's point. But that didn't excuse the fact that Jordan had totally blown Carrie off at the basketball game. Now that he thought he was some kind of jock, he was just psyched to hang out with the "in" crowd. And obviously Aimee didn't *like* him. No . . . she just wanted to use him for a good story—then toss him aside like a discarded chicken bone as soon as he quit the team.

And he *would* quit the team. Carrie was sure he'd come to his senses sooner or later.

Well . . . unless, of course, he really *was* becoming a jock.

II

"Hey, Jordan!" a familiar girl's voice called.

Jordan paused in the crowded cafeteria, clutching his lunch tray. For a second he couldn't tell where the voice was coming from. It definitely *wasn't* coming from his usual table. No, Carrie, Alex, Sky, and Sam were all sitting there, staring at him blankly. So where? It was way too noisy in here.

311

"Over here!" the girl called again, laughing.

Jordan pivoted on his feet—turning, turning . . .

Aimee?

Aimee Stewart was standing by the Amys' table, waving. At *him*. In front of the entire cafeteria. He blinked twice. It didn't make any sense.

"Come sit with us!" she yelled, pointing toward an empty chair beside her. "We have to finish the interview!"

Jordan stared at her. Okay. On the one hand, it was very bizarre that Aimee was paying so much attention to him. . . . But on the other hand, why fight it? He smiled. Now that he got a good look at Aimee, he noticed that her green dress was actually pretty cute. Funny. He never thought about things like that. Well, almost never. He took a few steps forward, then slowed.

Amy and Mel were sitting at the table, too—whispering to each other.

Hmmm. Something about the way they kept glancing up at him and smiling made him uneasy. Then again, Amy and Mel were the kind of girls who were always whispering about *something*. And they had been totally cool to him on the bus.

"Come *on*," Aimee urged. She patted the chair next to her.

Nah—there was nothing to worry about. Anyway, this was kind of a dream come true, wasn't it? He was being asked to sit with the Amys. Every guy at Robert Lowell would kill for this opportunity. Without another moment's hesitation he strode across the cafeteria and sat down beside Aimee.

III

"Do—do—do you *see* that?" Carrie sputtered. She jerked a trembling finger across the cafeteria at the back of Jordan's head, unable to control herself. "He's sitting with *them!*"

Sky shrugged. "You heard Aimee," she said calmly, digging into a plastic container of homemade salad. "She wants to finish the interview."

"So what?" Carrie hissed. Suddenly she realized she was grinding her teeth. But she couldn't help it. She was seething.

313

"This is the *second* time today Jordan dissed us for the Amys. We *always* sit together at lunch." Her voice rose. "It's like, now that he's a jock, he feels like he has to hang out with Amys because *all* the jocks hang out with the Amys, like Chris Tanzell and Johnny—"

"Uh, Carrie?" Sky interrupted, peering at her nervously. "You sure about all that?"

Carrie frowned. "Of *course* I'm sure."

Sky raised her eyebrows, then went back to eating her salad. "Okay," she mumbled with her mouth full. "I'm just saying that there's a slight chance Aimee actually wants to finish the interview."

"Since when do *you* stick up for Aimee Stewart?" Carrie cried.

"I'm not sticking up for her." Sky shook her head. "Jeez. I thought *I* was the paranoid one. Listen, just be thankful that we don't have to listen to any of Jordan's dumb jokes today," she added with a smile.

Carrie didn't say anything more. Her eyes wandered back to Jordan's table. Aimee and Jordan were laughing. Cracking up, in fact. They looked as if they were having a blast. Well, well, well. *Aimee* was certainly enjoying Jordan's dumb jokes. If Sky and Sam and Alex couldn't see how Jordan was turning into a grade-A jerk right before their very eyes, that was *their* problem. Not Carrie's. No . . . any last doubts about turning in that editorial were fading fast. If Jordan wanted to act like a jock, fine. He would just have to suffer the consequences.

IV

Jordan leaned back in his chair, unable to believe how *relaxed* he felt. Maybe he'd been expecting to be really intimidated or something. But eating lunch with Aimee, Mel, and Amy seemed as natural as . . . well, eating lunch with his friends. It was weird: Carrie and Alex and Sky were totally wrong about the Amys. As a matter of fact, he was actually beginning to understand why the Amys were the most popular kids at Robert Lowell. They didn't just *act* really cool. They *were* really cool.

"So what made you wait so long to join the basketball team?" Aimee asked, leaning toward him. "I mean, you're obviously

315

really good. You should have started playing in sixth grade. We would have won the championship by now."

Jordan could feel his face getting hot. *Oh, brother.* He didn't want to start blushing right now and making a complete fool out of himself. "Well, uh . . . to tell you the truth, I just didn't want to play on the same team as my brother Mark," he said quickly. He laughed once. "I mean, I don't know if you ever noticed, but I don't exactly get along with him."

"Why not?" Amy Anderson piped up. She exchanged a quick glance with Mel. The two of them giggled. "He seems fine to me. *Very* fine."

Jordan fought back the urge to sneer. *Fine?* He could think of another word. Okay . . . so maybe the Amys weren't all *that* cool. Aimee was definitely much cooler than the other two. Then again, he'd always known that Amy Anderson was in love with Mark. Of course, Amy also had a crush on Alex's older brother. She probably had a crush on every guy over the age of fourteen in the greater Seattle area.

"I just didn't want to embarrass him on

the court," Jordan finally mumbled. "It's tough when your younger brother can kick your butt, you know?" He flashed Amy a brief, phony smile. "I'm a sensitive kind of guy."

Amy just snickered. So did Mel.

But Aimee threw back her head and hooted with laughter. "Sensitive guy!" she cried. "Jordan—you're so *funny!*"

Jordan jumped slightly. *Wow.* None of his friends had ever told him that. In fact, they always groaned at his jokes. He *knew* he was blushing now.

Amy exchanged another quick glance with Mel.

"So now that he's gone, there's nothing holding you back, right?" Aimee asked once she'd gotten a grip on herself.

Jordan shrugged. "I guess not."

Aimee leaned closer. Her eyes bored into Jordan's own. "I'm glad," she murmured. "It looks to me like the Sullivan family saved its best for last."

V

Carrie squirmed in her seat, drumming her shiny black fingernails loudly on the table. If Aimee and Jordan sat any closer, they'd practically be *touching*. This was supposed to be an interview? Yeah, right. It looked more like a really cheesy teen romance movie. Things had gone too far. Way too far. What was Jordan *thinking* right now?

"Um . . . Carrie?" Alex said.

"What?" Carrie asked shortly, keeping her gaze riveted to Jordan.

"Are you all right?"

"Fine," Carrie stated.

"Uh . . . maybe we should all go outside," Sam suggested. "We can start recess a little early today. It's not raining anymore. . . ."

But Carrie had stopped listening. She held her breath. Aimee was draping her hand over the back of Jordan's chair. Carrie started shaking her head. Her stomach tightened. This couldn't be happening. Acting like a jock was one thing . . . but this, *this* was insane.

"Look!" Carrie hissed, pointing. "Look at that!" Her eyes darted wildly around at her friends' faces. "Aimee is, like, putting her arm around Jordan!"

Nobody said a word.

"Look!" Carrie repeated, a little desperately.

Slowly everyone at the table turned toward Jordan. . . .

"Eww!" Sky cried, wrinkling her nose. "You're *right!*"

Sam started laughing. "Jordan, you devil!"

Carrie's eyes smoldered. She didn't think she'd ever *been* so angry. For a moment, as she glared at Jordan, she almost felt as if she were looking at a complete stranger. She didn't even *know* Jordan anymore. The Jordan Sullivan *she* knew would never have gotten so warm and cozy with one of the three wicked witches of Robert Lowell.

She did know one thing, though.

Her editorial wasn't nearly harsh *enough.* Nope. Without another word she jumped up from the table and stomped out of the cafeteria. She had some business to take care of before recess started.

Jordan Sullivan: Robert Lowell's Newest B-ball Sensation

Six

Jordan felt perfectly loose when he strolled out onto the empty gym floor for practice Wednesday afternoon. He was still reeling from Aimee's article. Nobody had ever been that complimentary about him. *Nobody.* Of course, the self-portrait he'd drawn had helped a lot. He grinned. It had taken up most of the entire front page. But hey—maybe he deserved all this hoopla for once in his life, right? He *had* made the game-winning shot on Friday.

He shook his head, then picked up a ball and started dribbling. His life had changed more since Friday than it had in the past three years at Robert Lowell. Instead of being ignored by the Amys, he was practically best friends with one of them. Johnny Bates and Chris Tanzell weren't pushing him around anymore. Everywhere he went, people smiled at him, waved at him, asked him for advice. . . .

"Hey, Sullivan!" Chris Tanzell called from inside the locker room. "How does it feel to be a victim of your own stereotype?"

Jordan stopped dribbling. *A victim of my own stereotype?* What the . . .

"No, no—you got it wrong." Johnny Bates hooted. "The question is: How does it feel to be an egotistical snob?"

Egotistical snob? Jordan frowned. All right. Something very bizarre was happening. Either Johnny and Chris had each gained about forty IQ points in the last five minutes, or Jordan was losing his mind. Johnny probably didn't even know what a word like *egotistical* meant. He had trouble with any word over two syllables.

"What's going on in here?" Jordan demanded, dropping the ball and marching through the locker-room door. "What—"

He stopped in midsentence. The entire team was huddled around Johnny, laughing hysterically. He sat on one of the locker-room benches under a pale yellow fluorescent light, holding up a school newspaper for everyone to see.

Jordan pursed his lips. "What's so funny?"

"Come on, man," Chris muttered. "You

have to admit, this is pretty good."

"*What's* good?" Jordan demanded. "What are you talking about?"

"What do you *think* we're talking about?" Johnny groaned. "Your friend's letter, dummy."

"Letter?" Jordan repeated uneasily. "What letter?"

Johnny glanced up. "What—are you saying you haven't seen the editorial page?"

Suddenly Jordan realized that everyone in the room was staring at him. He shook his head. "No," he croaked.

There was a pause.

The next thing Jordan knew, everybody started cracking up again.

"Oh, man," Johnny mumbled, shaking his head. He pushed himself to his feet and handed Jordan the paper—pointing to an editorial. "I'm sorry, dude. Really. I thought you knew."

Almost instantly Jordan's eyes zeroed in on the name at the bottom of the letter. *Carrie Mersel*. He swallowed. Carrie had written a letter? Why hadn't she told him? What *was* this? Holding his breath, he began to devour the words.

To Whom It May Concern:

Recently some disturbing events at our school have caused me to do a lot of thinking about two four-letter words: *jock* and *hype.*

As everyone knows, jocks are the coolest of the cool. They're good-looking and popular—and they never let the rest of us forget it.

Nevertheless, I've always maintained that a good athlete doesn't have to be good-looking, popular, or full of himself. But once you get labeled as a jock, the label tends to stick. That's when the trouble begins. That's when you start thinking that you're better, cooler, and more popular than everyone else.

Take the case of a certain basketball star. I know this star very well. He doesn't possess any of those stereotypically "jock" traits. Not a single one.

Or at least he *didn't.* Not until after he won a game.

This leads me to the second word: *hype.* Sadly, this star came to believe his own hype. Now he thinks he *is* a jock. Moreover, he thinks that being a jock is a good thing to be. After all, jocks are cool, right? Being an egotistical snob is fine as long as you can put a ball through a hoop.

Perhaps it sounds as if I'm being harsh. But as a school we have to recognize our own power. We labeled this player as a jock. Days later he tried to become one. He became a victim of his own stereotype. We have to think twice before labeling people.

Thoughtfully yours,
Carrie Mersel

"I do—I do-don't *believe* it!" Jordan stammered. "This is *sick!*"

Johnny just kept laughing. "I told you, man."

Without thinking, Jordan crumpled the paper in his hands and hurled it to the floor—then bolted from the locker room. He had to talk to Carrie. *Now.* She'd obviously suffered some kind of complete mental breakdown. . . . Hopefully bus number four hadn't left yet. Jordan burst through the gym doors, nearly slamming into Coach Powell.

"Sullivan!" Coach Powell barked. "Where do you think you're going?"

"Can't talk!" Jordan gasped, sprinting down the hall toward the front of the school. "I'll be right back."

Ready to explode, Jordan picked up his pace. How could Carrie *do* this to him? He shoved through the crowd of kids at the front door and leaped down the concrete steps. Brick was just closing the bus door.

"*Wait!*" Jordan yelled.

The door squeaked open again.

Jordan stomped up the stairs.

"Hey, man!" Brick said cheerfully. "I thought you had practice—"

"*You!*" Jordan shouted, pointing down

the aisle at Carrie— who was sandwiched in the backseat between Alex and Sam. "Why did you do it? Why?"

Carrie started shaking her head. Her face was pale. "I . . . I . . ."

"Uh, Jordan?" Brick said, clearing his throat. "Are you gonna ride with us?" He chuckled nervously. "Because if you aren't, I'm gonna have to ask you to get off."

Jordan drew in a deep, quivering breath and nodded. "I'll get off," he panted. His heart sounded as if it were in the middle of some crazed thrash-metal drum solo. Yet even in his exhausted, frenzied state, he was able to make a decision. He had no idea *why* Carrie had flipped—but if she wanted a war, fine. She'd made the first move. Now it was his turn.

"Jordan?" Brick prodded.

Finally Jordan's breathing evened. "Sorry to hold you up," he said. He fixed Carrie with a calm gaze. "I just want to say one thing. I want to make one announcement. In front of this whole bus. As of right now Jordan Sullivan—the egotistical jock—is never talking to Carrie Mersel again. Ever."

And with that he marched back down the stairs and stalked off toward the gym.

Seven

Carrie paced back and forth across the tiny back deck of Sky's houseboat. She couldn't keep still. She'd been pacing for the past twenty minutes. Alex, Sky, and Sam just stood there, leaning against the rail and staring at her as if she were a complete lunatic. They'd barely said a word since Jordan's little outburst on the bus. Of course, Carrie couldn't blame them. They were probably still in a state of shock. They'd found out about the editorial at the same time as the rest of the school.

"Hey, Carrie?" Sky asked quietly, twirling her brown hair around her fingers. "Maybe we should go inside. I think it might start raining again."

Carrie paused for a second and glanced up at the gray skies. Sky had a point. The wind had picked up. Big, black storm clouds were rolling in from the west over the Puget Sound horizon. But Carrie was way too agitated to be cooped up in the little cabin right now.

"In a minute," she mumbled.

Sky sighed. "Look, Carrie—I have to ask you. . . . What were you thinking? Why *did* you write that letter?"

"Why *wouldn't* I?" Carrie grumbled. She started pacing again. "I mean, Jordan has totally changed. He's turned into a jock. There's no denying it. First he blows us off after the game on Friday—"

"He didn't blow us off, Carrie," Sam interrupted quietly. "Every single person in the gym was crowding around him at once. There was no *way* we could have talked to him."

Carrie shook her head. "But I was yelling his name!" she insisted.

"He didn't hear you," Alex murmured, lowering her eyes. She took off her wool cap and began fiddling with it. A powerful breeze blew a few wisps of dark blond hair across her face. "I was yelling his name, too, remember? He swears he didn't hear us. I asked him about it this morning. He was *looking* for us." She lifted her head and met Carrie's gaze. "But he couldn't even see anything. All those people were jumping around and shouting in his ear."

Carrie opened her mouth for a second, then shut it. So maybe Alex and Sam were right. Maybe Jordan hadn't seen or heard them even though they'd been screaming their lungs out. Maybe, just *maybe*, Jordan hadn't purposely blown them off. But that still didn't excuse the fact that he'd sat on the bus with Aimee. Or that he'd eaten lunch with her. It didn't excuse the invisible magnet that seemed to be constantly pulling Jordan toward Robert Lowell's Most Heinous Creature—and *away* from his friends.

"What were you going to say?" Sky prodded.

"Nothing," Carrie mumbled. She turned to face the oncoming storm. Her long black dress billowed in the wind. "It's just . . . that he's not acting like himself. What about the way he's been hanging out with Aimee Stewart? I mean, he's spending every single free second with her. First the bus, then lunch. And then he's got practice after school." She glanced at the others. "When are *we* supposed to hang out with him?"

"Carrie—the only reason he was hanging out with Aimee so much was because of the article," Sam pleaded. "Come on. You *know* Jordan. Do you think he'd really eat lunch with the Amys every single day?"

"That's the whole point!" Carrie countered, throwing her hands in the air. "I don't even know anymore! I *don't* know Jordan. At least I don't feel like I do."

Sam sighed. "Well, I still know him," he stated. "I spoke to him on the phone last night. He was psyched to hang out with all of us this weekend. He said so."

Carrie's hands fell to her sides. "He did?"

"Yup." Sam nodded. "He *was* psyched, that is. But now . . . I mean, after what you wrote . . ." Sam's voice trailed off.

"Um—what did he say, exactly?" Carrie asked, swallowing. Her throat was dry. All at once her anger seemed to be melting away. Now she only felt a vague sort of nervousness.

Sam shrugged. "Just the norm. He wanted to go to this novelty shop in Seattle to load up on stink bombs for this prank he's pulling on his brothers. Believe me, Carrie—he's the same guy he always was." He shook his head and laughed sadly. "The only difference is that he's really, really mad right now."

Carrie blinked. Her stomach squeezed. Jordan wanted to get his brothers with stink bombs? That certainly sounded like the same old Jordan. Maybe Sam was right. Maybe her letter had been a little over the top. Maybe she should have tried to talk to Jordan again before handing it in. . . . *Oh, man.* She shook her head. A terrible feeling was creeping over her—the feeling she always got whenever she made a huge and incredibly dumb mistake. She knew it well. Yup. She had already felt it about a million times in the past year alone. . . .

"Hey, Carrie—are you all right?" Sky asked.

Carrie's head drooped. "Not really," she moaned. She glanced up at Sam. "Why didn't you tell me about this earlier?"

"Because I didn't think it mattered all that much," Sam replied in a matter-of-fact tone. "I mean—how was I supposed to know you were going to write a letter to the paper?"

Carrie nodded. "You're right, you're right," she mumbled dismally. "I'm sorry. It's not your fault at all. I just wish there was something I could do to take that letter back. . . ."

"Maybe there is," Sky suggested.

Carrie raised her eyebrows. "Like what?"

"Like going to Sheridan School in Seattle to watch Jordan play basketball tomorrow," Sky said.

Carrie groaned. "That's not even funny, Sky."

"No—just listen," Sky went on. "It'll be the perfect way for you guys to make up. See, the four of us will probably be the only Robert Lowell fans at the game. And once Jordan looks up in the stands and sees that you went all that way just to watch him play, he'll be totally flattered, and . . . and then everything will be back to normal." She took a deep breath. "Right?"

Carrie shook her head. "Wrong," she answered quietly. Another gust of wind sent a shiver down her spine. She wrapped her arms around herself and stared out at the gray, choppy waters of the Sound. "I mean, no offense—but it's gonna take a lot more than watching a lousy game to patch things up. You read the letter. I don't know. I guess I should apologize first."

"Probably. But the game's worth a shot, too. Isn't it?" Alex put in. "Really. Maybe you should give basketball a chance, you know what I mean?"

Carrie dubiously cocked her eyebrow at Alex. "Give basketball a chance?"

Alex nodded. "Yeah. It's like, I used to be totally bored by basketball until Matt got into it. Maybe the same thing will happen to you."

Carrie had to laugh. "Yeah," she said dryly. "And maybe I'll win the Miss Teen USA pageant next year."

Sam chuckled. "Hey—stranger things have happened, right? I agree with Sky and Alex."

Carrie gazed at the three of them for a moment. "You *really* think that going to this basketball game will help?" she finally asked.

Sky lifted her shoulders. "Look at it this way, Carrie," she said gently. "At this point you have absolutely nothing to lose. You *have* to clear the air with Jordan."

Carrie nodded. Sky was right. The way things were going, it looked as if she'd already lost her best friend. Why didn't she ever *think* before doing something so ridiculous? Why was she always letting herself get so riled up? But even as these questions raced through her mind, she knew there was no point in asking them. The damage had been done. And if becoming a basketball fan would mean getting Jordan back as a friend . . . well, then Carrie Mersel would become the biggest basketball fan on the planet.

Later that evening Carrie stared at the old-fashioned phone in her room, trying to get up the guts to call Jordan. She knew that her friends thought if Carrie showed up at the game, it would fix everything, but Carrie wasn't so sure. And she didn't think she could handle waiting all the way until tomorrow afternoon to find out.

"Oh, stop being such a wuss," she told

herself. Before she could change her mind, she reached over, grabbed up the receiver, and dialed Jordan's number.

He answered on the first ring.

"Hello?"

Carrie's heart was in her throat.

"Jordan, it's Carrie. Don't hang up," she said quickly.

There was a short sigh. "I told you I don't want to talk to you anymore. Or am I such a stupid jock, I didn't get my point across?"

Carrie took in a sharp breath. She supposed she deserved that.

"Look, Jordan, I'm sorry I wrote that letter before talking to you," she began, waiting to hear the click of the line being cut off. Thankfully it wasn't. "I just freaked because you were hanging with the Amys and those morons on the team—"

"Carrie, they're not morons. And I *like* playing on the team," Jordan said severely. "And you'd see that the Amys are pretty cool if you'd give them a chance." He paused. Carrie chewed her lip. "You know what your problem is, Carrie?"

"My problem?" Carrie wasn't aware that she had a problem. She'd made one mistake. What was the monster trauma?

"Your problem is that you can't deal with change," Jordan said. "I decided that I wanted to try something new—something that—yes—forces me to hang around with different people—and you blow it all out of proportion. Just because you refuse to ever wear color or come out of the Ice Age and use a computer doesn't mean the rest of us have to live in a cave."

Carrie's mouth dropped open. Afraid of change? Living in a cave? Was that what he really thought of her? So she liked what she liked. Was that so wrong?

"Jordan, I . . ." Carrie trailed off. She had no idea what to say. She didn't even know what to *think*.

"I gotta go, Carrie," Jordan said, sounding tired. "I'll see ya."

The line went dead in Carrie's ear.

Afraid of change? Ha! *Well, I'll show him!* Carrie thought as she slammed down the phone, stood up, and paced around her room. She was going to go to that game with her friends tomorrow. She was going to show Jordan that she was capable of trying new things—of traveling all the way to Seattle on a smelly old bus so she could try something new. And she was going to show him that she could enjoy basketball—even if it killed her.

Eight

This is the most depressing thing I've ever seen, Carrie thought miserably, staring down at the basketball court.

Going to Jordan's first game had been halfway decent. At least Carrie didn't have to actually *go* anywhere—except the gym. But the bus ride to Sheridan School in Seattle had taken over an hour. And Sheridan's gym was totally . . . *dead*. It was like a cemetery in here or something. The only other people in the bleachers besides Carrie, Sky, Alex, and Sam were two tired-looking women who were obviously bored out of their skulls. One of them was actually knitting.

"Boy, they really pack 'em in here, don't they?" Sam whispered jokingly.

Carrie shook her head. "Maybe there's a reason nobody's here," she mumbled, glancing around at the rows and rows of empty seats. "Maybe Sheridan doesn't like to have people watch their games. Maybe we should just turn around and—"

"Don't even try it," Alex interrupted. She leaned forward in her seat and stared intently at Jordan and the other players. "We're here. Besides, the game has just started. As soon as we start making some noise, the energy is going to pick up. Trust me." She cupped her hands around her mouth. "Let's go, Panthers!" she shrieked.

"Let's go, Panthers!" Sky immediately joined in. "Let's go . . ."

Oh, jeez. Carrie winced. Yelling at a game where everyone else was yelling was one thing—but cheering wildly in a silent, deserted gym was just plain weird. Carrie looked back onto the court. Jordan was dribbling the ball, but his eyes kept darting up to the bleachers. He looked just as baffled as Carrie. She buried her face in her hands. Great. Jordan probably thought they had come here to make fun of him or something. There was no *way* this was going to help.

"All right, Jordan!" Alex suddenly yelled, leaping up. "Awesome shot!"

Carrie peered out from behind her fingers. Her eyes widened. *Wait a second.*

Jordan was suddenly *smiling* at them. He must have scored—because Chris Tanzell and Johnny Bates and some other guys were giving him high fives. He flashed a brief thumbs-up at Alex, then scurried back down the court. Carrie's lips twisted in a little grin. The change in Jordan's face was incredible. His green eyes were bright, his cheeks were rosy red, and his hair was flying all over the place. He actually looked as if he was having fun. More than fun, as a matter of fact. He looked as if he was having the time of his life.

"See?" Alex said, slumping back down beside Carrie and nudging her. "I told you they'd come alive if we made some noise."

Carrie nodded. The Panthers looked alive, all right. But she still didn't feel so thrilled. No . . . as Jordan ran up and down the court—patting Johnny Bates on the shoulder, grinning at Chris Tanzell—all her original fears came flooding back. A little over a week ago Jordan would have never even *talked* to those guys. Now he was obviously tight with them. He looked and sounded just like them—the way he was sweating and grunting in his black uniform. Everyone on the Panthers was the same. Including Jordan. He *was* a jock.

He's never going to be the way he was before, she said grimly to herself. *The more he hangs out with those guys, the more of a jerk he's going to become. Of course I'm afraid of change—if it means losing my best friend.*

She sighed and leaned forward, propping her elbows on her knees and resting her chin in the palms of her hands. It was sad. Watching Jordan play was almost like looking at an old photograph of a friend who had moved away. She could look at him—but the old Jordan, the one whom Sam had been talking about yesterday on Sky's boat—was long gone.

"What's wrong?" Sky murmured.

Carrie glanced up with a start. *Uh-oh.* She hadn't even noticed she wasn't watching the game anymore. She was totally spacing out, staring at the heavy black laces of her combat boots. "Huh?" she asked sheepishly.

Sky's forehead grew creased. "You look totally bummed right now."

Carrie shrugged and slouched back in her seat. "I guess I'm having a hard time getting into this basketball thing," she mumbled.

Sky's brown eyes flickered over Carrie's face. "That's not what's bumming you out, though," she prodded. "I can tell."

"Jeez," Carrie said dryly. She mustered a smile. "I've got to work harder on my lying skills."

"You *can't* lie around me," Sky said with a smirk. "You'd never get away with it. Now, what's up?"

Carrie took a deep breath. "It's just that . . . I know the letter I wrote was way too harsh. But still, it wasn't completely wrong. I mean, Jordan *is* a jock." She waved a hand at the basketball court. "Just look at him. He's becoming just like Chris and Johnny and the rest of those jerks."

Sky's eyes narrowed. "In what way?"

"In *every* way," Carrie replied glumly. She shook her head. "He's playing basketball, isn't he?"

Sky leaned back and raised her eyebrows.

"So playing basketball automatically makes you a jerk?"

"No . . . but if you're on the team, then you become a jock," Carrie stated slowly. "And once you become a jock, it isn't too long before you become a jerk."

Sky bit her lip—then burst out laughing.

Carrie frowned. "What's so funny?" she demanded.

"Carrie, listen to yourself!" Sky cried. "You're being totally prejudiced. You're basically saying that anyone on any basketball team is a jerk."

Carrie raised her shoulders. "Isn't it true?" she muttered, avoiding Sky's eyes.

"*What* are you saying?" Alex cut in.

"Carrie thinks that anybody who plays basketball is a jerk," Sky announced.

"That's *not* true." Carrie groaned, rolling her eyes. "I was just saying—"

"What about Matt?" Alex cut in. "*He* plays basketball. But you don't think *he's* a jerk. It's like that word you used in your letter. . . ." She scratched her wool cap. "Stereo . . ."

"Stereotype," Carrie finished.

"Exactly," Alex stated, pointing her finger. "You're stereotyping him."

"You guys—can we talk about this later?" Sam grumbled. "I'm trying to watch the game. We're here to watch Jordan, remember?"

Carrie didn't say anything. Alex was right, of course. Alex's brother, Matt, wasn't a jerk. And Carrie *was* stereotyping him. But Matt didn't really count. He was a year older, for one thing. He was in high school, for Pete's sake. He'd grown up and moved way beyond immature morons like Chris and Johnny.

"Look at it this way," Sky whispered, leaning toward Carrie's ear. "You know how the Amys always rag on you for wearing black all the time? Like you're a mental case or something?"

Carrie shifted uncomfortably in her seat. "What does *that* have to do with anything?" she asked.

"Because you're doing the same thing that *they* always do," Sky explained. "They think they know everything about you just because you wear black. They come up with all of these lame ideas about you for no reason at all. Don't you see? You're doing the same thing with all the guys on the basketball team." Her voice rose a little. "You don't even really *know* those guys. But I bet they're not all bad, right?"

Whoa. For a moment Carrie was too stunned to do anything but stare at Sky. *Was* she being like the Amys? She'd never thought about it that way. But she couldn't deny it. Every word out of Sky's mouth had been completely true. Making all kinds of judgments about those guys on the team—just because they happened to enjoy bouncing a lousy ball around—was no different than what the Amys did to her on a daily basis. She shuddered, suddenly feeling as if she were covered with some kind of diseased slime.

"See what I mean?" Sky prompted.

Carrie swallowed. "Yeah," she muttered. "I do."

"Look, I've got an idea," Sky went on. "After you watch the game, you write another letter to the editor, okay? Only *this* time you say that you were totally wrong to be prejudiced against jocks, and that basketball is actually kind of a cool sport, and that Jordan deserves to feel proud because he's such an amazing player."

Carrie thought for a moment. Incredibly enough, Sky's suggestion wasn't that outrageous. In a way it kind of made sense. The first letter had done a lot of damage—more damage than Carrie could have ever possibly imagined. So what could undo the damage—except another letter?

"What do you think?" Sky asked.

"I think you may be on to something," Carrie murmured. She nodded. Sky *was* on to something. Carrie's doubts began to disappear. Writing something for the paper could work. Because this time she would actually use her whole brain before she started to write—not just the angry part. As a matter of fact, she could even take her plan one step further than writing an editorial. Yeah. She could do something so totally crazy, so totally *unlike* anything she'd ever done before, that every single person at Robert Lowell would be completely blown away.

Particularly Jordan.

"So you'll do it?" Sky asked excitedly.

"I'll do something even better," Carrie stated. She smiled. "The *Observer* doesn't have an official sports column, right?"

"Uh . . . I don't think so," Sky said. "Why?"

"Because I'm going to make it my business to become Robert Lowell's first official sportswriter."

Sky started giggling.

Carrie wrinkled her brow. "What's so funny?"

"Carrie—you *hate* sports," Sky answered plainly. "Besides, you don't know a single thing about basketball. Coming to watch a game is one thing. You don't have to know anything about it to watch it—or even pretend like you're having a good time. But the thought of *you* writing a sports column is like . . . like *me* writing a meat-lovers' cookbook."

Carrie shook her head. "But that's the beauty of it!" she cried. "Don't you see? People will be totally shocked. And that's what I'm going for. It's exactly what you and Alex were talking about. People have this opinion about me—that I don't care about sports. But I'm going to break my own stereotype. I'm going to show the world that Carrie Mersel is not afraid of change."

"Afraid of change?" Alex said, raising her eyebrows. "Where did *that* come from?"

Carrie felt her face flush. "Jordan said I blew everything out of proportion because I'm afraid of change."

"When did you talk to Jordan?" Sky asked.

"I called him last night to apologize. He wasn't exactly thrilled to hear from me," Carrie said. "He said I live in a cave." Carrie hung her head slightly.

Alex and Sky burst out laughing.

"It's not funny, you guys!" Carrie protested. "And I'm going to show him he's totally wrong. And writing a sports article is the way to do it."

Sky controlled her laughter. "I don't know," she finally mumbled. "I mean, all the articles have to be in to the Amys by the end of the day tomorrow. Even if they *let* you write a sports column, how will you learn all the rules and stuff in time?"

Carrie grinned. "Come on, Sky. How hard can the rules be? You put the ball in the basket. Anyway, if morons like Chris Tanzell and Johnny Bates can learn all the rules, I'll be able to pick them up in no time." She laughed. "Trust me. I'm gonna be the best sports columnist Robert Lowell has ever seen. I'll write the article tomorrow during lunch. I just gotta figure out how to get it in the paper."

Friday:

Carrie's Ruthless Climb to the Top of the Newspaper Business

MORNING

8:46 A.M. Carrie strolls into Principal Cashen's office, requesting permission to create a new sports column for the *Observer*. Principal Cashen is confused. It's a great idea—but judging from Carrie's last editorial, he thinks it's . . . well, a little strange. Maybe she should think it over.

9:31 A.M. Carrie returns to Principal Cashen's office. She's thought it over. She promises she won't insult the players. After protesting for several minutes, Principal Cashen finally agrees. But Carrie still has to get approval from the editors in chief: Amy Anderson, Aimee Stewart, and Mel Eng.

10:15 A.M. Carrie spots Mel Eng in the hall by the lockers. She informs Mel that

350

Principal Cashen desperately wants Carrie to become a sports columnist. Mel shrugs. It's fine with her. It's one less thing *she'll* have to do.

11:43 A.M. Carrie bumps into Amy Anderson outside English class. She announces that she's going to write a sports column. Mel practically begged her to do it. Amy agrees—as long as Carrie swears she'll never talk to Amy in public again.

AFTERNOON

12:30 P.M. Carrie skips lunch and proceeds to the library, where she checks out a basketball rule book titled *Rules of the Game*. Unfortunately it's the size of a large dictionary. Oh, well. She doesn't need it, anyway. She'll just improvise her article.

1:17 P.M. Carrie finds Aimee Stewart in the courtyard and states that she's about to become sports columnist for the *Observer*. She's going to write about yesterday's game. Aimee snorts. Does Carrie even *know* anything about sports?

2:29 P.M. Carrie finds Aimee again. Carrie insists that she knows *tons* about basketball. Jordan taught her. After all, *she's* been friends with Jordan Sullivan her whole life . . . unlike *some* people.

3:15 P.M. Aimee finally agrees to let Carrie write her stupid column. As long as it's all right with Amy Anderson, it's all right with her.

3:16 P.M. Carrie dashes back to Principal Cashen's office, stating that the editors in chief have given her their wholehearted support.

3:19 P.M. Carrie submits her article to the Amys. Amy Anderson frowns. That was pretty quick, wasn't it? Carrie didn't even know she had a column until five minutes ago. She wrote it in five minutes? Carrie shrugs nonchalantly. What can she say? She works fast.

Nine

The moment Carrie got home Friday afternoon, she flopped down on her bed, snatched up the phone, and punched in Sky's number. "Guess what?" she said as soon as Sky answered. "You're talking to the *Robert Lowell Observer*'s newest sports columnist. I just submitted my first article."

Sky laughed. "Wow. *That* was fast."

Carrie snickered. "That's exactly what Amy Anderson said."

"Well . . . I guess I should congratulate you," Sky said slowly. "How did the article turn out?"

"Just wait till you see it," Carrie gushed, unable to contain her excitement. She sat up in bed and stared through a crack in the velvet curtains at the overcast skies outside. The weather might be lousy—but for the first time since her falling-out with Jordan, the dark clouds didn't match her mood. Nope. She was completely psyched. "Jordan is going to *freak*."

"I'll bet," Sky said quickly. "But I was just thinking . . ."

Carrie's eyes narrowed. There was a scheming tone in Sky's voice—a tone that usually spelled trouble. "What? What's wrong?"

"Nothing," Sky replied. "Except . . . I was just thinking about what you said the other day—Jordan saying you're afraid of change."

"Yeah . . . ," Carrie prompted.

"Well, I was thinking that you could do something else, too. You know, something that will show Jordan that you're totally behind him, like, one hundred percent. That your attitude has really shifted."

"Something else, huh?" Carrie raised her eyebrows, feeling wary. She could tell by Sky's eager voice that she already had something in mind. "Like what?"

"Why don't you change your look?" Sky said.

Carrie bit her lip. For a moment she wondered if she'd heard Sky correctly. "Change my *look*?" she asked.

"Yeah. Stop wearing combat boots. Wear another color besides black. Don't dye your hair—"

"Please," Carrie cut in dryly. "You're starting to sound exactly like my mom."

Sky giggled. "No, no. I'm being serious. Try going for a sporty-type thing. I mean, after all, you *are* a sports reporter, right? And if you do *that*, then you can show Jordan that you can do other things, *drastic* kinds of things—but still be your same old self. Just like he is. Does that make any sense?"

Carrie blinked a few times. "I'm not sure."

Sky cleared her throat. "What I'm saying is that you should give yourself a makeover."

Carrie's eyes bulged. A *makeover?* All right. Either Sky had recently developed a very bizarre sense of humor, or she had gone completely nutty.

"Carrie?" Sky prodded in the silence.

"A makeover," Carrie finally managed, trying not to laugh. "Like those girls in the Sweet Valley High books?"

Sky laughed. "Come on—"

"I don't believe this," Carrie muttered, twirling the phone cord around her fingers. She shivered—partly from a sudden chill and partly from the thought of changing her wardrobe. "You're serious, aren't you?"

"Just try it, all right?" Sky urged. Carrie could tell her friend was getting excited. "It'll be totally fun. It's supposed to rain tomorrow. We can go to the mall and load up on all kinds of great stuff. What better way to spend a rainy day than at the mall?"

Carrie didn't bother to answer. She could think of about a thousand better ways to spend a rainy day. But this *would* be something drastic. It might even be kind of amusing—in a very twisted way, of course.

"What do you say?" Sky prodded eagerly.

"Well . . ." Carrie turned the possibility over in her mind. Maybe Sky had a point. If Carrie did go for a "sporty-type thing," as Sky put it, then Jordan would be sure to notice. It would drive the point of the article home. He would see that she had changed her mind about jocks. He would see that she was taking her job as a reporter seriously—and not just doing it to make up for the letter.

"It'll be fu-un," Sky promised in a singsong voice.

Carrie chuckled. Shopping for a makeover. Jeez. Jordan had better believe she was serious about saving their friendship after something like this.

"Sure," she finally agreed. "Why not?"

Carrie's Nine-Step Makeover

Step One:
Saturday Afternoon (the Mall)

Under Sky's careful instruction, Carrie purchases a pair of blue jeans, a bunch of totally lame sweatshirts (totally lame in Carrie's opinion, anyway), a Supersonics cap like the one Alex used to own . . . and yes, a pair of those painfully trendy high-heeled sneakers she swore she would *never* buy.

Step Two:
Sunday Evening (the Bathroom)

Carrie spends over an hour in the shower, frantically scrubbing black dye out of her hair. When she wipes the steam from the mirror, she sees her hair in all its long, natural chestnut glory for the first time in over five months. She screams.

Step Three:
Monday Morning (the Breakfast)

Carrie strolls into the kitchen in her new red sweatshirt, jeans, and sneakers. Her dye-free hair is in a high ponytail. When Mrs. Mersel sees her, she bursts into tears. "My prayers have been answered," she whispers. Carrie fights the temptation to throw all her new clothes into the trash compactor.

Step Four:
Monday Morning (the Bus)

The moment Carrie climbs on board the bus, everybody falls silent. Once again Jordan is sitting with Amy Anderson. He gasps when he sees Carrie. Finally Brick breaks the silence by asking: "It isn't Halloween yet, is it?"

Step Five:
Monday Afternoon (the Cafeteria)

At the lunch table Carrie calmly explains her new look to Alex, Sam, and Jordan—

who's still giving her the silent treatment. She's tired of the whole "goth-rock thing." What's the matter with trying out some new outfits? Jordan just looks at her as if she's lost her mind.

Step Six:
Monday Afternoon (the Hall)

Carrie spots Jordan outside French class. Finally she'll get a chance to talk to him. Unfortunately he's chatting with Johnny Bates and Chris Tanzell. Carrie calls to him. Jordan offers a feeble wave and hurries in the opposite direction.

Step Seven:
Monday Afternoon (the Bus)

Basketball practice is canceled. Jordan dashes for the bus and barely makes it. "Sit with us!" Aimee Stewart calls. Carrie waits in the back with Alex, Sam, and Sky. Carrie prays Jordan won't sit with the Amys. But after a furtive glance toward the back, Jordan slumps down beside Amy Anderson.

Step Eight:
Monday Night (the Phone Call)

Carrie calls Sky. It's very clear this makeover stuff is *not* working. Jordan hasn't said anything to her about how open-minded and accepting of change she is. In fact, he's still giving her the silent treatment. Sky explains that these things take time. It's only been one day—and the article hasn't even come out yet. Maybe Carrie should wear the Supersonics cap tomorrow.

Step Nine:
Tuesday Morning (the Last Straw)

Carrie boards the bus, wearing her Supersonics cap and a matching green sweatshirt. Much to her relief, Jordan is sitting in the backseat. But as soon as Carrie sits down, Jordan hops up, mumbling something about how it's "too crowded back here." He sits with the Amys for the rest of the ride to school. Alex asks Carrie if she can have the cap.

Ten

Jordan plodded toward the cafeteria on Tuesday, feeling very much as if he were on his way to his own execution. Right at this very moment the newest issues of the *Observer* were being piled in the hall outside Principal Cashen's office. It would only be a matter of minutes before everyone had read Carrie's latest contribution. It would only be a matter of minutes before Jordan was humiliated before the entire school. *Again.*

How did this fight even start? He had no idea. All he knew was that Carrie wouldn't let it go. No . . . she had to become the *Observer*'s first sports columnist. He shook his head. Obviously that first editorial hadn't been enough. Carrie wanted more. She wanted to publicly rag on Jordan on a regular basis—week after week after week.

Why else had she bothered coming to

the game on Thursday? And why else did she keep wearing those incredibly freakish clothes? He didn't even feel like he *knew* her anymore. And he could just picture the first headline, too. Sullivan Stinks. *Oh, man.* Maybe he should just cut his losses and leave school right now.

"Hey, Sullivan!" a voice shouted behind him.

Here goes. Jordan slowly turned around. Chris Tanzell was storming through the hall. He had a rolled-up newspaper clenched tightly in his fist. *Uh-oh.*

"You wanna tell me what's going on here?" Chris yelled, shoving the paper into Jordan's hand. "Where do you get off with this stuff?"

Jordan swallowed. "Uh . . . what stuff?" he mumbled confusedly, unrolling the paper. His fingers were trembling. He'd never *seen* Chris so mad. "I haven't seen the paper yet—"

"Don't even try it," Chris snapped. "I'm not stupid."

Not compared to most household pets, Jordan thought, but he kept his mouth shut. His eyes scanned the page. "Sullivan

Wows Sheridan School." He frowned. *That* was the headline? That wasn't so bad. . . .

"You got your weird little friend to ignore the rest of the team, didn't you?" Chris growled. "Pretty swift, Sullivan. Only a dork like you would pull something like that."

Jordan had no idea what Chris was talking about. He shook his head and read the article.

Sullivan Wows Sheridan School
by Carrie Mersel

Like Vikings on the rampage, the Robert Lowell Panthers took no prisoners at Sheridan School this past Thursday.

The Panthers played superior basketball in every possible way, breezing to an easy forty-eight to thirty-two victory over the Bulls. Led once again by the brilliant play of Jordan Sullivan, they established a lead quickly in the first half. They never looked back. Sullivan's passing, shooting, and all-around hustle gave the Panthers the edge they needed throughout the entire game.

The Bulls were no match for Sullivan's trademark outside shot. Sullivan scored the final basket of the game, dazzling his opponents. Defensively he played a superb game as well. The Bulls' efforts to score were consistently thwarted by Sullivan. In the end they were broken, intimidated, and humiliated—and they had Jordan Sullivan to thank.

Does this mean that Sullivan will lead the Panthers to this year's championship? Probably. With Jordan Sullivan on the Panthers' side, it's hard to see how anything can possibly go wrong.

Come to the Panthers next home game against the Edgevale Hawks! Watch Sullivan in action!

Blood rushed to Jordan's face. He didn't know *what* to make of this. Part of him was flattered. But mostly he was embarrassed. Alarmed, even. Carrie hadn't mentioned any other player. Why? Jordan had played a decent game—but not *that* great. Why was the article entirely about *him?*

"It didn't even say that I was the leading scorer!" Chris yelled. "Sullivan, you hardly even *played* during the second half!"

Jordan glanced up. *Oh, jeez.* A crowd had started to gather around them—including Johnny Bates and a few other guys from the team. They all had papers. This was about to get ugly. Really ugly.

"Hey, Sullivan?" Johnny called to him. "What does *rampage* mean?"

"That's what we're gonna do to his

face," Chris spat, snatching the paper out of Jordan's hands. "You know, you got some nerve—"

"I had nothing to do with this," Jordan pleaded. He knew he sounded amazingly desperate and wimpy, but he couldn't help it. "I swear. Find Carrie and ask her. I mean it. I haven't even *spoken* to her in days. She did this all on her own. Just ask her."

Chris sneered. "Yeah. Like she's really gonna tell the truth."

"Well, uh . . . I don't know what to tell you," Jordan stuttered, stepping back. "She—"

"This is the biggest load of crap I've ever *seen!*" Johnny suddenly shouted. He hurled the paper to the floor. "You can't play defense at all, Sullivan!"

Jordan flinched. His eyes darted anxiously around the hall. Five or six guys were glaring at him now. This might be a good opportunity to make a run for it. He whirled—then slammed right into a mass of blond curls.

"Whoa, there!" a giggling voice squealed.

It was Aimee. Great. Perfect timing.

"Sorry," he mumbled, trying to push past her.

"Hey! Where are you going?" She grabbed onto his arm—then smiled at Chris and Johnny and the others. For some bizarre reason she was seemingly oblivious to the fact that they were about to pound Jordan into the floor. "What's up? What do you guys think of the article?"

"Oh, we just think it's *peachy*," Johnny grumbled sarcastically.

Chris snickered. "Yeah. We *loved* reading about a guy who sat on the bench for half the game."

Aimee raised her eyebrows. "Jealous, boys?" she teased.

Jealous? Jordan cringed. That wasn't going to make them happy. He forced a strained smile. "Look, I know the article was a little one-sided," he said quickly. "But there's nothing any of us can do about it now. So let's just eat lunch and forget about it. Huh?"

"Don't be so modest," Aimee scolded, letting his arm go. "If you were the star, you were the star." She laughed once.

"Your teammates will deal with it. No, the only problem with the article was Carrie's writing. You have to admit, it's *terrible*. Personally I think I could have done a much better job, but . . ."

Please shut up, Jordan begged silently. Aimee could be a real pain in the neck sometimes. None of the Amys ever knew when to keep quiet.

"The point is, you should be proud of yourself," Aimee finished.

Jordan nodded. "Right," he muttered. He started inching toward the cafeteria doors.

"Hey, Sullivan," Johnny called. He shook his head, grinning. "You're wrong about something."

"I am?" he croaked.

"Yeah. You said there's nothing we can do about it." His big, toothy grin widened. "And that's not true. We *are* gonna do something about it. You can count on it."

Eleven

"So did anyone find out what Jordan thought about the article?" Alex asked as she rummaged through the Mersels' refrigerator after school on Tuesday. "I didn't get a chance to talk to him all day."

"Neither did I," Carrie mumbled. She kicked her feet under the kitchen table. She was too antsy to sit still. Her high-heeled sneakers made little screeching noises on the white tile floor. She was definitely going to have to get rid of these sneakers. They were way too loud. "The only time I saw him was when he poked his head into the cafeteria. It was almost as if he disappeared after that." She glanced across the table at Sky and Sam. "Did you guys talk to him?"

Sky shook her head. "Not me."

"Me neither," Sam muttered. His dark brow grew furrowed. He leaned back in the chair and stared off into space. "It's weird. I *always* talk to him after sixth period. But today when he saw me in the hall, he just took off in the other direction. He looked kind of freaked, too."

Carrie chewed her lip, frowning. This was not good. She was starting to get seriously worried. He must have read the article, but why would he be upset? He should have come running to thank her. She had been sure that this stupid fight would be over by now. What more could she possibly do?

"Maybe he's starting to get sick of all the attention," Alex suggested. She closed the refrigerator door and opened the freezer. "Maybe he wants to keep a really low profile or something." She reached for a carton of chocolate chocolate chip ice cream. "You know—like Michael Jackson."

Carrie smirked. "Michael Jackson?"

"Yeah." Alex plopped down at the table and began spooning ice cream straight from the box. "You know how Michael Jackson is really shy?" she asked with her mouth half full. "He hides from people all the time. There's a word for it. He's a . . . um . . ."

"Weirdo?" Sky suggested, grinning.

Alex shrugged. "Well, *that*, too. But I was thinking—"

"Recluse," Carrie finished.

Alex pointed her spoon at Carrie. "Bingo!"

Sam shook his head. "You guys, there's no *way* Jordan is keeping a low profile, or becoming a recluse, or anything like that. Come on." He laughed. "If anybody loves attention, it's Jordan."

"So what's going on?" Carrie asked, almost to herself. "It doesn't make any sense."

Sky sighed. "Well, *I* think that Jordan . . . that Jordan—" She broke off. A piercing, high-pitched *beep-beep-beep* had suddenly filled the room.

Carrie rolled her eyes.

"What *is* that?" Sky asked, giggling.

"The phone," Carrie mumbled. She pushed herself up. There was no use explaining. Her mom had just gotten this brand-new cordless phone that sounded like a burglar alarm. Why? Carrie had no idea. She sighed and lifted the receiver off the wall. It was probably her mom right now, calling to announce that she was being held up at some vitally important meeting of the Gourmet Club.

"Hello?" Carrie asked flatly.

"It's Jordan."

Carrie nearly dropped the phone.

"Hello?" came the voice at the other end.

Everybody at the table stared at her.

"Who is it?" Alex whispered.

Carrie cupped a shaky hand over the mouthpiece. "Jordan!" she hissed.

"Jordan?" they all cried at once.

"Shhh!" Carrie removed her hand and turned toward the wall. "Hi," she breathed. Her heart was fluttering. "What, uh . . . what's up?"

"What's up?" He chuckled. "Not much. What's up with you? Long time, no talk."

"No kidding," Carrie muttered. She couldn't read the tone of his voice. Was he angry? Joking around? It was impossible to tell.

"Right . . . uh, anyway, I read the sports column in the *Observer* today," Jordan said. "I guess I should thank you."

Carrie shifted on her feet. He didn't *sound* as if he wanted to thank her. In fact, he sounded as if thanking her was about the last thing he wanted to do. "You're welcome," she said carefully.

There was a pause. "So. What made you want to write a *sports* column?"

Carrie hesitated. "I . . . uh, I realized that my editorial letter was a little harsh. The guys on the team aren't that bad," she answered. "I wanted to make up for it."

Jordan chuckled again. "That's funny. I don't know if you *were* wrong about the guys on the team."

"You *don't?*" Carrie frowned. "What do you mean?"

"Well, I think you were right about certain things," he said evenly. "Jocks *are* a little egotistical. It turns out they're also stupid."

Carrie's eyes narrowed. What was going on here? "Um, Jordan—"

"You see, a couple of the more stupid, egotistical guys on the team are a little mad," he went on. "They actually think that I *made* you write that article."

"They *what?*" Carrie cried. "Jordan, I didn't—"

"Let me finish," Jordan interrupted calmly. "The problem is, they don't understand why they weren't included in the sports column. I mean, some guys on the team played much better than I did. They played more minutes. They scored more points. So they're a little confused. And so am I."

Carrie drew in her breath. She couldn't believe this. "Jordan, I . . . uh, I guess I wasn't paying as much attention to the other guys as I should have," she mumbled, struggling to organize her thoughts. "I . . . uh . . . how mad are they?"

"You don't want to know," Jordan muttered.

"Well, well—what can I *do?*" she asked frantically.

"I'm not really sure," he replied. "Let me just ask you something, though. You weren't *trying* to make them mad, were you? I mean, you didn't do this on purpose . . . you know, to get me back or anything?"

"Of *course* not!" Carrie exclaimed. "I did it because . . ." She held her breath. What could she possibly say? "I did it because I was sorry and I was worried you were never going to talk to me again," she finally admitted.

He sighed. "Well, I guess it worked, then. You got me to talk to you again."

Carrie gulped. "Jordan—you aren't still mad at me, are you?" she murmured.

He didn't reply.

"Jordan?"

"Now's probably not the best time to ask me that," he grumbled.

She winced. How could he be so mean? "I'm *sorry!*" she cried desperately. "What do you want me to say?"

"I don't know," he moaned. "All I know is that my entire team wants to kill me because you left them out of your article."

"Well, the next time I'll include them," she promised. "I swear."

"Okay, okay." His tone softened a little. "Listen, you know we have a game against Edgevale on Thursday, right? Just tell the truth about the game. That's all I want you to do."

"You got it," she breathed hoarsely.

"Good. I'll talk to you later, Carrie. Good-bye." The line clicked.

Carrie blinked. Was that it? After all that time, all the energy she'd spent, all the effort she'd gone to in order to make him believe that she wasn't afraid of change, Jordan *still* hadn't forgiven her. On the other hand, she couldn't really blame him. If ten hulking meatheads wanted to pulverize *her*—well, she might feel the same way. She hung up the phone and slowly turned to face the others.

All three of her friends were gazing at her, waiting.

"So?" Sky eventually asked. "Did you guys make up?"

Carrie shrugged. "I don't really know," she said with a sigh. "But the way I see it, I have one last chance. I'll know after Thursday's game."

Twelve

I

Carrie was starting to get nervous.

The Panthers were losing. They were actually *losing*.

In all her worries about today's game— over how she would compliment each and every member of the team, over how she would learn all the rules by this afternoon, over how she wouldn't make a lifelong enemy of Jordan—she never once considered the possibility that the Panthers might lose.

How on earth could she write a beautiful, glowing article about a loss?

She glanced around the gym. The bleachers were totally silent. Everybody was wearing the exact same grim, stone-faced expression—including Alex, Sam, and Sky. The atmosphere was even worse than it had been at Sheridan School. At

377

least *that* gym had been empty. But this gym was packed, and nobody was talking. Even the Amys hadn't so much as uttered a peep. Carrie rubbed her hands on her blue jeans. Her legs were so *itchy* in these things. Maybe she should just treat the whole game like one of her horror stories. There didn't seem to be much difference.

The whistle blew for a time-out.

"Hey, Carrie?" Sky said. "Can I ask you something?"

Carrie shrugged. "Sure."

"Why isn't anybody passing the ball to Jordan?"

"I don't know," Carrie lied. But she knew very well why. She just didn't want to admit it—to herself or to anyone else. The guys on the team weren't passing the ball to Jordan because they were majorly angry with him. And it was all her fault.

"Looks to me like they're doing it on purpose," Sam muttered.

"On *purpose?*" Sky frowned. "But why?"

Sam shrugged. "Beats me."

Carrie slumped deep into her seat. At least they didn't know the truth. She could hardly bear to watch. Even if everybody on the team was mad, losing didn't make any sense. Jordan was a good player. When time was running out, you were supposed to use your good players.

She glanced at the scoreboard. Only two minutes were left.

So why couldn't the guys on the team just stop acting like morons for once and get Jordan the ball?

II

"All right, guys, listen up," Coach Powell snarled. "In case you haven't noticed, we're down by six points. What the heck is your problem?"

Jordan groaned inwardly. He was exhausted. Sweat bathed his face and arms. His lungs were heaving. And even though he'd been running around like crazy out there, nobody seemed to notice he was even on the court. Nobody had thrown the ball to him. Not once. He was actually a little ticked off himself. So what if they were mad about Carrie's article? Didn't they want to win?

"Hey, Tanzell—are you daydreaming or something?" Coach Powell asked. He jerked a thumb at Jordan. "Sullivan here has been wide open about a dozen times." His voice hardened. "When he's open . . . *throw him the ball.*"

Chris lifted his shoulders. He didn't seem the least bit concerned. "Sorry," he muttered.

"You better be," Coach Powell grumbled. He picked up a little chalkboard and began drawing Xs and Os. "Now here's what I want you to do. . . ."

Jordan shot a quick, nasty look at Chris. But Chris just smiled.

And in that instant Jordan knew that Chris *wasn't* going to throw him the ball. Ever. Even if it meant losing the game. Jordan's teammates *didn't* want to win.

III

"Let's go, Panthers!" Carrie shouted along with the crowd. *Finally* it seemed as if the people in the bleachers were showing some signs of life. Maybe they could breathe some life into the players, too. The Panthers could still win, couldn't they? They were only down by six points. Anything was possible. "Let's go, Panthers!"

Carrie kept her eyes pinned to Jordan. He was scrambling across court, waving his hands furiously. Johnny Bates was dribbling the ball. But he didn't even *look* in Jordan's direction. Instead he threw up a wild shot that completely missed the net. The ball bounced out of bounds.

A whistle blew.

Carrie's jaw tightened. *That's it*, she said to herself. *Maybe I started it—but this whole thing has gone way too far.* She cupped her hands over her mouth and took a huge breath.

"Hey, *stupid!*" she shrieked. A few people in the stands turned to look at her—but she didn't care. She was furious. If the Panthers were going to win, they *had* to get the ball to Jordan. "Johnny Bates!"

Johnny paused for a moment on the floor and squinted in Carrie's direction.

"Yeah, *you!*" Carrie hooted. "Instead of taking a lame shot, why don't you pass it? There's no *i* in *team*, dummy!"

Alex, Sky, and Sam giggled. But they were the only ones laughing. Everybody else looked mortified. Except for the guys who were playing for Edgevale, of course. *They* seemed to think it was funny.

"That's an *awesome* line," Alex stated.

"Totally," Sky agreed. "Did you make that up?"

For a moment Carrie was tempted to take credit for it. But then she shrugged. "Nope. It was the only thing I learned from that book—*Rules of the Game*," she said.

IV

Jordan allowed himself a little smile as he ran back down the court. *No* i *in* team. It was Coach Powell's favorite expression. He had to hand it to Carrie—she always knew *exactly* what to say. He glanced at Johnny. The guy was fuming.

Jordan couldn't have been happier.

If his teammates hated him, fine. He could handle the nasty looks in the locker room. But they were freezing him out of the game. When Johnny took that pathetic shot instead of passing the ball to Jordan, it was confirmed. Aimee was right. They *were* jealous. So to get revenge, they were pretending as if Jordan wasn't even on the team. They were willing to lose just for the sake of making Jordan mad.

How lame was *that?*

Jordan struggled to get into his defensive position—but before he could, Edgevale scored another basket. The score was now forty-four to thirty-six.

Jordan glanced at the clock. Less than a minute remained.

The game was pretty much over.

Oh, well. At this point Jordan didn't even care. Why would he even want to play on this team? Basketball wasn't worth this much trouble. It was supposed to be fun.

He should have trusted his instincts. He had known right from the start that he didn't fit in with these guys. The Robert Lowell Panthers were all a bunch of fools. Come to think of it, Carrie had been right, too. The players on this team did think they were better than everyone else. They sure thought that they were better than Jordan.

So there wasn't much point in playing with them, was there?

V

Even when the final buzzer sounded, Carrie still couldn't quite believe that the Panthers had lost. Sure, deep down she knew the game was over. She knew they'd been beaten. But for some reason it just didn't seem to make sense. Maybe it was because she hadn't seen them lose until now. She didn't know. She could only stand there, gazing at the scoreboard while people quietly filed out of the gym.

"Carrie?" Sky murmured, tugging on the sleeve of her sweater. "You coming?"

Finally Carrie allowed her head to droop. "Yeah." She sighed. "I'm coming."

"I can't believe they ignored Jordan that whole time," Sam muttered. "They would have won if they hadn't ignored him."

"I know." Carrie groaned. "I know."

"Hey, Carrie—look at it this way," Alex offered. "At least you won't have any problem focusing on other guys besides Jordan for your article. Jordan had nothing to *do* with this game."

Carrie nodded. Alex was right. Jordan might as well have been in another time zone. She *couldn't* write about him.

But the whole reason she'd even invented this stupid sports column was for Jordan. If he wasn't involved, she had absolutely no interest. None. In fact, the thought of heaping false praise on Chris Tanzell and Johnny Bates was enough to turn her stomach. They had *cost* Robert Lowell the game.

She didn't want to make Jordan mad . . . but at the same time could he blame her for despising the guys who'd treated him like garbage?

No. She didn't think he could.

And that meant there was only one thing left to do.

Thirteen

"So let me get this straight," Principal Cashen said, leaning back in his leather chair. "You want to stop writing for the *Robert Lowell Observer*."

"That's right," Carrie replied.

He stared at his desk for a moment. "Does Amy, Mel, or Aimee know anything about this?"

Carrie shook her head. "No, Principal Cashen. I haven't told them yet. In fact, I just made up my mind yesterday afternoon after the game. But I doubt they'll mind."

He glanced up. "What makes you think they won't mind?"

Carrie shrugged. How could she answer that? *Because they hate my guts and the feeling is mutual?* No—that wouldn't do. "Well, to tell you the truth, we don't see eye to eye on a lot of things," she said.

Principal Cashen nodded gravely. Carrie squirmed in her hard-backed wooden chair. She never understood why there was no couch in here. Shouldn't a big-time principal have a couch in his office? This place was definitely big enough for a couch. Of course, there was probably a reason. Maybe he *wanted* people to be uncomfortable. That was probably why he kept his office dark, too— like all the rest of the teachers at Robert Lowell. It was like they were all vampires or something.

"Can I ask you a question, Carrie?" he said after a moment.

"Sure," Carrie replied, even though she was a little nervous. Whenever somebody asked if they could ask you something instead of just asking the question, you *knew* it was going to be bad.

"Why did you want to write a sports column at all?"

Carrie just stared at him. Yup. That was bad. She couldn't blame him, though. After all, Jordan had asked her the same thing.

"Carrie?" Principal Cashen coaxed.

"I—uh, I thought it might be fun," she managed, smiling anxiously. "I figured it would be a change from the kind of stuff I usually write. Plus I thought I could write about sports differently than most people because . . . um . . . because—"

"Because you're not interested in sports?" Principal Cashen finished dryly.

Carrie's face reddened. *Oh, brother.* She should have known he'd see right through her. He *was* smart. She always managed to forget that. As terrible as it seemed, she had a hard time taking a pudgy, balding guy in a really corny suit all that seriously.

"I don't mean to put you on the spot," Principal Cashen said. He cleared his throat. The faint beginnings of a smile curled on his lips. "May I make a suggestion, though?"

"Sure," Carrie mumbled, looking at her lap.

"Why don't you write something *else* for the paper? Why don't you create a column that really interests you?"

Carrie's head jerked up. "You'd let me do that?" she asked, baffled.

Principal Cashen chuckled softly. "Yes, Carrie, I would. Principals aren't ogres, you know. We're in the business of educating and encouraging young people." He raised his eyebrows. "If you can believe it."

"No, no—I didn't . . . um, I mean—"

"Look, the point is that you're a talented writer," he gently interrupted. "I was very pleased when you expressed an interest in writing for the *Observer*. I just think you need to direct your energies in the right place."

Carrie shook her head, too overcome with a strange mixture of gratitude, shock, and embarrassment to speak. Finally she took a deep breath. "That's . . . uh, nice of you to say," she murmured.

He shrugged. "It's true."

Carrie met his gaze. "What kind of a column could it be?" she asked curiously.

"That's up to you," he replied.

"Hmmm." She smiled. "I don't know if the Amys—I mean, Amy Anderson and the others—would be too thrilled about my writing a column."

"Why not? They let you write a sports column, didn't they?" Principal Cashen leaned back in his chair. "Besides, I think it's a good idea for the *Observer* to have . . .

well, differing points of view. Amy and her friends tend to be pretty one-sided about things. Even if they aren't thrilled, they'll have to live with it." His face grew stern. "Of course, anything you contribute *does* have to be in good taste."

"Of course," Carrie replied quickly. Her smile widened. "Well, I don't know how I can refuse after that. You've got yourself a columnist."

"Good." He pushed back his chair and gestured toward the door. "I don't want you to be late for your bus. We can discuss the specifics later."

Carrie hopped out of her chair. "Sure. Thanks a lot, Principal Cashen. I mean it."

"Oh—there's one more quick thing, too," he announced, holding up his finger. "You're friends with Jordan Sullivan, right?"

Her stomach abruptly twisted into a knot. In all the talk about the column, she'd totally forgotten that Jordan was the reason she was here in the first place. *Was* she friends with Jordan Sullivan? She didn't even know how to answer that question. "Why?"

"Because I was very impressed with

that self-portrait he drew for Aimee's article," he said in a businesslike tone. "I was thinking that it would be wonderful if he wanted to contribute drawings to the *Observer* on a regular basis. If you see him, just mention it to him."

Carrie nodded. *Wow,* she thought. Jordan would *love* a regular cartoon. Or would he? The knot faded, leaving an odd emptiness in its place. She didn't even know anymore. She and Jordan didn't even *speak* to each other anymore. Whenever he saw her these days, he just stared at her as if she were a total lunatic.

"I'll tell him," she finally murmured. *But I don't know if he'll even listen to me,* she added silently.

No. It was time for this silliness to end. He'd have to listen to her. She'd make sure of it. In fact, she would go to his house this very afternoon. She'd wait there for him until he was done with basketball practice. She wouldn't let one more day pass without a face-to-face talk. They'd grown too far apart.

If he wanted to keep playing basketball, fine. That was part of who he was. But he couldn't forget the other parts. He couldn't go around pretending to be somebody else. After all, *she'd* learned that she couldn't be somebody else, right? She was no sports columnist. She never was. She was just herself, for better or worse. Jordan would just have to deal with it.

Just like Carrie would have to deal with his basketball.

If she could learn to deal, so could he.

Fourteen

"You want to *what?*" Coach Powell cried.

"I want to quit the team," Jordan repeated quietly, standing as straight as he could in front of Coach Powell's desk.

Coach Powell leaned forward and looked Jordan directly in the eye. He took a deep breath. His forehead grew wrinkled, as if he were thinking very hard about what he wanted to say. "Is something bothering you, Jordan?" he asked. "Do you want to talk about it?"

Jordan shrugged, but he was struck by something. Coach Powell had never called him by his first name before. It made Jordan feel more relaxed, somehow. And that was good, considering that he could hardly breathe in here. But it was almost as if Coach Powell were finally admitting that Jordan was an actual living, breathing *person*. It was kind of nice.

"I just don't think I'm cut out to play on this team," Jordan said simply. "That's all."

Coach Powell nodded. "You're upset about yesterday's game, right?"

Jordan lowered his gaze. "A little," he admitted.

"Well, that's perfectly understandable," Coach Powell stated. "Listen. I don't know what's going on between you and the other guys on the team, but whatever it is, I'm sure we can work it out—"

"There's really nothing to work out, Coach Powell," Jordan interrupted as politely as he could. He lifted his head and brushed his bangs out of his eyes. "I appreciate it and all, but nothing's going to change how I feel."

Coach Powell leaned back in his chair and gave his head a thoughtful scratch. "Is something *specific* bothering you?"

Yeah, Jordan thought. *The whole team. They make me ill.* He paused. There had to be a more delicate way to explain things. But explaining things had never been his strong point. He suddenly wished Carrie were here. *She* could tell him what to say. Nobody else had a better way with words. Like what she'd said to Johnny . . .

"Well, let me put it this way," he said after a few seconds. "You know how you're always telling us that there's no *i* in *team*?"

Coach Powell's eyes narrowed. "Yes?"

"I just think . . . I think that the guys on the team really wish that were true," Jordan finished awkwardly. "That *I* wasn't part of the team. You know what I mean?"

All of a sudden Coach Powell burst into laughter: "Ahee, hee, hee!"

Jordan's eyes widened. He wasn't trying to be funny. He'd never seen Coach Powell laugh before, either. It was kind of scary.

"You know what, Jordan?" Coach Powell asked, shaking his head. "You may be one of the smartest players ever to walk in here."

Jordan blinked a few times. "What?"

"It's true." He laughed again. "You know—if half the guys on the team used their brains as much as you do, we'd be guaranteed to win the championship."

Jordan just stared at him. *Jeez.* He was shocked. This wasn't like Coach Powell at all. He handed out compliments about as often as the cafeteria handed out edible food. Jordan had no idea what to say. In fact, he was starting to get a little embarrassed. He started backing toward the door. "Well, thanks for your time. I really should be going. I have to catch the bus—"

"Wait!" Coach Powell raised his hands. "Just hold on one more second. Look, I know that some of the guys have a hard time sharing the spotlight. But try to see things from their point of view. Most of them have been playing together for the past three years. You just joined the team a few weeks ago. There's bound to be some tension, right? They're not *all* bad, Jordan. They're just human."

Jordan started shaking his head. Human? That would be pushing it a little in Johnny and Chris's case. "I know what you're trying to say," he said. "But really, my mind is made up." He reached for the doorknob. "Thanks again."

Coach Powell sighed and folded his hands across his lap. "All right. If your mind is made up, it's made up. But we really could use you, Jordan. You've got a lot of talent." He pointed a finger at his head. "Especially up here."

"Thanks," Jordan mumbled. Now he

was *really* embarrassed. He pushed open the door.

"But do me a favor, okay?" Coach Powell asked.

Jordan hesitated in the doorway. "What's that?"

"Join the basketball team when you get to high school." He flashed a wry grin. "Somebody's gotta keep all your older brothers in line."

Jordan chuckled. "You got it."

"Good. I'll see you later, Jordan."

"See ya." He closed the office door behind him.

Wow. Jordan wandered out into the crowded hallway, shaking his head. Kids bumped into him as they ran toward the front doors, but he hardly noticed.

He couldn't believe how painless that had been. He'd been dreading that confrontation all day. But Coach Powell totally understood where he was coming from. He didn't get angry or act disappointed—or even try to push Jordan into staying. He *knew* Jordan would have been miserable on that team. And he respected Jordan's decision.

That was pretty cool.

"Hello? Jordan Sullivan? Anybody home?"

He glanced up. Aimee was right there.

Oh yeah. He'd told her to wait for him outside Coach Powell's office. He wanted her to be the first to know that he'd quit.

"Hey," he said. "Sorry. I'm kind of spaced right now."

Aimee raised her eyebrows. "I noticed." She giggled. "By the way, you're walking in the wrong direction. Basketball practice is *that* way."

"But I'm not going to basketball practice," he replied with a smile.

"Why not?" She stared at him. "Are you sick or something?"

"Not at all." He laughed. "In fact, I haven't felt this good in a long time. I just quit the team."

Aimee froze. "You *what?*" she cried.

"I quit," he said casually. "It's no big deal—"

"But *why?*" she demanded. "Did somebody make you?"

Jordan paused. "No," he said, a little taken aback. That was sort of a weird question. "I just wasn't happy," he explained. "I'd rather shoot hoops with my friends on my own time than practice every day. And playing on that team meant hanging out with—"

He broke off. Aimee's face was all shriveled—as if she'd just taken a bite of some really old cottage cheese or something. She looked disgusted.

"What's the matter?" he asked.

"Jordan—playing on that team is the best thing that ever happened to you!" she snapped. "You can't just quit!"

Jordan frowned. "I can't?"

Aimee put her hands on her hips and rolled her eyes. "Of course not, *stupid*. Don't you see? If you quit the team, you go back to being what you were before." She sneered. "No, even worse. Quitters are the lowest forms of low. Quitters are losers."

Jordan just gaped at her. For a second he almost felt like laughing. Coach Powell wasn't mad, but Aimee Stewart was. Either she was insane, or stupid, or incredibly conceited—or all of the above. Did she honestly think that those words would make him want to rush back and join the Panthers? "And what was I *before?*" he asked.

"You know what I mean," she muttered.

"No." He smiled. "No—please explain it to me." He had a feeling he knew *exactly* what she meant—but he wanted her to say the words herself.

She glowered at him. "If you quit, you go back to being just another a *dork*, like all the rest of your dumb friends."

Jordan nodded. *Ah, yes.* Aimee thought that basketball was the only thing in Jordan's life that saved him from being a hopeless failure.

But he'd always kind of known what Aimee thought.

He knew something else now, too. He *would* go back to being like all his dumb friends if he quit the team. Yes—once again Aimee was absolutely right. And if quitting the team made him a dork in her eyes . . . hey, he could live with that. Plus he'd have the added bonus of never having to talk to her again. Carrie would be proud. That's because Carrie was a true friend. She'd made a fool out of Johnny Bates in front of the entire school—all for Jordan. She'd always hated the whole idea of basketball, anyway.

Or did she?

Jordan sighed. Who knew what Carrie was thinking these days? She had told him that she was writing the sports column to apologize for being so harsh in her first letter. But what was up with her hair? And the jeans and sweatshirts and baseball caps. What was *that* all about?

I have to talk to her. I have to get everything out in the open once and for all.

Without another word he turned and hurried toward the front doors. He couldn't afford to miss the bus. Not today.

"Where do you think you're going!" Aimee shouted after him. "I haven't finished talking to you yet."

"That's okay," he called over his shoulder. "You wouldn't want to talk to me, anyway. I'm going back to being a dork."

Fifteen

Carrie didn't think she'd *ever* felt more lonely or self-conscious. Nope. The backseat was totally empty. Well, except for *her*, of course. She'd sunk as low as a person could sink. She was hunched in the backseat of bus number four, staring down at a pair of heinous high-heeled sneakers. It was like a form of torture or something. Why couldn't Brick just start the lousy engine and get out of here?

Maybe she should have gone with Alex, Sam, and Sky. They were on their way to the high school to watch Alex's brother play basketball right now. But Carrie had refused to go. After all, she'd seen enough basketball to last the rest of her life and beyond.

As usual, of course, she hadn't been thinking. Anything was better than this. She had never realized how huge this seat was. She could lie down across it if she wanted to. Actually, that might not be a bad idea.

"Hey, man!" Brick called. "I didn't expect to see *you*."

What now? Carrie thought dismally. She raised her eyes.

"Jordan!" she gasped.

Her mouth fell open. What was he doing here?

He marched down the aisle and slumped beside her. His bangs immediately fell in his eyes. He brushed them aside and smiled. "What's up?"

For a moment she was unable to speak. She just shook her head. This was impossible.

He peered at her closely. "What's the matter?"

"I . . . I don't get it," she murmured at last. "Why aren't you at practice?"

"Would you believe me if I told you that I quit the team?" he asked.

Carrie struggled for a moment to process his words. Quit the team? "No," she answered. "I wouldn't."

He laughed. "That seems to be what *everybody* thinks."

"Hey, Jordan!" Brick yelled from up front. "Are you here to stay or what? I've gotta start this thing."

"Go ahead," Jordan called.

The bus roared to life and bounced out of the semicircular driveway.

Only then did it hit Carrie: *He really must have quit.* Why else would he have stayed on the bus?

"What made you do it?" she asked, unable to tear her eyes from him.

He shrugged, slouching in the seat. *"You saw the game yesterday,"* he mumbled. "If the guys on the team don't want me to—"

"Jordan, I have something to tell you," Carrie suddenly blurted. "I can't write a fair article about yesterday's game like you asked me to. I can't write anything more about the guys on the team, or the game, or anything having to do with basketball."

Jordan hesitated, staring at her. Afternoon sunlight flickered across his face as the bus began the long climb up Pike's Way. "You can't?" he finally asked.

She shook her head. "No. I'm not the sports columnist anymore."

"Whoa." He sat up straight. "What happened?"

She grinned slightly. "The same thing that happened to you. I quit."

"You *did?*" he exclaimed.

"I had to." She turned and gazed out the window at the passing pine trees. "You know that old saying, If you don't have something nice to say, don't say anything at all?" she muttered. "That's a very polite way of summing up how I feel about the Robert Lowell Panthers. I had nothing nice to say. So there was no way I could keep writing a sports column."

"Yeah, after what happened yesterday, I'm not exactly having happy thoughts about the team, either," Jordan said ruefully. "It's so annoying. It turned out those guys actually fit the stupid stereotypes."

"What do you mean?" Carrie asked.

Jordan shifted in his seat. "When I was having fun and playing well, the guys didn't seem so bad," Jordan said. "But when they got angry about your article, they wouldn't even let me explain. They turned into total meatheads, just like you said."

"So all jocks *are* jerks?" Carrie asked, confused.

"No, not at all," Jordan answered. "I mean, I'm still thinking about playing on the high school team next year because I really do love basketball, and I'm sure some of the guys will be cool. It's just a lot of the guys on the Panthers do happen to be, well, *really* stupid."

Carrie laughed once. "You can say that again. I couldn't believe the way they were freezing you out." She shook her head. "But guess what? I have some incredible news."

"What is it?" Jordan asked, looking interested.

"I went to Principal Cashen's office to quit the paper for good. But he ended up convincing me to stay. He says I can write my own column." She flashed a wicked smile. "About *anything*."

Jordan's face brightened. "Carrie, that's *awesome!*"

"That's not all, though," she went on, unable to wipe the smile from her face. "He told me to tell *you* that he wants you to start doing cartoons for the *Observer* on a regular basis."

Jordan drew back his head. "Get out of here."

"I'm *serious*," she said. "He saw that self-portrait you did. He said he was really impressed."

Jordan didn't say anything for what

seemed like a long time. He just kept glancing at her, then at the floor, then back.

"What?" she asked worriedly. "Aren't you psyched?"

"Listen, Carrie, you're not pulling my leg, are you?" he asked cautiously.

"Pulling your leg?" Carrie cried. "Are you *kidding?*"

"Well, to tell you the truth, I don't know *what* to think anymore," Jordan murmured. His bangs fell in his face as he lowered his eyes again. "I mean, I hardly feel like I know you right now, you know? Everything is so *weird.*"

Carrie nodded. For a moment she was half tempted to throw her arms around him and hug him as tightly as possible. But she managed to control herself. After all, she didn't want him to gag or anything. She took a deep breath. "I was feeling the same thing about you. That's how this whole thing started, remember? I was freaked out by the way you were acting like a total superstar and hanging out with the Amys—"

"Don't remind me," Jordan interrupted, grimacing. "I mean, I can't believe I actually hung out with Aimee Stewart. As Sky would say: *Eww.*"

Carrie grinned. "Actually, she did say that. . . ."

"The point is that it's over," he piped up. "I'm willing to forget about that letter you wrote if you're willing to forget that I ever hung out with Aimee Stewart." He extended a hand. "Deal?"

Carrie grasped his hand and shook it so vigorously that Jordan's entire body wriggled. "Deal."

"Whoa!" he yelped.

"Oops." Carrie let his hand go. "Sorry."

"Can I ask you something, though?" Jordan brushed his bangs aside and looked her in the eye. "Why did you decide to stop dyeing your hair?"

Carrie blushed slightly. "What? You don't like the natural look?"

"No, no . . . it's not that," he said quickly. "The natural look . . . is, um, interesting."

"Yeah, right," Carrie muttered with a smirk. "You sound about as convincing as one of those infomercials for dandruff shampoo."

Jordan chuckled. "You're right. I guess I kind of miss the old Carrie, you know? That's what freaked me out so much. The way you totally changed."

"Wait a minute," Carrie said, sitting up straight. "*You* were freaked by the way *I* changed. What're you, like, living in the *Ice Age?*"

Jordan brought his hands to his face. "Ugh!" he groaned. "I can't believe I said that to you the other day! I was just so mad. You can wear whatever you want. We're still friends even if you never wear black again."

"Really?" Carrie asked. She pointed down at her horrible high-heeled sneakers. "Well, what do you think of these?"

Jordan didn't say anything. His smile was totally forced.

"My thoughts exactly," Carrie stated. "In fact . . ." She reached under her seat, yanked the laces untied, and wrenched the sneakers from her feet. Then she calmly placed them at her side. She wiggled her toes in her socks. "Ahhh," she said, closing her eyes. "That's *sooo* much better."

"I couldn't agree with you more." Jordan sighed and leaned back in his seat.

"There's one more thing, too," he said solemnly.

"What?" Carrie asked.

Jordan bit his lip. "No matter what

either of us does in the future—I mean, even if one of us decides to take up sumo wrestling or something—let's promise that we'll always be friends."

"And we'll never, ever say that one of us fits a stereotype again," Carrie added.

"Never," Jordan agreed.

Carrie smiled, even though at the moment she felt like bursting into tears—not that she would allow herself to do anything so gushy. Jordan would think she was crazy. But it was pretty amazing that even when they'd been drifting apart, they'd both been feeling the same things about each other. It was almost like there was a psychic bond between them or something. *Oh, brother.* Now she was starting to think like one of those tabloid magazines. Maybe she *was* crazy.

"Promise?" Jordan asked.

"Promise," Carrie managed after a moment.

"Good. So . . . Principal C. really liked my drawing?" Jordan asked.

Carrie threw her hands in the air. "Yes!" she exclaimed, laughing. "*Jeez.* How many times do I have to tell you?"

Jordan cocked an eyebrow. "Just making

sure." He looked out the window. The bus was turning off Pike's Way onto Whidbey Road. Before Carrie knew it, the bus squealed to a stop in front of an enormous, disgustingly modern white house. *Yikes.* She couldn't believe it. She was already *home.* She jumped up and snatched her sneakers off the seat. "I guess I'll see you—"

"Hey!" Jordan suddenly cried. "I got it!"

Carrie hesitated. "Got what?"

"Why don't you and I do something for the paper *together?*" His face brightened. "You can write the column—and I'll draw the illustrations. What do you think?"

"What do I *think?*" Carrie laughed. "Genius. Pure genius. What do you have in mind?"

Jordan tilted his head and wrinkled his brow. "I don't know."

Carrie thought for a second. There was no way they could figure out something right this second. She glanced around the bus. Her eyes happened to fall on the pair of sneakers in her hand. She'd have to save these for Halloween.

Hold on.

That was it! Not the sneakers—but what

they represented. Namely being a poser. She didn't have to wait for Halloween. The sneakers were *already* part of a costume Carrie had worn. They represented all the stupid stuff she'd done these past couple of weeks—all the roles she'd tried to play and failed at playing. How could she have ever worn these? They were so *ugly*. Oh, well. It didn't matter. What mattered was that if Jordan could forgive her for the sneakers, he could forgive her for anything.

"Maybe it should be about all the posers at our school," she suggested slowly. "You know, all the people who try to be something they aren't." She raised her eyebrows. "After all, it's something we're both familiar with, right?"

Jordan's green eyes sparkled. "You bet . . ."

"So what do you say we get started?" She reached out and yanked him up. Excitement was bubbling up inside her. This was going to be good. After all, they were the two most brilliant kids at Robert Lowell, right? Well, maybe not. But who cared? They were *partners*.

"It's time to seize the day, my man. Opportunity is knocking!"

Poser Patrol

by Carrie Mersel
and
Jordan Sullivan

Yes, folks—it's that time of year again.

It's the time of year when the days get a little shorter. The time when the wind blows a little colder. And the time when certain members of the student body (who shall remain nameless for the sake of their protection) lose their minds and start acting like total idiots.

As you may or may not know, this problem has a clinical name. It's called "posing." And it affects at least two out of every five members of the Robert Lowell student body.

Perhaps you think we're exaggerating.

Hardly. As two former posers, we're in a perfect position to evaluate others. You see, *we've* both been down that dark road. *We've* both lost our minds. So it's only fair that we perform a public service and describe these terrifying symptoms in our fellow students.

Take the case of a certain girl we all know and love. We'll call her Bootsy. Anyway, Bootsy recently had a huge crush on a certain boy with certain, shall we say . . . talents. She *worshiped* him.

But as soon as this boy found out that certain people with similar talents happened to be total jerks (who shall also remain nameless), he decided to keep his talents to himself.

Then—poof! Bootsy suddenly forgot that he existed.

Strange, isn't it?

Does she still really like him? Doubtful. Did she ever like him? Questionable. Did she only pretend to like him because it made her look good? Now *there's* an idea. . . .

Sadly, we cannot answer these questions with absolute certainty.

After careful study we've come to the conclusion that Bootsy is too confused to answer them herself.

Watch out! You could be next. And trust us, nobody wants to be like Bootsy.

Make sure you don't miss the first book in the
FRIENDS 4 EVER series . . .

Kate Andrews

Three is never a crowd for Carrie, Alex and Sky!

Carrie, Sky and Alex are best buddies. They love
hanging out together – sharing secrets, sorting out
problems and having heaps of fun. OK, so they
have their differences. Like Carrie wouldn't be
seen dead in Sky's technicoloured tops, and nothing will ever make Alex swap her trendy trainers
for Carrie's slick, chic look.

But one thing they do have in common is their
hatred of 'The Amys' – three snobby, ultra-pretty
girls who reckon they're way better than everyone
else. But when Alex starts thinking it might be cool
to be mates with them, Carrie and Sky are totally
shocked. Things have always been bad between
them and 'The Amys', but they're about to get
much worse . . .

JOHN LEKICH

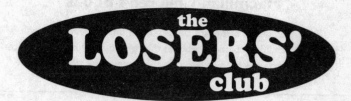

Best friends Alex, Winston and Manny are found-
ing members of The Losers' Club – a group of
so-called losers who meet to moan about their loser
status. But now they've decided that enough is
enough. Throwing darts at a life-sized photograph
of Jerry Whitman, school bully, just isn't satisfying
their desire for revenge. A school competition gives
them the perfect opportunity to humiliate Jerry, but
it's going to take some meticulous planning and a
lot of guts to WIN for the first time ever.
Meanwhile, Winston's loaded parents are away
and the three friends have the run of his mansion
home. Chaos is just around the corner . . .

**A laugh-out-loud, massively entertaining novel
about a bunch of the most unlikely heroes ever,
who are ready to expose exactly who the *real*
losers are . . .**

A selected list of titles available from Macmillan Children's Books

The prices shown below are correct at the time of going to press.
However, Macmillan Publishers reserves the right to show new retail prices
on covers, which may differ from those previously advertised.

Kate Andrews

| Friends 4 Ever | 0 330 43355 5 | £4.99 |
| Friends 4 Ever: What M8S R4 | 0 330 44205 8 | £5.99 |

Linda Aronson

| Plain Rude | 0 330 48254 8 | £4.99 |

John Lekich

| The Losers' Club | 0 330 42092 5 | £4.99 |

Meg Cabot

| Teen Idol | 0 330 43300 8 | £5.99 |

All Pan Macmillan titles can be ordered from our website,
www.panmacmillan.com, or from your local bookshop
and are also available by post from:

Bookpost, PO Box 29, Douglas, Isle of Man IM99 1BQ
Credit cards accepted. For details:
Telephone: 01624 677237
Fax: 01624 670923
Email: bookshop@enterprise.net
www.bookpost.co.uk

Free postage and packing in the United Kingdom